Give Me Your Tomorrow
by

John Brassey

First published in 2014

Copyright © Text John Brassey
Printed by CreateSpace, an Amazon Company

The author asserts the moral right under the Copyright, Designs and Patents Act 1988 to be identified as the author of this work.

All rights reserved. No part of this publication may be reproduced, stored in a retrieval system, or transmitted, in any form or by any means without the prior written consent of the author, nor be otherwise circulated in any form of binding or cover other than that in which it is published and without a similar condition being imposed on the subsequent purchaser.

Any characters in the publication are fictitious and any resemblance to real persons, living or dead, is purely coincidental.

Lyrics from *'If I Were A Carpenter'*
Words &Music by Tim Hardin
Copyright © 1966 (Renewed) TRIO MUSIC and ALLEY MUSIC CORP
All Rights for TRIO MUSIC Administered by BUG MUSIC, INC., A BMG CHYSALIS COMPANY
International Copyright Secured   All Rights Reserved
Reprinted by Permission of Hal Leonard Corporation

'If I Were A Carpenter'
Words and Lyrics by Tim Hardin
© Copyright 1965 Alley Music Corporation.
Robbins Music Corporation Limited.
All Rights Reserved. International Copyright Secured.
Used by permission of Music Sales Limited

Cover design by Spiffing Covers
Text design byRed Button Publishing

Table of Contents

Chapter One	5
Chapter Two	10
Chapter Three	15
Chapter Four	20
Chapter Five	28
Chapter Six	34
Chapter Seven	40
Chapter Eight	48
Chapter Nine	50
Chapter Ten	58
Chapter Eleven	65
Chapter Twelve	72
Chapter Thirteen	74
Chapter Fourteen	83
Chapter Fifteen	88
Chapter Sixteen	92
Chapter Seventeen	101
Chapter Eighteen	114
Chapter Nineteen	121
Chapter Twenty	127
Chapter Twenty-one	132
Chapter Twenty-two	138
Chapter Twenty-three	147
Chapter Twenty-four	153
Chapter Twenty-five	168
Chapter Twenty -six	172
Chapter Twenty-seven	176
Chapter Twenty-eight	182
Chapter Twenty-nine	188
Chapter Thirty	191
Chapter Thirty-one	198
Chapter Thirty-two	202
Chapter Thirty-three	207
Chapter Thirty-four	213
Chapter Thirty-five	223
Chapter Thirty-six	229

Chapter Thirty-seven	233
Chapter Thirty-eight	236
Chapter Thirty-nine	240
Chapter Forty	244
Chapter Forty-one	247
Chapter Forty-two	251
Chapter Forty-three	258
Chapter Forty-four	260
Chapter Forty-five	265
Chapter Forty-six	270
Chapter Forty-seven	272
Chapter Forty-eight	275
Chapter Forty-nine	277
Chapter Fifty	281
Epilogue	283
Author's Note	284
Acknowledgements	285
About the Author	286

Chapter One

Alfie: April 1969

I've been here a week now; I still can't believe it. This time last month I was dodging Freddie Hodge and his bullyboys on Gladstone Street; today I'm dodging German snipers on a street with three hundred steps on a Greek island. Yessss! Corporal Alfie here; reporting for duty. Well, not reporting really, as I'm on my own and I've got nobody to report to, but it's flipping fab here. If only Hodge and his lot could see me now.

Every day I've got a little bit higher up the street towards that little white stone church at the top. It's called the Kali Strata – the street that is, not the church. Mum says that good morning is '*Kalimera*', so I suppose Kali Strata is 'Good Street' and it's flipping good for exploring. She says that all these huge empty houses are ruined palladium villas. 'Like *Sunday Night At The London Palladium*?' I said and she just laughed. Not that I would know anything about *Sunday Night At The London Palladium* – Granddad would have had a fit if I'd put the telly on on a Sunday.

Most of the palladium houses are wrecked. You go in through the door and look up and see the sky, and sometimes there's a tree growing where the roof used to be and there's no sign of any Jerries – there's nowhere for them to hide. But this one looks a bit different. I've been counting. I think it's about number forty-five which is funny because we lived at forty-five in Gladstone Street. Boy, is it different.

Okay. Here goes. I have to run between the houses to keep in the shade because that sun is flipping hot – it makes the day when Granddad took us all to Llandudno, when he sat on the beach with a hankie on his head and we all came home as pink as a stick of Llandudno rock, seem like the Ice Age.

It's still got a door on, this one. Unusual. But it's the usual routine: back to the wall; crouch down below window level. My back's wet through. My shirt's sticking to me; it's the sun, not nerves – honest. Now, quickly. A kick on the door. Blimey it's heavy: it hardly budged; I'll have to use my shoulder. Ow. I'll have a flipping big bruise on that shoulder tomorrow. Creak. So much for surprising Fritz. Wow.

There's a few slats out of the window shutters and now the door's open I can just about see. What was that? Come on, Corporal Alfie, pull yourself together. You're not frightened of a lizard, are you? What if it was a scorpion?

Eurgh: a cobweb. This one's a giant one; it's flipping enormous. It just brushed my face, like that creepy stuff they had on the ghost train at Southport. Blimey: look where it's coming from. That old chandelier looks like a spirit ship, the *Marie Celeste* or something. I wonder if one of those giant Symos spiders Mum's been telling me about wove that web.

I'm not supposed to be calling her Mum at the moment. It's 'Sis' or 'Maggie'. It's our little game we're having with Bobby Charlton and all the locals. Mum says she'll sort it out when we're settled in, but she says remember Gladstone Street. How could I forget Gladstone Street? I'll call her Grannie, Aunty or even flipping Sandie Shaw if it means not going back there and having to dodge Hodge. Dodge Hodge! I'm a poet now.

Okay. Deep breath. Tiptoe. Sneak to that room on the right. Better chuck a grenade through the door first. Boom! Wave the dust away. No. All's clear.

All right, now where? Wow: look at that staircase. Huge stone steps. And that iron stair rail is like something out of a town hall or museum or something – all twisted metal branches and iron leaves. Mum would like that. She likes old stuff. She seems to like Bobby and he's pretty old.

Are you going up, Corporal Alfie? I'm not sure. There goes that blinking scuttly thing again. What if it *is* a scorpion? Come on. Be brave. You're Corporal Alfie VC,

Give Me Your Tomorrow

and you don't get the flipping VC for being scared of creepy crawlies unless it's the Very Cowardy Custard – but that would be the VCC. I put a hand on the rail. I take a first step. Uh-oh. That rail's a bit wobbly. Crash. Oh no! The whole thing's come down and I'm stood here with the noise ringing in my ears and covered in white dust; I look like I've just come down from that chandelier to haunt the place.

Hang on. *That* bang wasn't a flipping scorpion. That was coming from upstairs. Blimey. I don't like this. Time to scarper.

I come back into the daylight and all I can hear is ring, ring, ring, clang, clang, clang. It must be twelve o'clock. I think there must be two hundred churches in this place. At least it sounds like it. Mum will be shouting me soon.

'Alfie. Alfie. Time to head back now.'

Speak of the devil. I'm down those steps in world-record time. I'm not Corporal Alfie now. I'm a fox being chased by a pack of baying hounds. Will I make it in time? Or will I be ripped to pieces?

Phew. Here she is.

I jump the last couple of steps and Mum catches me. She's got a big smile on her face. She's pleased to see me.

'So how many Germans did you flush out today, Corporal?' she asks.

'None, Mum. I didn't get a sniff of one.'

She takes a hankie out of her pocket and dampens it on her tongue before rubbing my face with it.

'Look at you. They'll think I've been sending you up chimneys,' she says.

She takes my hand and we head off back to the cottage. There's only one route. Round the harbour we go. I skip to keep up with her. She's not very big, Mum – she's not much taller than me and I'm nearly five feet tall now – not bad for a nine-year-old – but she can sure walk fast in those Jesus sandals. I think she does it to get past all those fishermen and the waiters in the tavernas. I wonder if they know that she can speak Greek and she knows what they say about her. I ask her what they are saying and she always says 'Nothing' or 'They are having a joke'; but I can tell she doesn't like it as she slows back down again when we get away from the town and onto the path.

I leave her now. I fly along the track. Arms out – I'm a Spitfire seeking out enemy bunkers and clearing the way for the Lancaster bombers. Neeeeaaaoooo. Boom. Just closed in on a bunker. Direct hit. Got to be careful now. There's lots of flipping potholes on this patch. Nearly home.

Home's a whitewashed cottage. It's in a fab spot. We're right at the end of a headland surrounded by sea that's as blue as an Everton jersey. *And* we've got our own island. Mum says the sea is 'pellucid', whatever that means. She's always using big words, Mum.

We've got three rooms and Mum says we're going to be here for a year. A year without school. Yippee. Well, maybe. Mum says that she's going to teach me to start with and, if we settle in, I can go to Greek school after the summer holidays, but that's not for at least a few months.

I've got the smallest room. There's enough space for a bed and a chest of drawers. Mum's got a room with a double bed. She's got a wardrobe and French windows. The windows open onto a stone terrace and there's a canvas canopy like a big sail over it so the terrace is like the deck of Bluebeard's galleon. Ahoy captain. Redcoats on the starboard bow. Raise the Jolly Roger.

Bobby loves those French windows. He made more fuss of those flipping windows and that terrace when he showed us around than he did of anything else. We've got one more room. When you come in through the front door you come into it. It's a big space with a big black fireplace – maybe Mum *will* send me up the chimney. At the back there's a sink under a window where you can see the path back to the harbour. Mum says the path looks like a scar running down a pirate's face. I think it looks like a path. We've got a wooden

Give Me Your Tomorrow

kitchen table with a red-and-white checked cover, four dining chairs and a comfy lumpy (I'm a poet again) red sofa. The ceilings are low but we aren't that big so we're not going to bump our heads. We've got an oven, but it's not electric like at home and I have to bring in sticks and wood for it. Oh and we've got a bath. It's tin and it hangs on the wall.

We've got to be careful with water, Mum says. She says that it comes from the water tank up on the hill and that a lorry will fill it up once a month, but I haven't seen a lorry yet and I haven't seen any rain apart from that day when we arrived. You should see the flipping toilet! Pawhh. It's in a little stone shed outside at the end of the garden (it's not really a garden) and there's just a plank with a hole in it. I have to hang on with one hand when I go or I could end up falling in. I have to hold my nose with the other. Mum says Granddad would call it a thunder box.

But we have got electricity. We've got a generator that Bobby filled with petrol. We've got no TV but I've got my radio and Mum's got her record player, and she says they will have the same batteries here in Greece so I don't need to worry about them running out. That would be flipping awful.

So here we are. Mum says it's still the Swinging Sixties and she may not have gone to San Francisco and she's not wearing a flower in her hair but now she's free she's going to 'fly like a bird'.

Chapter Two

Maggie: One week earlier

Almost there. It's only been a couple of days but it seems like a month since we left Liverpool, and now I'm here on the good ship *Symos* – or good ferry *Symos* – ostensibly reading a magazine but really trying to take everything in. We're on the top deck in the cheap seats (where else would you find Maggie Johnson?). At least *I* am on the top deck. I don't know where Alfie is. Gone to explore. Alfie gone exploring? Surprise, surprise.

The boat is full and I'm sitting on one of the two-seater benches on the port side with my back to the rail so I can see everything that's going on. Fascinating, it is. The centre of the deck with all the rows of long benches facing the front is packed with locals chattering away beneath the shade of the canopy. So animated they are, with their extravagant hand gestures and their faces full of character lined like road maps. It's a million miles from Kirkdale. All those black dresses with black headscarves – it's like a widows' convention up here. There's a fair few priests too with their long beards and stovepipe hats. Maybe they are monks. There's a monastery on the island (I've been doing my homework). I think there may be just one or two more of us. By us, I mean pale-faced northern Europeans – not English. I haven't heard an English voice since the stewardess wished us luck as we left the plane.

No wonder nobody else chose to sit here. Those fumes from the funnel remind me of the time when Dad drove through the Mersey Tunnel and his window jammed open and me and Alfie were gasping for air like a couple of trout fresh out of the river.

I love the rhythmic thrum of the engine: it seems to come and go in time with the waves; it's almost hypnotic. There are plenty of kids on the deck too. At least there were a few minutes ago.

I turn towards the staircase and see Alfie's head

Give Me Your Tomorrow

coming into view. As he reaches the top he starts to march forward. He's singing.

'The animals came in two by two, hurrah, hurrah. The animals came in two by two, hurrah, hurrah. The animals came in two by two – the goat, the sheep and the chickens too ...'

I smile as I see beyond him. I'm fascinated by the small band of ragamuffin followers that he has acquired. They're skipping along in step with their new leader.

'Here comes the Pied Piper.'

Alfie stops. 'What?'

I point. 'Look behind you.'

He turns to see the group of little Greeks whose curiosity has been piqued by the sight of this strange, foreign, singing, freckled boy.

'Shoo,' he says gently. There's not a nasty bone in my Alfie.

The children giggle, but they get the message and set off back to their families.

'What's with the song?' I ask him.

'It's like Noah's Ark down there, Mum. They wouldn't let me onto the bottom deck, but I could see it from the steps and it's got loads of crates of stuff in the middle and then there's a couple of pens full of goats and sheep and crates with live chickens in. There's a few dogs tied up too, and at the back there's two old bangers like out of the Keystone Kops and a brilliant five hundred Norton that looks brand-new.'

'What's on the other deck?' I ask.

'It's just seating and there's a man selling drinks at a little bar.'

'Do *you* want a drink?'

'No, I'm okay for now,' he says, sitting down beside me.

Facing the front in the nearest seat to us there's a young man. Thin-faced and with a pencil moustache, he's immaculately dressed in a black suit and white shirt with a red-and-silver striped tie. He's wearing shiny black shoes and a black homburg hat.

Quite a looker, I think, and I blush as he turns, smiles and, doffing his hat, says, '*Kalispera.*'

Damn. I wish he hadn't seen me looking. I smile shyly and suddenly find my feet very interesting. I notice a small case beneath his seat with a shiny new motorcycle helmet resting on top.

Oblivious to our shared glances, Alfie stands in front of me and, flexing his tiny biceps, sings, 'I'm Popeye the Sailor Man, toot toot.'

I respond automatically; it's an old game. 'You come from the Isle of Man, toot toot.'

Straining to see over Alfie's shoulder, I realise that I've already been passed over by my potential admirer, who is now engrossed in conversation with a dark-haired beauty in the seat in front.

I shrug. 'Sit down now, sunshine. I think that's the island.' I point straight across the boat.

'Blimey, Mum. It's hilly.'

I have a little smile to myself. 'Blimey' was banned in our household. Dad had explained that it was a contraction of the blasphemous 'God blind me', shortened to 'Cor blimey' and then to just 'Blimey'. Disgraceful! But I'm setting the rules now, and Alfie will be allowed the occasional 'Blimey' and 'Flipping heck', although that's the limit. Any really bad stuff and he'll know about it.

As the distant island comes into view, Alfie studies the barren and mountainous terrain, sparsely dotted with an occasional speck of green. 'You sure that's it?' he asks.

'No. It can't be.' I say. 'It looks uninhabited. I can't see any houses.'

I turn to an old lady seated behind the young man. She's carefully guarding three chickens crammed into a tiny wooden cage on her knee. I point. 'Symos?'

The woman gives a gap-toothed grin and nods. '*Nai.*'

My heart sinks a little. It's not quite the beauty that I had been expecting, but at least the sky and the sea are blue and, even though it is only April, it's much hotter than a late spring day in England. The sea has been calm and the sky has been clear throughout the journey, yet as our destination moves ever closer we see banks of dark thunderclouds gathering above the island's mountaintops.

'That sky looks a bit worrying,' I say.

But Alfie's not listening. His attention has been grabbed by a far more interesting distraction. 'Mum, look!' he says, rushing forward to the front of the deck and leaning on the rail. He points down to the sea.

I leave my seat to join him and my eyes follow his arm to where he is pointing, just ahead of the bow. For a second I see nothing and then, 'Wow. How beautiful!'

Fellow passengers line up along the rail gesturing excitedly in the direction of the waves, anxious to catch a glimpse of the silver creatures as they break the surface in unison. They watch spellbound as, in perfect harmony and symmetry, these sailors' companions with their fixed smiles lead the ferry towards the fast-approaching island as if towing us to port on invisible gossamer threads.

'Well, that's a lot different from Liverpool,' Alfie comments.

'What do you mean?'

'We've got the Mersey Pilot. Symos has the Aegean dolphins,' he jokes.

As the ferry approaches a headland, the dolphins make one final leap before turning away, one right, one left, to find another diversion. As they do so, I'm sure that the creature on our side of the boat gives us a playful wink.

'That was just magic,' I say. 'And, speaking of magic ... look.'

As we passed the headland, the boat had changed course and veered starboard into a channel. By now the black clouds that had covered the mountain have rolled across the whole island, but there are one or two small gaps tinged with silver edges through which shafts of sunlight shine like spotlights. And there at the end of the channel, caught in the spotlights, is a harbour filled with boats. Rising above it, banks of fine honey-coloured Palladian houses are lit up one by one as the sun's rays move across the scene.

Any disappointment that I had felt on our first view of Symos evaporates as I take in the beauty before me.

Alfie stands wide-eyed and open-mouthed. For once he is lost for words.

Chapter Three

Nico

I am always the first to arrive to meet the ferry.

Today is no different; I am standing in my usual position at the disembarking point. It will be half an hour before the ferry docks, so there is time to relax. I sit on a bollard.

'Good afternoon,' I say as Mrs Constanides arrives and stands in front of me, holding that dog-eared white card that reads:

> DOMATIA
> ROOMS WITH HARBOR VIEW
> ZIMMER FREI
> CHAMBRES A LOUER

The old lady acknowledges me briefly and then concentrates on the ferry, which has rounded the headland and is now in view.

Mrs Constanides's card never ceases to amuse me. I know those crummy rooms. They are in a back street reached by a very steep climb up the hill. Standing on the toilet seat and peering through a pane of dirty frosted glass would be the only way of taking in a view of the harbour. 'Always respect your elders', that's what Momma says, and however much it annoys me, Mrs Constanides is certainly my elder. So too are Mr Sioufas, Mr Fotouplos, Mrs Stefanidis and the thirty others who, as always, muscle their way to the front clutching their precious cards.

As the ferry is about to dock, the sky turns to night when the first bolt of lightning strikes the mountains and the clouds spill their load in a tumultuous burst. For a bunch of geriatrics, the island welcoming party can certainly move with some speed, and I smile as they flee the quayside to the lean-to waiting room.

Unfazed by the rain, I stand alone with my own

welcoming card. There's no 'Zimmer Frei' for me. I hold my large magazine-cover-sized photo of the cottage in front of me. The photo is wrapped in a protective layer of heavy transparent plastic as I have lost the precious negative for this particularly brilliant and irreplaceable shot. Despite its thick protection, there is no mistaking my sparklingly white single-storey villa overlooking the clearest, brightest and gaudiest blue sea you could ever dream of seeing. It would not look out of place on the front of the most exclusive travel magazine.

The gangplank is lowered, and as the deluge continues unabated, my shirt and my trousers cling to my skin and my hair is plastered to my forehead. But I am not going to be deterred. This is the first time I've been at the front and I am going to make the most of it. I look up to see the first passenger at the head of the gangplank anxiously awaiting the stevedore's final all-clear – a pretty young woman of perhaps around eighteen or nineteen. Maybe she'll need a cottage.

I see her say something to a child she's with and then, using a magazine as a makeshift umbrella, she rushes headlong down the gangplank towards me. It looks like she has got her eyes on my photo and wants to make sure that she reaches me before her fellow travellers see the wonderful property that I've got on offer.

'British?' I ask – although it could not have been more obvious if she had come down the gangplank waving a Union Jack and singing 'God Save the Queen'.

'Yes,' she responds.

'Welcome to Symos, young lady. You like my cottage?'

What a relief. We can communicate. And, even more of a relief, the deluge has stopped and the sky is already starting to lighten again.

'I love the *look* of your cottage. How much is it?' It is a guarded response.

I pull her gently to one side to allow the other disembarking passengers to pass, and as I do I notice the soft whiteness of her skin.

'Good. The price is very good.'

'Yes, but how much?'

'How long you want to stay?'

'Six morns,' she says holding up six digits.

I'm confused. 'Six morns?' That's not a word I know. Six nights maybe, but I have never heard of six morns.

'No, no,' she says, shaking her head. 'Six months! Months!'

I cannot believe my luck. After being jostled out of position through respecting that cantankerous old bunch time after time, week after week, I have finally found my rightful place and with it has come the perfect tenant. They can all fight among themselves for the rest of the year now. I cast an eye on the group of oldies busily assailing the other passengers with their sales pitches.

'Six months,' I repeat. 'Six months!' My face creases into a smile. I can't hide my delight. 'Oh yes,' I say. 'A very good price. A very, *very* good price.'

She hasn't asked all the usual sensible questions, such as: 'Where is the cottage?' 'How many rooms?' 'What about the cooking facilities?' She must have fallen in love with the photo (well, it is a beautiful place; who wouldn't?) and her instinct has told her that the place is going to be just right.

'Wait!' she says, turning back towards the gangplank. The child is sitting patiently on a pile of luggage at its top. She waves to summon him down. He looks puzzled and shrugs as if to say, 'What about the stuff?'

'Your brother?' I ask, looking at the little boy. He's about ten.

'Yep, that's Alfie.' She seems a little flustered by all the noise going on around us. 'That's him.'

'Nicos Karteras – Nico,' I say.

'And I'm Maggie Johnson.'

We shake hands. I think she's just as nervous as I am.

I call a porter across, tip him a few drachma and ask him to bring down the Johnsons' baggage. As the porter loads his trolley, Alfie comes down to join us at the foot of the gangplank.

Maggie ruffles Alfie's hair. 'Alfie, this is Mr Karteras. He's going to be our landlord. And Mr Karteras, this is Alfie, my lovely little brother.'

I bow politely and offer my hand. 'Welcome to Symos, Master Johnson.'

And so the deal is done right there on the quayside: no more than ten minutes after the gangplank has been lowered by the ferry crew, I've got tenants. And I don't have to go through that uncivilised scramble for another six months. Six months! Hallelujah.

As we shake hands, we are disturbed by the throaty roar of a motorcycle as a smart young man disembarks the ferry and flies along the quayside in style.

'Wow!' says Alfie.

Maggie smiles and her eyes follow the bike along the harbour with a face that says 'Wow!' too.

'Wow,' I respond unenthusiastically. Bloody show-off! I think.

As night is drawing in, it's too late to take the track to the cottage, so I agree to find the pair a room in lodgings and walk them down to Mrs Andreas's on the quayside. It's clean and welcoming and Mrs A never interferes, no fussing. In the morning I will be back to take them to the home of their dreams.

~

What a day! What a wonderful day! It was about time that I had some luck. It's the best thing that's happened since I don't know when. Perhaps things have finally changed for the better since Easter. It was only a couple of weeks ago that we did the Apollo Extravaganza on Good Friday and since then I've heard about nothing but. It seemed to touch everyone on the island, even if it wasn't enough to stop the mob elbowing me out at the ferry. 'Wow, Nico,' they say, patting me on the back and offering to buy me a Metaxa or an ouzo. 'How did you come up with the idea of that rocket flying straight at St Spiro's spire?' they ask, or 'How did you divert it at the

Give Me Your Tomorrow

last minute?' or 'How did you get the whole harbour to light up like it was floodlit?' I've even had a couple of old folk blaming me for damaging their hearing aids. 'Look,' I say. 'If you think that was special, wait until you see what I've got planned for the moon landing. The days when all you got was a few sparklers, a tonne of dynamite and two months of your ears feeling like they're inside St Spiro's bell tower are gone.'

Thank God for that display. It took six months to prepare, and if I hadn't had that to keep me busy, I'd have been on my own in my tiny bedroom under a very, very black cloud. But even I have to admit that it was a bit special. I thought last year's display with the old boats burning like funeral pyres was original, but this one made that look like something a Turk could have created. And now not only have I got the summer fireworks for the Apollo moon landing to prepare, but the cottage is rented for six months. Six months! And what a tenant! She's very young – no more than twenty I guess. Very pretty, blonde hair, tiny – less than one metre fifty probably. Pity she's got her little brother with her. Don't know why I'm thinking that; she's way too young for me and why would she be interested in a podgy forty-year-old? Why indeed? At least there'll be a bit of money coming in now.

Maybe her brother likes fireworks. What a shame they arrived in Symos a week after the show. They could have seen for themselves the brilliance, artistry and nerve – yes, nerve – of Nicos Karteras, the master fireworks maker. But at least I had some luck when God created His own fireworks as the ferry docked and old Fotouplos and his gang ran for shelter. One chance, that's all I needed. Like a monsoon it was. Thank you God. Over in a few minutes but it must have dumped a month's worth of rain on the island. Most of it on me.

Chapter Four

Maggie

After a restless night, we awake to the light streaming through the shuttered windows. I leap out of bed, draw back the curtains and open the shutters to let the full power of Greece into our lives. I'm dazzled and screw up my eyes. Not quite a rainy Monday in Liverpool.

Last night we stayed in a small bed and breakfast right on the Yiossos quayside. I gaze down at a procession of small boats heading into the harbour, their decks piled with boxes of glistening silver cargo that just a few hours earlier had shoaled in moonlit waters. Other craft laden with bread, fruits, vegetables and bottles are heading out the opposite way, perhaps filled with provisions for the isolated settlements we saw dotted around the coast.

The noise, the light and the movement! Fascinating. I catch a glimpse of Nico sitting waiting on a black iron bollard an hour ahead of the allocated time. At least I think he's an hour early. Have I got the time right? I check my watch. Yes. He's way too early. He looks up and I think he catches sight of me before I turn away. Oh dear. Not a good start. What on earth will he think if he saw these winceyette pyjamas? I'm embarrassed, but relieved that he's keen, and punctual, and hasn't had a change of heart.

The room that we shared last night is high-ceilinged and clean; two wrought-iron and brass beds and a huge mahogany armoire leave room for little else other than a marble-topped table that supports a Victorian ceramic washbasin and a jug of clean cold water. There's an enormous electric fan which Alfie's convinced came from a helicopter. It gives the room a degree of comfort, but it will be a scorcher today compared to home. Somebody has hung a long yellow flypaper under the fan and it's coated with a liberal sprinkling of the local fauna. I shiver as I see some of the stuff it has snared. I suppose we'll have to get used to that sort of thing. The family groups in the large brown-framed sepia photographs peering sternly down on us from the walls would think me a real sissy if they had seen me standing on the bed last night while Alfie chased some monstrous bug around the floor. He was trying to catch it alive under a glass but it wouldn't fit, and (ahem) *unfortunately* he managed to decapitate it.

There's a knock at the door. Nico has arranged for Mrs Andreas to deliver breakfast to the room – that must be it.

'Alfie, answer the door.'

He opens the door but there's nobody there.

'Must have been a ghost, Mum,' he says and then looks down. A tray loaded with the freshest bread, some butter, jam, two glasses of orange juice and two tiny cups of treacly black coffee. The food is welcome and we devour it like a couple of ravenous beasts.

'I've made a jam buttie,' says Alfie. Home from home.

'Eat up, sunshine,' I say. 'There's a long day ahead.'

Dressing is easy. There's not a huge choice – an outfit of white vest and socks, black plimsolls and grey-flannel shorts held up by his favourite snake-head-buckle belt for Alfie. I choose a multicoloured long-sleeved cotton kaftan over flared white cotton trousers and a pair of tan sling-back sandals with a low heel. I top the outfit with a small red peaked cap. We deliberately travelled light. Although we plan to be away for well over six months, we can add to our wardrobes during the stay; I wanted plenty of room for my books, my portable record player and my small collection of LPs, and of course Alfie's toys, books and radio.

'Ready, sunshine?' I ask, giving the room a final check over for forgotten possessions.

'Ready, Mum. But Mu-um? Before we meet Nico, what was all that "little brother" stuff?'

I tighten my lips and raise an eyebrow in thought. After a pause, I say, 'Remember Gladstone Street?'

Alfie nods. He needs no further explanation.

John Brassey

Before leaving the lodgings, I seek out Mrs Andreas to thank her for her hospitality and pay for the stay, but Nico has already settled the account. We spill onto the harbour and fill our lungs with the scent of sea, fish and kerosene.

'*Kalimera*, Nico,' I greet our new landlord warmly, more confident of my linguistic skills after a sleep, albeit a fitful one.

'Good morning, Miss Johnson. Good morning, Master Johnson,' is the pleasant response.

'Alfie and Maggie, please,' I correct him.

'Sorry.' Nico smiles. 'Good morning, Maggie. Good morning, Alfie.'

With more time and with sunshine replacing the murk of the previous evening, I am able to study Nico more closely. He's about five foot ten. I barely noticed those kind brown eyes last night. They're unquestionably his redeeming feature; Nico is certainly no Greek god. His black hair has receded, leaving the top of his head bald, and attempts have been made to conceal this with a flimsy comb-over. His face is clean-shaven. Indeed, there are few signs on his round and double-chinned face of the five o'clock shadow that many of his compatriots seem to wear all day. His shoulders and chest are not broad, but his waistline is. I guess that he is about fifty. He's dressed in the white short-sleeved shirt and black trousers that seem to be the uniform of many Greeks; he could be a waiter, a banker or a clerk in a post office. His neatly manicured hands, with no sign of the usual nicotine stains that I've noticed a lot during our short adventure, aren't those of a fisherman or labourer.

Before we set off, Nico goes into a shop. A few minutes later he returns.

'A gift for you, Alfie,' he says, proffering a large sponge.

As presents go, I bet Alfie thinks that this one is on a par with the embroidered handkerchiefs and socks that his nana considered an appropriate Christmas present for a little boy when everyone else at school was getting an Action Man. But he is well brought up (thank goodness) and puts on a grateful expression.

For a second he probably wonders if Nico is trying to tell him that he needs a good wash, but then Nico continues, 'This *is* Symos.'

I can almost see the cogs working in Alfie's brain. 'What on earth is Nico talking about?' he'll be thinking as he looks up at me with that puzzled expression of his. He's not old enough to get what Nico's trying to say. All he can see is a sponge, and even if it might be slightly island-shaped, he won't have a clue.

Nico crouches down so that he is at eye level with Alfie. He points around and above the harbour at the magnificent Venetian style-buildings in a sweeping gesture.

'See these?' he says. 'All of these and these and these are built from sponges. Every one.'

This will confuse him more. 'Sponge houses?' Alfie screws up his face and whistles. 'What happens when it rains?'

I'm laughing at his incredulity. I need to step in. 'Nico means that they were all built with money from selling sponges.'

'Ah.' The penny drops. Alfie takes the sponge from Nico.

'Yes, Alfie. The most important animal in Greece,' says Nico.

'Animal?' Alfie thinks out loud. 'It doesn't look like an animal to me. It looks like a giant Crunchie bar with the chocolate licked off.'

'Now *you'll* be confusing Nico. He won't know about Crunchies. And even if he does, it's only you who licks all the chocolate off.'

But Nico is clearly passionate about sponges. It's obviously more than just a passing interest. 'Yes. We hunt this animal.'

This is becoming even more of a riddle. Alfie's attention moves beyond the houses of the harbour to the barren, rugged hillsides 'Do you chase them with dogs?' he says and I smile, imagining a crowd of Greeks with rifles and a pack of hounds chasing a panting sponge across the dusty terrain.

'We hunt them in the sea,' Nico says and quickly adds, 'We dive for them.'

The penny finally starts to drop for Alfie.

It's time to clear things up for him or we'll never get to this cottage. 'Nico's right, Alfie. It *is* an animal,' I say. 'I've read about them and I'll tell you more when we get time. And speaking of time, let's get going.'

And so starts our adventure proper. Despite his less than athletic physique, Nico manages to manoeuvre the trunk that holds most of my worldly goods onto his shoulder and wedges my hard-cased suitcase beneath his arm. Alfie has his army-surplus haversack filled to the brim with plastic soldiers and cowboys and Indians, a radio, comics, a yo-yo and a small but well-thumbed library of books (plus a sponge). This leaves me with a small battered suitcase in each hand.

Our intrepid trio heads seaward on foot along the harbour, away from the town. Like me, Alfie's clearly fascinated by the tavernas, the sponge emporia, the fishmongers and their associated noises and smells. 'Oh look,' I say. 'An Odeon like in Liverpool.'

Alfie runs to the cinema to examine the posters. Dad hardly ever let me take him to the pictures, although even *he* couldn't find a reason for us to miss *Mary Poppins*. Alfie skips back. 'It looks more like the Fleapit than the Odeon' he says. 'Perhaps I'll take you one day ... when you can speak the language,' I joke.

There's no time to take everything in. Despite his physique Nico is moving at a fair pace. He's puffing and panting a bit and there's a huge wet patch on the back of his shirt, but in no time the sights, sounds and smells of the harbour have faded into the distance. At the old concrete pillbox guarding the entrance to the harbour, the road swings left and, after passing the immodestly named Grand Symos Hotel, it soon deteriorates into a dirt track. The track climbs gently and the sun, not yet high in the sky, has yet to completely dry the ground from last night's deluge, so we aren't signalling our presence with a dust cloud visible for miles. Early-morning April Symos temperatures are comfortable for the walk ahead.

Nico speaks very little. He is gasping a bit and his lungs must be pumping under the weight of the trunk, but he is doing his best to appear as if his ordeal is perfectly effortless and doing his utmost not to show his exhaustion. Every now and then he pauses to point out some insignificant flora and sneak a few deep breaths. I spare him embarrassment and feign real interest in gnarled olive trees and clumps of lavender. He keeps his utterances to the obvious and near monosyllabic as he walks. 'Cinema', 'Fish' and, at the pillbox, a brief imitation of heavy gunfire for Alfie's benefit is the level of conversation.

In fairness, we are pretty quiet too. It's hot, it's sticky, the path is rocky and the luggage is taking its toll. The track is narrow and warrants strict concentration. It narrows further as we pass below the water tower. Puffs of smoke come from a couple of small dwellings perched on the hillside below – evidence that we have not yet left civilisation completely behind us.

Nearing the top of the slope, Alfie turns to study the route we've taken. Although the climb has been gentle, he looks surprised 'Blimey M–aggie' – well done, son – 'look how high we've come.' We can see right across the harbour to a similar hillside directly opposite. That hillside is covered in neo-classical houses leading right down to the quay where the Rhodes ferry docked less than twenty-four hours earlier, and along the spine of the hill is a chain of six ancient windmills. The harbour is still busy with boats and on the horizon we can see a much bigger white vessel, a cruise liner probably taking well-heeled tourists on a tour of the Med. High above the harbour on a mountaintop we can make out a tiny church and a not so tiny TV mast.

Nico seizes the opportunity presented by Alfie's pause. He puts down the trunk and, despite attempts to appear nonchalant, he rests on a convenient large boulder with palpable relief. 'Take a rest,' he says. 'When you see what I show you in a moment it will take all your breath away. I have done this walk a thousand times and every time I feel the same' – I wonder if the extra two or three stone he has around his waist might contribute to that feeling – 'and I want you to share it,' he adds.

Nico points out a couple of colourful crickets and a bright-green lizard that darts across the path, but he's breathing normally now and picks his load back up and gestures for us to walk ahead. Just as our heads are almost level with the path summit he calls out, 'Stop! Stop!'

We do as we are told and come to an immediate halt.

Nico stands behind us and I feel a large soft palm across my eyes. He does the same to Alfie. 'Now ... forward,' he says.

As we take that final step he removes his hands. He's so proud of the revelation that he has presented to us, I can tell. He squeezes our shoulders and lets out a satisfied sigh. And it's not difficult to understand why he has taken such pleasure in his unveiling. Even Alfie, who is not exactly artistic, will appreciate that this is something special.

'Is that the cottage?' Alfie asks excitedly.

No need for Nico's confirmation. I squeeze Alfie's hand; there is no mistaking it from the photograph.

'It sure is, sunshine. It sure is.'

Stretching ahead and down through the barren scrub and bare white rocks, the path leads to a white cottage perched right on the edge of the headland. Apart from the cottage, the headland and a tiny island ahead of it there is nothing but blue, the deepest azure of the sea and the lighter sky blue. Even the mountains of Turkey in the far distance are a hazy blue blur. The sea is flat with just the odd white cap of spume and the occasional wake from a fishing boat heading back to port, low in the water from a successful trip.

Island would be a grandiose title for something that is little more than a plug of rock sitting in front of the cottage. It is as if God had made the headland and then, finding He had a little material left over, had dropped the surplus into the sea just off the coast. Although still distant, we can see that the only feature on this barren limestone cube is a single flat-topped tree.

Within days, no doubt, Alfie will be flying down this track towards the headland on some mission to clear German bunkers or leading a cavalry charge on a tribe of Sioux, but today he needs to watch his footing and follow closely in Nico's footsteps. On the way down to the cottage we spot plenty more of the island's wildlife, but Nico seems to have got his second breath and there's a fresh spring in his step. Lizards of all colours and sizes are prolific and most of the larger slabs of limestone dotted along the path feature one basking in the morning sun. It's not a surprise. I read how Gerald Durrell was inspired to pursue a life in zoology by the fauna of Corfu; but for Alfie, who has spent most of the last five years in Kirkdale and whose greatest adventure in his nine years was a trip to the Great Orme at Llandudno, the profusion and array of island creatures is spellbinding.

And the noise! As the sun has climbed higher and the day has grown warmer, the sound of the Mediterranean has grown with it. Alfie is mystified. He has no idea what is creating that incessant, throbbing, chirping sound and is looking everywhere for the culprits. It sounds as if every rock and every bush conceals an invisible person holding a rigid plastic comb in one hand while using the other hand to drag a knife across the teeth. Again and again and again and again. The hundred-decibel mystery will be one for him to solve during our stay.

Enchanted, exhilarated, watched by a multitude of lizards and serenaded by a host of cicadas, we make our way carefully and slowly towards our new home, which happily seems a million miles away from the last.

Chapter Five

Nico

Two miles and the trek is finally over. The white cottage, so perfect from a distance, looks a bit rundown outside on close viewing, but Maggie seems a nice young woman and I can help her to smarten things up. Where else would she find anywhere with such peace and such an amazing view?

I unlock the door, brush away a few cobwebs and put down the trunk and suitcase on the stone floor. Maggie and Alfie drop the rest of their luggage and, after a couple of minutes getting their breath back, start to explore their new home. I hear her say to Alfie what sounds like 'It's a little squaleed' but squaleed's not a word I know. Perhaps she means 'a little gem' or 'a little diamond'. She can't complain about untidiness. I've given it a thorough tidy after last year's disastrous tenants.

When they arrived on Symos, the hippies numbered just two. Two tall, slim American girls wearing jeans, T-shirts and bandanas spotted my photo and followed the same track as Maggie and Alfie. A deal was done, and those two pretty faces, those sirens had me wrapped around their fingers for two weeks. They were real beauties and were so nice whenever they wanted anything from me. Carol was a blonde like Maggie (but so unlike Maggie); Joan a brunette. I thought maybe, just maybe, they saw something in me.

There are very few young women left on this island. Most families left before the war when the sponge industry collapsed, and unless I want to marry cousin Agatha (and I don't) I've no chance of romance. Retiring sea captains and sailors tend to come back to set up home, and young people with ambition tend to leave. This leaves us with an island of old men and a shortage of women. So why am I still here? To care for my mother. It's my fault she's a widow and I owe it to her to stay. I can't abandon her. So I haven't joined my old friends and relatives in Australia and the USA.

Those women! They had me for their lapdog for two weeks. I would struggle along the path laden down with provisions, following the two of them sauntering along carrying nothing but a couple of flowers. Like fragrant carrots on sticks, blatantly raising my hopes with charm and flattery that dwindled with every step we got closer to the cottage and evaporated completely upon arrival.

'Nico, you're an angel. Nico, you're a star,' they would say, while I – a love-struck fool carrying three bags and somehow balancing a case of wine – struggled behind them.

'It's no problem, ladies. No problem!' I would wheeze. My only minor compensation? A couple of miles to concentrate on their incredibly cute little bottoms.

'Nico, darling, about the rent ...'
'Yes?'
'Will next week be okay?'

That's what they were like. And stupid me – what did I say?

'No problem, ladies. No problem.' Exhausted, I would have no breath left for talking and simply follow like a bee enticed by the prospect of honey.

But there was no honey.

'Thanks so much, Nico,' they'd smile as I struggled onto the terrace and carefully placed my burden on the table. 'See you soon. Bye now.'

And without even a glass of water or time to catch my breath, I would be bundled back through the gate and off on the long path back to Yiossos.

I tried to impress. 'Any jobs need doing, ladies?' 'Would you like me to take you around the island in a boat?' And they brazenly played upon it. 'We'll see.' 'Maybe next time.' After just a week, they negotiated another week for free, pointing out some minor damage by way of justification. And I'm sure that damage wasn't there when they moved in.

'You know we asked about delaying the rent, Nico?'
'Yes.'

'Well, look, Nico, this window's broken.'
'If you forget this week's rent, we'll call it a quits.'//

And I fell for it! What a mug. A pushover all my life. 'Here to please' was, and still is, my motto. I lived up to it, but even I started to realise that sometimes I was being taken for a ride.

A couple of weeks into the girls' stay, I was sipping an ouzo in a quayside taverna and watching the Rhodes ferry dock. I noticed Carol waiting near the gangplank and then saw Joan stroll down to join her. Maybe they wanted to watch the landlords' and landladies' mêlée, or to check timetables? And then I saw them. A couple of long-haired young men lolled down the gangplank and onto the island. The girls were clearly delighted. Hugs and kisses all round.

One of the men was dressed in a pair of jeans with stars and stripes patches, the other in blue-denim dungarees. Both had guitars slung over their shoulders. I spluttered into my ouzo. This had never been part of the deal.

I thought that if they had been Greek youths with hair like that they would have been open to whistles and howls of derision as they walked along the harbour, before being summarily marched to the local barber for swift and severe correction. But they were visitors and I believe strongly in promoting the image of Greek hospitality to strangers. We're renowned for it throughout the world. So I kept my thoughts to myself, though horrified at the desecration of a national flag on a pair of jeans. I imagine that a pair of Greek-flag jeans would easily result in a charge of treason and quite possibly a stretch in jail.

So, with sinking heart, my faint hopes of a summer of romance disappeared just a few weeks after they had been raised.

Hippies had been visiting the Greek islands for a number of years and had been tolerated, if not exactly welcomed, on some islands. Those who arrived on Symos tended to depart within a few days; the land is

Give Me Your Tomorrow

barren and the lack of fresh water makes camping impossible. But somehow, *somehow* I, Nicos Karteras, had managed to give a group of them a toehold on our island. Was this all of them? How many more might arrive on the next ferry? How popular would I be on Symos if I were to house a commune of long-haired layabouts?

Now I thought about it, the girls were constantly 'borrowing' money from me to use the payphone in the Grand Hotel.

'Oh, Nico, there you are. Nico, we've been looking for you. Do you have any of those fifties we need for the phone?'

And I always obliged, offering a handful of coins.

'Nico, darling, you're an angel.'

I smiled and kept my hand open for a note to replace the coins, but the girls would turn and, giggling to each other, head for the hotel with a parting shot: 'Thanks, Nico. You're so cool.'

'That's another two days' rent,' I would think.

They never seemed to have any change, and I had probably returned quite a few more days' rent in helping them to fund their calls. Had I paid for them to summon a horde of hippies to descend on our idyllic whitewashed cottage?

On arriving to collect the rent later the next day, the door was opened by one of the men. I could hear giggles in the background and, peering behind the young man's shoulder, I caught a glimpse of Carol. She was totally naked. The man's manner was distinctly strange and I smelt an unfamiliar pungent sweet odour that reminded me of the priest's incense.

'Hey, man. You Nico?' The man was slurring his words as if drunk. A thin hand-rolled cigarette hung from his lips. 'Good to meet you, man. I'm Tom. The chicks have told us all about you. Want a drag?' He offered me the cigarette.

'No, thank you, I've come for the rent.'

Tom was very slow in his response and looked at me

vacantly. 'Rent? Yeah, man, rent. Hmmm.' He slapped his jeans pockets.

I am not stupid. I may not have experienced it myself, but I knew straight away what was going on. That was enough. There's no way I was letting the Karteras family be associated with drugs, even as innocent dupes. I'd already brought shame on us for renting to the 'sinful cohabiting Americans' (it's a small island; news travels fast). If these drugs were discovered, life would be impossible for us.

But as well as wishing to preserve the Karteras family reputation, I didn't want to see the foreign visitors end up in jail. The hippies had to go, but they had to go without anyone knowing about the pot and without any big rows. I'm not a tough guy. I would do anything to avoid confrontation. And so I formed a plan.

The island abounds with fauna – the lizards, the cicadas, the birds. But another bountiful resident of the island is the Symos spider. This hairy beast is harmless but extremely scary to anyone with even the slightest degree of arachnophobia. About four inches across and easily covering the palm of a hand, the thick-legged creature is very much like a tarantula in appearance. Few visitors ever see the spiders, but having spent my entire life on the island, I know exactly where to find them. With the assistance of a few of my fireworks helpers, I soon found plenty. And when I had built up a collection of thirty of the fearsome arachnids, I put my plan into action.

I realised that the daily routine at the cottage revolved around little more than rising after noon, the occasional dip in the sea, some token cooking of vegetables, playing guitars, smoking marijuana and going back to bed. The hippies knew our Greek drug laws and the serious penalties for those caught, but they made no attempts to conceal their smoking pot from me. They guessed that I'm not the sort to shop them and they tended to have a stoned look for a lot of the time when I was around working on the fence around the villa, although they made sure that they were totally clear-headed whenever they needed to visit the town for provisions. So I waited until such a visit. I was pretty sure that the enforced abstinence would lead to a binge that evening – and I was right.

It was dark when I arrived back at the cottage. I could hear the drawling voices, the giggles and the irregular strumming of the guitars, and I could smell the marijuana smoke wafting from the open windows. Thirty of my very ugly, hairy arachnid friends should certainly do the trick.

And so came the release. Peering cautiously through the rear window, I could see that all four of my guests were sitting together on the stone floor with their backs resting and heads lolling against the sofa. They were clearly spaced out. Fifteen spiders were gently dropped into the room and they immediately scuttled across the floor in the direction of my guests. I then crept around to the front and let the remaining fifteen scurry in through the open front door, directly towards the hippies' bare feet.

It was a matter of less than a minute before the first 'What the fuck? Man! What the fuck?', followed by screams and a speed of activity previously unseen in any of them. In a flurry of stars and stripes jeans, blue dungarees, guitars, bandanas and a couple of rucksacks the foursome were smoked (or perhaps I should say spidered) out of the cottage and managed to make it to Yiossos harbour in record time with only the moon to illuminate their path. The last I heard of them was that they had been seen around the ferry terminal complaining loudly about what sounded like 'badtreep, man, badtreep'.

I brush a spider's web from my arm and smile as I recall my last tenants' hasty departure. Thankfully, Maggie doesn't look like a hippy, and with a little brother with her I can see that she will be no trouble at all.

Chapter Six

Alfie

It doesn't take long to explore the three rooms, and we are soon making plans.

My room is at the back of the house and my small window looks out onto the fenced plot behind and, in the distance, the mountain above the harbour.

I've got a single bed. It's not bouncy like the one at home – so no acrobatics here. The bed's got wooden slats under the mattress. It's a flipping heavy bed and I can't budge it.

'What do you think, Alfie? Comfy?' Mum asks.

'Fab,' I say. Even if it's as comfy as a flipping bed of nails, I don't want to disappoint her. I decide that nobody could possibly believe there's room for a POW to squeeze below its bottom rail and start an escape tunnel, but, defying all the laws of science and with a good deal of breathing in, I soon manage to wriggle my way under. It's yet another brilliant place to play.

Mum says the three-drawer pine chest is more than adequate for my small supply of shorts, underpants and vests and I can keep my collection of toy soldiers in the bottom drawer too. My books can stand on the top, alongside a photo of Nana and Granddad.

On the wall above the chest in a wooden frame there's a big faded brown photograph of a family – a man with a big moustache dressed in a smart suit with his wife (I guess) in a long dark dress over a light blouse with an old-fashioned collar and three kids, two boys and a girl. The kids are dressed up too. Sunday best. It has to be. They must have had their photo taken before going to church. 'What do you think of "The Sundays"?' I ask Mum. She smiles. She knows what I mean. 'Careful what you say, sunshine,' she says, 'they may well be Nico's relations.'

There's another piece of art in the room on the wall above my headboard. Mum says it's an icon. It's not all a painting but some of it is a painting. It's Mary and baby Jesus and it looks like it's made of gold and silver foil with the only painting just a cut-out of their faces. It's flipping old.

Mum also has one of these over her bed. Hers is Christ on the cross and again there is a gold-foil halo and silver body and background with Jesus's face the only painted part of the picture.

In the living room there are no icons, thank goodness. I don't want to feel like we're living in a church. But there are more of those big brown family photos. On one side of the fireplace there's a whiskery old man and on the other there's a lady who looks like our old headmistress. She's got a stare to kill a boy at fifty paces and her flipping eyes follow me all around the room. I'll have to behave in here; probably two more of the Sundays.

We finish exploring the lodgings pretty quickly – there's only three rooms, after all. We step back into the sunshine to check out the outside. Nico is standing by the little white fence that surrounds the property. Mum says it's a 'picket' fence. And I say, 'Did Nico pick it?' She pats me on the bum and groans.

Nico says, 'You will not find another fence like this in Symos. I see one in an American magazine about Cape Cod.' He swells up and looks like a kid at school waiting for the teacher to tell him what a good boy he's been. 'All stones,' he says, pointing to the ground. And he's got a point. It must have been some job hammering those posts in.

'Wow, Nico. What a lovely fence,' Mum says. She's great like that, Mum. Always knows what to say. A diplomat, Granddad calls her, whatever that is.

Nico beams. She's worked her magic again.

At the far end of the fenced area behind the property (it's not really a garden, as it is no different to the land outside the fence) is the toilet. Mum says there's no need for Nico to explain and tells him that Granddad and Nana once took her on holiday to a cottage in the Lake

District where water came from a well at the end of the garden and the toilet was just like this. 'Be careful when you use the thunder box, sunshine,' she says. 'I don't want to be fishing you out of there.'

Outside the French windows in Mum's room there's a terrace. The picket fence carries on around this terrace, which is a good thing as it stretches to the very edge of the headland, about thirty feet above the sea. Above the terrace, on four thick wooden poles, is an awning. Nico says he made it from old sails. Mum says it gives a wonderful cool shade.

Nico says he made the terrace by clearing all the plants growing from the rocks and using the stone base. He filled all the gaps between the rocks with cement so it looks just a bit like the crazy paving that Granddad put in the backyard. The view from the terrace is unbelievably fab.

There's a round iron table and four big heavy castiron chairs on the terrace. Mum's very impressed with these white painted chairs. They're all decorated – the backs with roses and the legs with fierce lion heads at the top and clawed feet at the bottom. The rose pattern is on the table too. That's got lion legs as well. Mum says, 'Oh. I think these are from England. Coalbrookdale perhaps.' She bends to look at them closely. They're only furniture, Mum, come on – there's a flipping island to explore. 'Yes, Coalbrookdale,' she says, 'antiques.'

'You like?' says Nico, seeing Mum's enthusiasm. She nods. 'They're beautiful.'

'From Kali Strata,' he says.

I'm getting bored. Now *here's* something more interesting. A pair of flat slabs of rock sit at either side of the front door of the cottage.

Mum says, 'Look, Alfie. Teardrops.'

I see her point. They do look a bit like teardrops. Like those big ones that clowns paint on their faces. Both have neat holes at the narrowest point and through each hole is a long rope tied firmly with a very complicated knot. Their ropes are looped into big coils that hang from heavy iron hooks in the wall.

'What are those, Nico?' asks Mum.

'*Skandalopetra* – bellstones.'

Nico sees that she doesn't understand and explains.

'For sponge hunting.' Nico moves towards the door and lifts one of the heavy *skandalopetra*. He holds it at arm's length in both hands and bends into a diving position.

Mum twigs. 'It helps the diver to sink quickly.'

'Yes, very fast. And when he has caught the sponges, he signals' – Nico tugs twice on the rope; Mum nods – 'and his friends pull him back up.'

'This *skandalopetra* is very, *very* important to Symos,' Nico continues. He certainly loves his sponge hunting; he seems different, more excited, more lively when he mentions it.

'*Skandalopetra*, bellstones, whatever. They'll always be teardrops for me,' says Mum.

Directly opposite the terrace is the island. At last. Enough about old stones and furniture. Let's go and see Treasure Island, or maybe Never Never Land, Crusoe's Island or Kirrin Island, or all of them rolled into one. I wonder what smugglers' caves, pirate treasures or naked savages it might hold.

Nico leads us through a gate in the fence onto a bridge that links the island to the headland. The gap between the two is only thirty feet, but Nico tells us that the bridge took him ages to build. But he's done a really good job. It's a rope bridge, just like you read about in adventure stories in the *Eagle*. Mum and Nico go first and I follow. I try to get the bridge to swing, but it's almost as steady as a solid one. The planks are close together, the rope supports at each side are almost as high as me and Mum and there are plenty of sturdy strands holding the top rope to the bottom. The bridge is so well made that the three of us cross comfortably without the scary swaying that I hoped for – despite my best efforts.

Once we're across, the island is little more than a

cube of rock with a sheer thirty-foot drop all around. There is no picket fence on the island.

'We'll need to establish a few rules over here, young man,' Mum says.

'Okay, M–aggie.' It's hard to stop the 'M' word slipping out, but I bite my lip and it stays in my throat. 'Whatever you say.' Having a private island is all my dreams come true. Oh Freddie Hodge – if you could see me now!

'Well, firstly, no closer to the edge than this.' Mum points the toe of her shoe and scratches a rough line in the dirt about three feet from the cliff edge.

Pretty generous. 'Sure, M–aggie,' I say.

The island is exactly the same height as the headland and the only feature is the tree that we could see on the walk down to the cottage. It's an old olive. (See, I *was* listening on the path.) It's got a flipping thick trunk and an extremely flat top and it doesn't spread far. It stands in the dead centre of the island. It reminds Mum of prehistoric stone circles that she's seen in history books. 'Its central position has a very ritualistic feel to it,' she says, whatever that means.

'That tree is weird,' she adds.

'How do you mean?' I ask.

'Well, I bet if you measured you'd find it's in the dead centre of the island.' She looks at Nico. 'The tree. Dead centre, isn't it?'

'Dead? Death?' Nico doesn't understand. 'What has the tree to do with death? No. No. Not death. It is an olive. The tree of peace,' he says.

'Sorry, Nico. Dead centre means the middle,' Mum says.

'Ah yes. The meedle.'

Beyond the tree, Nico shows us steps hewn into the rock. These lead down to a tiny cove with a small shelving pebble beach. Cast-iron rings have been fixed into the stones along this rocky staircase and a thick rope links these to form a strong handrail. More rings are anchored into the boulders at the foot of the climb.

Nico explains that a boat can moor here.

'Here. You can tie boat.' He lifts one of the rings and lets it fall back with a clang.

'Here okay to swim?' says Mum, doing a fair impression of the breaststroke.

'Yes. Is okay. But ten metres, no more.' He points to a spot about thirty feet away. You can see the pebbly beach shelving gently and then disappearing into blackness at that point. We get the message.

'Alfie!' Mum shouts. 'If we ever go swimming, we go no more than twenty feet from the beach. Okay?'

'Okay, Maggie.' I've finally got the hang of it.

Sadly, there are no caves for me, but there is more than enough for my thoughts to run riot.

We cross back over the bridge. Nico points out the deep clear blue sea below. 'Thirty metres deep,' he says.

So the price is fixed and Nico hands me the keys. 'For the man of the house,' he says. I'm starting to like Nico.

'We'll soon get this place habitable,' Mum says, watching Nico start back down the path. 'Once we get rid of the cobwebs and wash the bedlinen, we can start to settle in.'

I'm not sure whether my first job will be searching for Captain Hook or meeting Man Friday, but I'm going to have plenty of time to decide.

Chapter Seven

Nico

As soon as I feel that the young English have all they need to settle into the cottage, I take my leave and head back along the path towards Yiossos.

It's usually a difficult walk to manage twice in one day, especially if one trip sees me laden down like a donkey, but I've got a fresh spring in my step. I feel like I've won the jackpot on the lottery. It would be great to have anybody rent the place for six months – but such a charming young woman! I've won the lottery and it's Christmas at the same time. I don't want to raise my hopes, but maybe Maggie ... Don't be an idiot. You saw how she looked at that show-off on the bike. I'm not in her league.

I reach my favourite boulder. It's midway between the cottage and the town and it's always a welcome sight when it comes into view. It's got a natural hollow that lets me rest my back as well as my backside. I feel like Zeus sitting here surveying his realm. I see the fishing fleet heading out of the distant harbour like a flock of swallows heading south for winter. But today I'm the one with all the sun. My head feels like I just baked it in Momma's oven. Sweat is running down my forehead into my eyes. I soon won't be able to see properly. I bought two sponges when I got that one for Alfie. One was to give to Maggie, but I didn't want her to get the wrong idea – a strange man buying her presents – so I changed my mind. I reach into my pocket, find the other sponge and mop my eyes and forehead.

I'm lost in thought. I hold the sponge and turn the golden honeycomb over and over. Sponges. Such simple creatures; but creatures that have moulded all of my life and most of everyone else's on Symos. Who was it that discovered hundreds of years ago that cleaning that smelly black mess would turn it into such a fabulous tool, like a butterfly emerging from an ugly chrysalis?

'Sponge down the chariots,' Odysseus would have commanded his servants. Just like old Captain Savvas – he used one to spruce up his vintage Cadillac down at the harbour. Mum says that when I was an infant she used to soak one in honey and it kept me quiet for hours. And Yianni reckoned they're why his girlfriends never got pregnant. I reckon there's a much simpler reason for that. Poor Yianni.

~

It was early June 1945.

When my father – my dear Tata, Yianni and I left Yiossos behind us just after dawn and sailed out into the open sea, there was no leaving party, no music, no church bells – just the three of us in Tata's red-and-green hulled fishing skiff with a small dinghy in tow.

Hitler and Mussolini had done their utmost to destroy much of Europe and the Mediterranean countries and islands. Five years of strife had resulted in almost every boat in the Aegean being commandeered for martial use. Sponges were a luxury and luxuries were forgotten during those bitter and violent years. So when we – the Karteras men – set out to hunt for sponges on that glorious June morning, we soon found that once barren over-fished sponge beds had enjoyed five years of peace and replenished themselves. We would not have to sail hundreds of miles to find gold.

I was sixteen. My brother, Yianni junior, was twenty-one and like Tata had spent the last five years fighting alongside the Greek resistance forces against the occupiers. But that violent experience was behind us now; this sponge diving trip was to be our first step back towards normality.

The Karteras family have sponge diving in their blood. Photographs of barrel-chested men, whose torsos held lungs of enormous capacity, line the walls of our family home. From as early as I can remember Yianni and I practised leaping from the headland at our uncle's whitewashed cottage into the thirty metres of crystal-clear water below, carrying bellstones to speed us to the deep. As we reached our teens we could hold almost four minutes' worth of breath and both of us developed the trademark diver's chest. We were good at what we did.

But my life was shattered at thirteen when I got sick. Tuberculosis. What Momma called one of the strongest thirteen-year-old lungs in Greece collapsed, and I was left gasping on the one that was left. Thankfully, I recovered from the TB; it may even have saved my life. Some of my school friends were rounded up by the Nazis and never seen again. The Germans didn't come to the hospital, at least not while I was there. But my days as a diving wonder boy were finished and the islanders started feeling sorry for me – the chubby, weak kid who could usually be found with his mother.

This was the first time that I had left her side for years. Tata navigated the skiff to a favourite spot that had been so productive for the family, a location passed down over generations on a chart we guarded like our own secret pirate treasure map.

He cut the engine. 'Okay, boys. This is it,' he said.

We were in open sea; the islands were just a hazy blur on the horizon.

'Nico, have a look and see what you can see.'

He handed me the bucket with the bottom replaced by glass and Yianni pulled the dinghy alongside. My brother helped me into the dinghy, then passed the bucket down to me and pushed the little boat away from the skiff.

I peered down into the clear, calm waters in search of the black sponges as the two boats drifted slowly along. And it took no time before I shouted, 'Drop anchor! Sponges to starboard! Sponges to port! Drop anchor!'

The sponges were back. They were back in their thousands.

'Let the diving begin,' Tata shouted cheerfully.

I marvelled at his magnificent body – a huge chest, the broadest shoulders and toned arms with bulging biceps above tautly muscled legs. I was sure that nobody would kick sand into this Charles Atlas's face. There was no embarrassment at his nakedness. Tata plunged in feet first, a knife between his teeth and net tied around his waist, holding the *skandalopetra* tightly to his chest as he plummeted to the depths. Four or five minutes later, as I, the *Kolaouzieris* – the dive overseer – for the day, hauled him and the bellstone back to the surface, Tata emerged with his net full of sponges.

Yianni junior was a near mirror image of Tata: not quite as developed as Yianni senior yet, but well on his way to becoming so. His technique involved diving headlong to the sea bed, *skandalopetra* ahead of him at arm's length; he believed this gave him a head-start in cutting sponges as soon as he reached the sandy floor twenty-five metres below.

Dive followed dive; by late afternoon there was a decent haul of sponges in the hold.

As they looked proudly at their catch, Tata hugged Yianni. 'Well done, son. Well done.' He patted my big brother on the back. 'That's quite a catch. And well done you too, Nico,' he said, turning towards me.

'Yeah. Well done, brother,' said Yianni, slapping me firmly on the shoulder. 'You found a fantastic spot and you handled the dives perfectly. Don't you want a try?'

I would have liked nothing more than to travel once more to the seabed and look at the wonders it held, but that could not be. My weak lungs would never be able to hold enough breath.

Seeing my face, Yianni realised his thoughtlessness. 'Sorry, Nico. Sorry.' He held my shoulder and gave it a sympathetic shake.

I smiled. The moment passed. 'It's okay. Now you two go and find us something decent to eat; I'm starving,' I said.

Tata went first and jumped in with a whoop. A couple of minutes later he broke the surface – a mass of red claws, blue pincers and frantically waving legs the proof of his success.

'How's that?' he said.

'Well, that's enough for me,' I joked. 'What about you

two?'

My brother dived in and returned with two more crabs and another lobster.

Tata said, 'Okay. Last dive of the day. Let's see if I can get us your favourite. I've seen a few today.' He leapt again.

I wasn't *Kolaouzieris* now and hadn't been carefully monitoring the time, but this seemed like one very long dive. I started to worry. I peered into the deep.

'He's taking his time, Yianni,' I said, walking around the deck glancing anxiously into the waves.

'Don't worry, Nico.' But Yianni's assurance was not convincing. He joined me and we both looked down edgily. The seconds felt like minutes and the minutes passed like hours.

Splaaaashhh! The sea erupted on the other side of the boat and we were soaked in spray.

Our worry was short-lived. We saw a huge grin spread across Tata's face before he filled his lungs with an enormous gulp. He lifted his right arm, wrapped in a writhing suckered mass, high out of the water and I knew that my most prized delicacy would be on the menu that night.

This was to be a short journey; one night at sea only. The cabin was small with just enough room for the three of us to sleep: one at each side of the small cabin and the smallest, me, across the front. The bunks doubled as seats and a foldaway table fitted snugly in the centre. There was a small double gas burner powered by liquid gas.

I was the cook. I had spent plenty of time with Momma and knew how to prepare seafood.

'The octopus is going to be tough,' I said. 'Momma usually pulverises them before cooking them.'

'Here, give it to me,' said Yianni, taking it from me and going outside.

I heard my brother smash the octopus down against the skiff's back rail time and again to tenderise it, in the way that he had seen the fisherwomen flailing them

Give Me Your Tomorrow

against the rocks around the entrance to the harbour.

'If that's tough now, I'm blaming the cook,' he said, smiling, as he handed the softened mess back.

After we finished feasting on the very freshest seafood followed by galaktoboureko, our favourite custard-filled filo-pastry sweet soaked in light lemony syrup, lovingly prepared by Momma especially for the journey, Tata told us boys of a surprise that he had in store for us.

'You know how Yianni and I both said that we had seen hundreds of enormous sponges on a deep shelf out of reach?' he asked.

'Yes,' I said, wondering where this was going. Those sponges were usually found at a depth of at least fifty metres.

'Well, they're not out of reach now.'

'What do you mean they're not now?' Yianni junior asked.

'Look!' said our father.

Tata took the mattress off his bunk and raised the hinged flap below it. Reaching into the locker, he pulled out a large white bundle of rubbery material, followed immediately by a magnificent silver and glass ball. It needed no introduction.

'A *skafandro*!' I said my mouth dropping open. 'A diving suit!'

'Tata, that's a Siebe Gorman helmet, isn't it?'

'It certainly is,' said Tata.

Siebe Gorman! Makers of the world's best and most famous diving equipment. The white rubbery suit had the stars and stripes emblazoned across its left shoulder and breast.

At first my brother was almost lost for words, but then they came in a rush.

'Where did you get it, Tata? That's worth a fortune. You couldn't afford it.'

I was asking questions too. 'And why has it got an American flag on it?'

'Okay. Okay. Too many question at once. Sit down

and I'll tell you all about it. And tomorrow we'll give it a try.'

I couldn't help but admire the beautiful suit, but my heart sank when I heard the words 'we'll give it a try'. I knew everything about diving. Naked skin divers faced the perils of sharks, jellyfish, turbulent currents, sea urchins, self-inflicted perforated eardrums and, most dangerously, the failure to correctly calculate the amount of time the air left in their lungs would give them underwater. But *skafandro*-using divers, full of bravado, those matadors of the sea whose swagger attracted both children and young women in equal measure? They had much more to endure.

When the *skafandro* revolutionised the industry, marking the end of two thousand years of naked diving, everything was not quite as simple as it seemed. It was, in fact, probably the most dangerous piece of professional equipment in the industrial world. The hero worship divers attracted and the huge wages they were paid were deserved; payments made in advance were a sensible idea as many did not return, with scores losing their lives and their bodies ending up interred on the notorious white rock island just off the coast of Egypt, reputed to hold more bones than the San Stefano ossuary. Such was the devastation that when the fleet came back to the island in the autumn, it became traditional for the divers' womenfolk to wait on the quayside dressed from head to toe in black, in anticipation of the dark news to come.

The cause? Not the suits themselves. They were invariably high quality and well designed, expertly made in England. The problem lay in a mixture of the failure to understand the bends, that most agonising side effect of deep diving, and, when the condition was understood, the flaunting of that knowledge in a quest for riches.

Breathing compressed air at depth causes lethal nitrogen bubbles to form in the blood stream. By timing an ascent carefully, divers can allow these bubbles to dissolve harmlessly. In the beginning, nobody knew anything about this effect, and being hauled rapidly to the surface decimated the first divers. An extremely painful death or agonising and severe crippling soon followed. Even when the cause and remedy were fully understood, the number of accidents and fatalities remained at unacceptable levels. Action to ban the suits was taken and laws were successfully passed. But financial pressures led to the flouting of the rules and to their eventual overturn.

The divers relied on maybe the youngest crew member – just a boy – to be the *Kolaouzieris*, who would keep an eye on the glass sand timer which governed their dive and their ascent. It was not unheard of for him to distractedly miss the timer. A series of signals by way of a number of tugs on the ropes allowed the divers to communicate with the boat. A misinterpreted signal (was that one pull or two?) could have fatal results.

The supply of compressed air depended upon the cabin boy cranking a handle. Airlines could kink. Handles could seize. And when the mechanism was replaced by kerosene-driven compressors, it was possible for a diver to be poisoned by fumes. Valves could fail, depriving the diver of air or inflating the suit to a grotesque balloon that flew to the surface and above the waves. It sounds hilarious, but it was no fun for the mourning family. The dangers of the *skafandro* were so great that it is no surprise its wearers were viewed as risk-taking heroes of the highest order.

For almost all of my life I had listened to Momma's endless campaigns against the *skafandro*. 'Dangerous', 'reckless', 'idiotic', 'mad' and 'stupid' were just a few of the more respectable words that she had used about the diving suit. And having lost her own father, my Bampa, to diving and seen two uncles crippled by it, Momma's distaste for the suit was fully justified.

I awaited Tata's explanation with a mixture of excitement and dread.

Chapter Eight

Maggie

As Nico disappears into the distance, I almost pinch myself with delight at how things have turned out and at the beauty of where we are.

'So, Alfie, what do you think?' I ask.

Alfie pauses a moment. He's rarely lost for something to say. He looks around the terrace and across to the island before he turns back.

'What do I think?' A broad grin lights up his face, 'I think it's all a dream and when you wake me up Freddie Hodge will be kicking his football against our door again, waiting for me to leave for school.'

I gently pat his cheek. 'Wake up, sunshine. Get your satchel, you're late.'

He laughs. Yes, he laughs. Poor kid, I haven't seen him laugh like that in ages. He says 'I've come to Never Never Land ... or Camelot ... or ... or ... anywhere I want it to be.'

I'm so, *so* pleased to have brought this magical playground into his life. All the world's a stage and there couldn't be a better stage for a child with such a head full of ideas. I remember those day trips to Southport when we got off the train at Birkdale and walked half a mile to the sand dunes that stretched southwards for miles along the coast. The dunes were full of small valleys and sandy amphitheatres, and Alfie would watch the local children enviously as the Little Bighorn materialised before his eyes and a cap-gun-waving Custer vainly attempted to repel hordes of Sioux armed with bows and fearsome sucker-tipped arrows.

Poor Alfie. He was always an unseen onlooker to those adventures from his hiding place amid the spiky clumps of marram grass and was never Custer, Sitting Bull or even a Red Indian brave. But now, on Symos, he has his own wonderful magical playground in which he, Alfie Johnson, can and will be whoever and whatever he wants to be.

'Mum, it's just fantastic.'

I smile. 'I can't tell you how happy that makes me, Alfie. It's not been easy coming here, you know, but I'll make sure that we never regret it.'

I've read all about those Symos spiders, but the cobwebs in the cottage don't seem to hold any nasty surprises and Alfie manages to turn the few house spiders we find into terrace spiders. It has been a long day and I'm exhausted but we've got to eat, so I prepare something for us from the small box of provisions kindly provided by Nico's mother. Sitting at the antique terrace table, cold chicken, some tomatoes and lettuce and a gooey honey pastry that Alfie says looks like shredded wheat are washed down with fresh orange juice.

I put Alfie to bed. I start to read his bedtime story. It's *Swallows and Amazons*, but in less time than John, Susan, Titty and Roger would take to hoist their mainsails Alfie's in the land of nod. I peck him gently on the cheek. 'Night night, sunshine.'

I go to my room and fish out my diary. This journey has a purpose. This journey is planned, and if it is going to successfully change our lives then I've got to keep to that plan. I turn to the blank April and May pages in the diary and write 'LEARN GREEK' on each one. That's stage one. I'll fill in the other months when I've reached that target.

I close the book and take my record player to the terrace and set it on the table. As the sun sets behind the cottage and darkness creeps over the scene, the lilting melody of Simon and Garfunkel's perfect harmony begins and with it quiet but relieved tears come into my eyes.

Chapter Nine

Nico

We got our answers as Tata spun his tale.

He took us back to the time of the Nazi occupation, when the Germans had used divers to sabotage harbours, to lay mines and to carry out surveillance. One night in 1943, Tata's team of resistance fighters was patrolling the Symos coastline in a small rowing boat that they kept concealed in a secret grotto.

'We know it,' we both chimed in as soon as Tata mentioned it.

There were five of them in the boat, he explained – Tata and four handpicked men who were equally at home both on the sea and in it. As night drew in and the sky blackened, the silent group came upon a German patrol boat.

The enemy boat was anchored just inside the mouth of Yiossos harbour, but with no moon the resistance team could not see clearly what was going on. They knew that it was an enemy vessel. They knew every seaworthy craft on Symos and even in darkness they recognised this as old Pallas's large wooden fishing boat, commandeered from its Yiossos mooring by the Nazis, who had cruelly made the octogenarian pay the ultimate price for his feeble attempts at resistance.

'Poor Pallas,' I said.

'Evil bastards,' added my brother.

Tata continued with his tale, describing how they were rowing as close to the Germans as they dared when suddenly a dazzling spotlight on the starboard side of the patrol vessel's bow blazed into life. He immediately thought that they were doomed, but fortunately for him and for his men the Germans were concentrating the powerful beam down into the water rather than in their direction. Our men were all experienced sponge-divers and they realised that the Germans were involved in an underwater mission – the harbour was about to be mined.

'They were using the *skafandro*!' I jumped in.

'Wait, you're running ahead. Let me tell you the story.' Tata smiled at my enthusiasm. He had a good yarn to tell. There was a long evening ahead. He wanted to savour it.

All five of the fighters stripped down to their underwear. They reckoned that the German crew would be about ten strong, so each Greek would have two enemy sailors to deal with. Tata lowered their anchor overboard as quietly as possible and, knife between his teeth, edged himself slowly into the water. They had automatic weapons on board but could not risk them in the water; there was no choice but to leave them on the rowing boat. His companions followed one by one.

As the last Greek, Hercules, hit the water with a splash, Tata feared that they would be spotted.

'Typical Hercules,' said my brother, blowing out his cheeks and sticking out his stomach.

Tata smiled and explained that luckily the German boat was running a compressor that drowned out any noise that the resistance team made.

They had managed to anchor just ten metres away from the patrol boat. The sea on the Germans' starboard side was brightly lit and as the Greeks dived below the surface they could make out the shaft of brilliant light and could see the German diver's airline and lifeline in the middle of the beam. If they were doing things properly, at least two of the crew would be involved in supervising the dive and another would be manning the searchlight. Tata reckoned that left the one man in the sea and maybe six more on board.

He decided that, to minimise risk, he should board first and if his companions heard no obvious commotion or the sound of his being discovered within a couple of minutes then they too should climb the anchor chain. He was lucky. Not only were there three Germans involved in supervising the dive, three more were looking on as if hypnotised by the spotlight that reflected moon-like on the surface.

The anchor and its chain were on the port side of the stern. Tata pulled himself up the thick metal links and slipped silently onto the deck. The first German was just a dark shadow. The harbour and all of Yiossos was under blackout and it felt as if they were in open sea instead of being less than a mile from home.

The young sailor was supposed to be on watch but was more interested in the cigarette that he was puffing contentedly. Its small orange glow gave Tata a clear idea of where the lookout's throat was, and within seconds of boarding he was behind his youthful enemy and slitting his windpipe with a razor-sharp blade.

At this point, Tata paused in his storytelling, lit a cigarette and drew a deep breath. 'Yeah. Not much older than you, Nico. And I killed him.' He seemed thoughtful as he reflected on the memory.

'It's not your fault, Tata. You had to do it. It's war. An eye for an eye. You know that,' said Yianni.

'I know.' Tata nodded. 'But it doesn't make it any easier.'

The victim's machine gun was retrieved and his bloody corpse lowered carefully and quietly to the deck. Tata crept back to the anchor chain to help the rest of the team aboard. Together they lifted the dead German and rolled his lifeless body out of sight beneath a tarpaulin.

Next they decided to create confusion by disabling either the compressor or the spotlight, or ideally both.

'The compressor, Tata. You had to go for the compressor first,' I said.

'You're right,' said Tata. 'That's exactly what we did.'

The compressor was running noisily and unattended and Stavros was assigned to it. He crept along the deck and simply cut its fuel pipe, leaving it to pump kerosene out onto the wooden boards. The compressor spluttered a couple of times as if it too was in its death throes and then fell into silence – a silence that caused commotion among the crew.

The two German *Kolaouzieris* started to haul their diver on board, another swung the spotlight around in the direction of the compressor and a fourth ran towards it. The beam shone above Stavros, who lay flattened on the deck in wait for the sailor and caught him with an upward lunge of his knife – a lunge that went straight through the German's tunic and into his ribcage. This assault did not escape the beam and was acted out in the full glare of the spotlight; the Germans were now in no doubt that they were under attack.

Three of them rushed towards the compressor, their shouts alerting the remaining crew. Two emerged from the small cabin below deck and the commander jumped down from the steering platform. Tata picked up the first guard's still smouldering cigarette from the deck and moved towards the fuel line. His aim had to be good; this had to be a perfect throw and it was. The cigarette hit the pool of kerosene on the deck. A circular fire flashed, followed in a split second by a huge blast and fireball as the kerosene tank exploded.

'Booom!' Tata waved his hands expansively to convey the enormity of the blast.

Three of the enemy caught the full blast of the exploding tank. Two were blown into the sea and the third leapt overboard, hoping that the water would provide relief from the flames. But such was the volume of kerosene on their clothes that the fire simply continued to blaze away on the surface.

'Two years on and I still hear their screams every day.'

With no one now in control of the spotlight, it had swung down on its bracket, lighting the inferno on the sea surface. The crewmen, unarmed and sitting ducks while hauling the diver up, knew that without the compressor they were fighting a lost cause and abandoned their comrade, cutting his air and lifelines and leaving him to sink to a watery grave at the mouth of Symos harbour.

The fire had taken a firm hold on the patrol boat and

was running across the whole deck from port to starboard. With the Greeks on the stern side of the flames and the Germans towards the bow, it had created a natural frontline – a frontline that gave a false sense of security and offered no protection as the resistance fighters discovered when a burst of machine-gun fire penetrated the line and riddled Stavros's body. A quick look told Tata that there was no hope.

'Poor Uncle Stavros.' Stavros had been a lifelong family friend who we had loved dearly.

Tata nodded sombrely, then continued. Georgiou, Hercules and Costas were still there to support him. He gave the machine gun to their best marksman, Costas. They needed to work fast. They had done their job in disabling the patrol boat and stopping the Germans' dive but they couldn't get back to their own boat without being easy targets in the German spotlight. Costas took the beam out with a quick burst of fire, leaving the scene in blackness apart from the blazing deck.

The fire had spread below deck and the patrol boat was starting to list. It swung in the current and for a moment the small Greek boat became visible in the glow from the inferno, bobbing gently and peacefully oblivious to the mayhem just ten yards away. The German leader pointed it out to his comrades and it was clear that with their vessel likely to sink they were viewing it as a potential escape route.

Two Germans started to remove their boots – swimming in them would be impossible.

'Idiots!' said Yianni. 'How could they waste time taking boots off in the middle of a gun battle?'

'Exactly,' said Tata.

Defenceless in their anxiety to escape, they had made themselves easy prey and a rifleman of Costas' experience could not miss, even with an unfamiliar weapon and in extremely low visibility. With the sides now even, a short gun battle ensued. Georgiou took a bullet to the head and was killed instantly.

More head-shaking from me and Yianni.

'A good man,' I said.

'A very good man,' my brother echoed.

But Costas was more than a match for the enemy and succeeded in finishing the job. The Greeks, Tata declared proudly, had defeated the German patrol boat.

Our cheers rang around the cabin. 'Whoo!' shouted my brother.

Tata held up a cautionary hand and continued. With the enemy boat ablaze like a beacon at the breakwater, it would not be long before other Germans came to investigate. Costas and Hercules scoured the boat for weapons and ammunition while Tata opened a locker on deck at the stern. There in all its splendour was the magnificent white *skafandro*, complete with the beautiful steel Siebe Gorman helmet.

Tata swam to the rowing boat and, nearing total exhaustion, hauled himself aboard. He brought the anchor up quickly and rowed across towards the sinking German vessel. With traces of kerosene still ablaze on the surface it was hazardous, but he, Costas and Hercules managed to carefully lift their two dead colleagues onto their small boat before transferring across their booty. The resistance fighters looked back to see the fruits of their endeavour as the patrol boat slipped silently below the waves. They returned to their hideout in silence.

'Great story, Tata. I knew you were brave but I never knew that you were so bloody foolhardy.

Tata tutted. 'Language, son,' he said to my brother while tilting his head sideways in my direction. 'Language.'

'I don't mind, Tata,' I said.

'It doesn't matter if you mind, son. I'm the one who says what goes on this boat.' He smiled.

'Okay, so you got a fantastic German white *skafandro*,' I said. 'So why has it got American stars and stripes across it?'

'Good question, son. A very good question. I got that suit back to the grotto and I was looking at it for ages.

Every time I saw that black cross and the eagle carrying a swastika I felt sick. Those brutes had murdered my closest friends Stavros and Georgiou and plenty more besides. I couldn't stand looking at it. It was like a wart on the nose of a beautiful woman. It was stuck on with some sort of latex glue. The suit was thick. I didn't want to damage it but after picking away at it—'

'Like a scab,' I said.

'Yeah. Good description. Like a scab. I managed to pick it off.'

'Did you burn it?' asked Yianni junior, lighting a cigarette for himself and inhaling deeply.

'I wanted to, but I was in Yiossos when the Brits arrived and I got talking to a Brit.'

'So when did you learn English?' said my brother.

'Very funny,' said Tata. 'Okay, I got into a conversation with a Brit using sign language. It seems that he collected war badges and stuff and he'd got nothing from diving detachments and he really wanted it.'

'They're okay, the Brits,' I said.

'Yeah, they're okay. So anyway, he pulled out this enormous stars and stripes and offered to swap. And that's what I did.'

'So is the stars and stripes waterproof?' I asked.

'Don't know,' said Tata. 'We'll soon find out.'

'Tata, you're not going to use it?' I was worried. 'What would Momma say?'

Knowing all we knew about the *skafandro*, I couldn't understand why my father was contemplating putting on the suit and making a dive into sixty metres.

'What Momma doesn't know, Momma won't mind. And you two aren't going to mention it, are you?'

There was a steely determination in Yianni senior's voice and I knew that there was no point arguing. If my father wanted to wear it, my father would wear it.

Yianni Karteras senior was completely confident. He knew the risks. He had studied decompression charts. His assistants were not stupid cabin boys. We were his own sons who loved him dearly and we would never let him down.

Chapter Ten

Nico

The weather was even kinder the following morning: the sea flat calm, the sky cloudless and the sun blazing as only the Greek sun can. I spotted a pod of dolphins about half a mile away and imagined from all the activity that they were into a substantial shoal of mackerel. I pointed the activity out to my brother.

'Yianni, look at that!'

'If they're still around after Tata's dives, we'll see if we can catch a few to take home to Momma,' said Yianni.

'What's she going to do with a couple of dolphins?' I asked straight-faced.

'Very funny,' my brother groaned and nudged me playfully in the ribs.

After moving the boat a hundred yards north to be directly above the deeps that we had spotted the previous day, Tata rigged a strong wooden boom from the mast at the front of the boat and carefully looped the airline through a large iron eye beneath its tip. A coil of rope tied firmly to a capstan was the only other accessory and that too was looped via a pulley onto the boom and through the metal eye. The end of the airline was connected to a hand compressor and it was to be my duty to keep it turning.

Tata went below and arrived back on deck wearing the white *skafandro*.

I whistled. 'If Momma could see you now,' I said, 'she might change her mind about the *skafandro*.'

He cut a magnificent figure against the backdrop of blue sea and blue sky clad in the white suit, with the bold and colourful stars and stripes covering his left breast and shoulder. Most diving suits were made in drab brown or yellow waterproof material, but the white suit made a real statement. This was a status symbol, making its wearer somehow bigger and more important.

'You'll never change your momma's views on the *skafandro*,' he said. 'And that's why she'll never know about this ...Will she?'

We both nodded.

I looked at the deck. I felt uneasy. The ninth commandment came into my mind: 'Thou shalt not bear false witness.' But then the fifth popped into my head: 'Honour thy father and thy mother.' I wondered which was most important: fifth or ninth? Father or mother? Parents could really make life difficult.

Young Yianni locked the beautiful precision-made helmet's fixings firmly into place. Our father was silenced.

A few hugs all round and then Tata plunged into the clear waters with a wave.

I had no time to look down through my glass-bottomed bucket to watch my father's progress. I simply kept turning the compressor handle smoothly and slowly while my brother kept watch on the time. Tata kept the dives short and I kept the ascents long and safe. We'd seen enough cripples in Yiossos and attended too many funerals in our lives to make any mistakes. The sponges he surfaced with were huge: twice the size of those in the previous day's haul and twice as plentiful in the deeper waters.

But on that glorious morning, the dolphins were not the only ones to spot the enormous mackerel shoal that had come to feed in those warm rich waters. The vibrations from the dolphin feeding frenzy had triggered the sensors on another group of large predators.

Had Tata been in the boat at the time he would probably have told us that they presented no danger. 'Leave them,' he would have said. 'They'll be gone in a minute'. Attacks on divers were almost unheard of and the huge shoal of fish that he had seen for himself was more than enough to satisfy their hunger. But he was not in the boat. He was just starting a fresh decompression stage and suspended fifty metres down, perhaps enjoying himself watching the tiny brightly coloured fish inspecting him through his solid glass mask in a sort of aquarium role reversal.

It was me who spotted them first. 'Shark!' I screamed at my brother while I kept up the rhythmical cranking.

Yianni junior saw the dark shadow move under the boat, followed by another and another. There were four in all and they swam from front to back and side to side as if making a critical examination of the paintwork on the hull.

And that would have been it. Investigation over, they would have moved on to that inviting mackerel feast a couple of hundred metres away. That would have been it – if my brother hadn't seized a sharpened boat hook and lunged at one of the black shadows as it emerged port side, the trademark triangular fin sticking out of the water.

The hook punctured the shark's flank and a crimson tide covered the surface. Sensing blood, the others returned. Yianni was still holding the boat hook while the shark writhed in agony on its barb.

I continued turning the handle as smoothly as possible, but this was not easy with my brother locked in mortal combat with a killer fish and my father suspended fifty metres down, marvelling at the beauty of the submarine world and blissfully unaware of the commotion on the surface.

If young Yianni had let go of the boat hook things might have been different, but he held it tightly and as the shark took a desperate dive downwards Yianni slipped and followed the fish into the water. As he floundered, he screamed for my help. But how could I help? If I stopped cranking, Tata would suffocate. If I ignored my brother's cries, my brother could lose a limb or die from a shark attack.

'Nico! Nico! Help me!'

The words ran through me and I realised that without Yianni's help it might be impossible to haul Tata back onto the boat while keeping his air supply running. Our father was a naked diver. He was certainly the best in

Symos and possibly the best in Greece. He could hold his breath for almost five minutes. Yes, he could hold his breath for almost five minutes.

So I stopped my cranking and rushed to the side of the boat. I threw a lifebelt to Yianni junior, who gratefully grabbed it at the third attempt and pulled it over his head. But there was something strange about his pallor. His olive skin was turning white and there was so much blood in the water. After a difficult struggle he finally managed to get the ring around his body. As he leaned back I saw the tear in his thigh. It was pumping blood and with each bloody gush life was draining from Yianni's face.

And so Yianni Karteras junior's life ended from blood loss. He was unlucky that a razor-sharp shark tooth had severed his femoral artery, but the death was his own reckless fault, although I would make sure that my big brother would forever be a hero on the island of Symos – a hero who died trying heroically to fight off a shark attack while his weak and sickly sibling had looked on helplessly and hopelessly.

Realising I could do no more to help Yianni, my thoughts flew quickly to Tata. Only a minute or two had passed, so although I hurried back to the compressor, I was confident that Tata would still have lungs full of air.

But in thinking about Tata's amazing lung capacity and his ability to hold his breath for almost five minutes, I had made the gravest misjudgement of my life. I had overlooked the fact that to breathe unaided for so long, my father had to prepare for the feat by first expanding his lungs and filling them with a huge volume of oxygen. With the compressed air, he was just breathing in and out normally.

So when Tata's air supply suddenly stopped, there were no huge lungfuls to keep him going. He had at most a hundred seconds to look around him. The helmet prevented him from looking upwards, where he would have seen the life-and-death struggle being acted out on the surface. I imagine him now: looking slowly around at the mass of sponges that might have brought him riches; watching as his brilliant aquatic companions sped away to investigate something far more interesting; studying the quality of the wonderful white of his *skafandro*, which would have been the envy of every man on Symos; and thinking of his wife, Anna, my Momma. That was all the time he had before slipping out of consciousness and into eternity.

I resumed cranking the compressor. Smoothly and steadily. I was convinced that Tata would have realised that there was a problem and would be taking gulps of the air as it came at him sporadically. Between turns of the compressor I had to haul on the rope that led to the boom. After raising my father another few metres, I stood on the length of rope that I had retrieved to prevent it from slipping back and then returned to the compressor. Very slowly and gradually, between bouts of cranking and hauling, I brought Tata to the surface.

As the silver helmet broke through the ruddy brine into the atmosphere, there was no movement from inside the *skafandro*. I kept hauling until my prize was almost level with the top of the boom. I locked the rope into position around a capstan and swung the boom towards the skiff. Lowering my father gently to the deck, I rushed forward and unlocked the beautiful helmet. As soon as the helmet was off and I saw the blue lips, there was no mistaking it.

My wonderful father, my hero, Yiannis Karteras, was dead.

Cushioned by shock, I turned to action. I lowered Tata's body to the deck. Then I turned my attention to my brother's body, which was still suspended from the lifebelt. Using a second boathook I manoeuvred Yianni junior sufficiently close to allow me to get a grip on an arm. Releasing the boathook, I hauled my lifeless brother aboard. The gash in Yianni junior's leg was severe but his body was otherwise unmarked. I laid the body alongside my father's.

I was gently removing my father's diving suit when

reality hit. My body was wracked with great gasping sobs as I suddenly realised the enormity of what had happened. For a few minutes nothing had sunk in and I had worked on autopilot, but now, alone in the gentle swell, looking down on the bodies of the most important men in my life, I realised how isolated I was.

I removed the *skafandro* and placed it back beneath the bunk. Conscious of their nakedness, I dressed each corpse in a pair of black swimming trunks before covering the bodies with a canvas tarpaulin.

Like most of the boys on the island, I could handle boats and navigate using the sun, moon and stars. The day was clear and I would be back in the harbour long before nightfall. As I weighed anchor and started back on my saddest voyage, I wondered how I would break my tragic news to Momma and to the island. Yianni junior's fate would be clear to all. There was no mistaking the telltale signs of shark attack on his near-severed leg. But what about Tata? How could I explain the unmarked peaceful body alongside my brother's gored one?

Momma was one of the island's fiercest critics of the *skafandro*. She had suffered more than most with family losses and a life made difficult by nursing its victims. She had been at the forefront of the protests that had sprung up demanding the banning of the diving suit. She would never countenance her husband using one of those monstrosities. I did not want my father's memory to be blighted by his failure to heed Momma's warnings and to respect her deepest convictions. Momma doted on her husband. She idolised him. And as far as I was concerned, that was how it always should be.

So all traces of deep-sea diving – the compressor and the huge deep-water sponges that would have raised suspicions among experts – were despatched to the deep. But I could not bear to part with the beautiful white *skafandro* with its colourful stars and stripes, and it remained hidden beneath Yianni's fishing gear in the cabin.

A self-blaming story was fabricated during the wretched journey home – a story that I thought would just about pass muster. It would pass muster as long as the officials did not seek an autopsy, which would show there was not a drop of water in Tata's lungs. If that happened and a doctor realised that this was death by suffocation, I would have a lot of questions to answer. But I was sure that an inquest was extremely unlikely. If it happened, I would tell the truth. If it didn't, I was committing myself to a lifetime of deception.

Chapter Eleven

Maggie

I've decided that the best way to improve my Greek will be to spend each morning in Yiossos buying just enough provisions to get me and Alfie through to the next day, when I will return and do the same again. With my A-grade A-level I can read signs and a few newspaper headlines and I can order a simple meal in a taverna, but if I am going to become fluent I need regular contact with the people.

But before I make my very first trip alone into Yiossos I've one important job to do, and I settle down at the wooden table to do it. I write:

Dear Mum,

We have arrived safely on the island of Symos and if you want to write you can do so care of our landlord, Nicos Karteras, Symos, Greece. Nico seems to know everybody and I am sure that your mail will reach us.

I was undecided on exactly where we would end up but had settled on the Dodecanese Islands. My final decision was made for me by an old mariner in the ferry booking office in Rhodes and as soon as the harbour came into view, we realised that he was right and we had made a perfect choice.

I am sorry if you feel that I have let you down, but, as I tried so hard and so many times to tell you and Dad, I am not running away. I am trying to make a new life for us. A life of independence away from the claustrophobia of the brethren.

I know that you won't want to hear this, but I remember that cottage in the Lake District with Dad fishing for our supper in the tarn, you collecting bilberries on the hillside, the adder in the grass, the pouring rain, the thunder box (we've got one here) and most of all the sound of you and Dad laughing.

That's a sound that I haven't heard since you got involved with religion. I haven't known you visit the pictures, buy a new dress or go to a dance. No. Your life has just been God, God, God. And God (sorry) am I sick of it. I am not saying that everything about the church is bad, but we are isolated. I have been unable to make friends, as all those non-believers outside our circle are seen as sinners.

Your quest for eternal life might be a realistic hope and maybe on Judgement Day you and Dad will have the last laugh as the rest of us are condemned to eternal damnation, but if that is the next time that you both laugh, is that a quest worth being on? Because if you are not right and your chosen religion is not 'The Truth', you will have spent half a lifetime in prayer and piety for nothing. What sort of life will that have been for either of you?

Alfie has been the victim of endless taunts – imagine how it is for a nine-year-old in a playground jungle. Your total avoidance of any mention of reproduction during my adolescence resulted in Alfie (and I am strangely grateful for that), but nobody should suffer the torment of being told that his mum is a slut and his granddad is really his dad (yes, scandalous and untrue as it is, that's what some of the children have been saying).

And that's why we have escaped here. Not for a glorified holiday but to make a serious change. I plan to develop a business from my experience here and to give Alfie happiness in what remains of his childhood.

Thank you, Mum, and thanks to Dad too for supporting

me. I'm sorry if I have let you down. I love you both dearly but I don't love the church and I want no part of it ever again.

Forever yours,
Maggie x

I read and reread what I have written on the flimsy airmail paper.

In Liverpool I wanted for years to rail against the church and everything that it did to us and everything that it stood for. I wanted to shout it from the rooftops; to tell Mum and Dad exactly what I thought of multiple Sunday services, Saturday gatherings and daily readings. But I was a product of that church and that church produced a subservient, timid and cowed congregation whose sole aim in life was achieving eternal salvation. It was said that the meek would inherit the earth, and apart from one or two of the leaders the brethren were universally meek. My subservience precluded me from opening my mouth and speaking my mind and it is only now – now that I am thousands of miles away – that I feel able to express my views freely in the safe medium of pen and ink.

Before leaving England, I studied the Greek islands as thoroughly as I could during snatched breaks and late evenings at the huge reference library in William Brown Street. My research was comprehensive and covered not just the topography of the islands but their culture and traditions, their industry, their climate, fauna and flora and, most importantly, their history. If I, an unmarried young mother, was going to gain any respect whatsoever in Greece, I felt that I would really have to earn it. And now I'm not an unmarried mother but a big sister looking after my brother. I'll have to sort that out quickly, but I have to admit that if single unmarried mothers are as popular here as they were at home, maybe I'll just play along for a couple of weeks until I settle in. I've got to be tough, but there's no point in making things harder than they need to be.

After weeks of studying I narrowed my research down to the Dodecanese. I felt that the islands, being completely unexploited by tourism, had the potential to fulfil my plans.

And at the harbour ticket office in Lindos on Rhodes the time came to choose a destination from my shortlist. What I told Mum in the letter was true.

~

We were standing in the ticket office scanning the ferry posters with their photographs of blue skies and crystal seas.

A wiry, white-haired old man with a leathery weather-beaten face sculpted by a lifetime at sea approached us. He wore a captain's cap, but it was clear that his days on the bridge were long past. He touched my arm.

'Nice tourists,' he said. He indicated a group of distinctly unwashed long-haired hippy backpackers sitting on the floor of the office, despite an abundance of perfectly satisfactory seats, and mimed a spitting gesture as if to say 'unlike them'.

I warmed to this old man. He had a winning smile and posed no threat.

'Where are you from?' he asked.

'Liverpool. It's in England.'

'Ah, Leeverpool, Leeverpool. Roger Hunt. Tony Hateley. Lime Street. The docks. Yes, the Dock Road,' he said wistfully.

'You've been to Liverpool?' asked Alfie.

'Many, many times. I was a captain.' He pointed to his cap. 'I sailed Athens to Liverpool. Liverpool to Athens. Tins of fish to Liverpool. Crates of soap to Athens. So! Where you going?'

'We're not sure. Kos, perhaps.'

The old man repeated his spitting mime. 'Pah.'

'Kalymnos?' I said.

The old man simply rolled his eyes.

'What about Symos?' I responded.

Bull's-eye! The gushing began. 'Ahhh, Symos. Excellent choice. Most excellent choice. The most beautiful harbour in Greece. The finest churches in the Dodecanese. The magnificent houses of Yiossos. The beautiful Kali Strata. The sponges. Oh yes, you must go to Symos. Magnificent Symos. Sun, swim, food, wine. Perfect. As the harbour comes into view for the very first time it will be something that you will never forget.'

As he spoke, the old sailor pursed his lips and pinched them between his thumb and forefingers, making the sign normally used by chefs or diners to demonstrate the deliciousness of the food on the table.

Symos had certainly been on our list of potential islands, but the old man had sold it to us.

'Where are you from?' I asked him.

'Symos, of course.'

'Of course.'

~

Now, here on the island, installed in a near fairy-tale cottage in a glossy-magazine location of all blue, blue and even more blue, my new life has begun.

'Okay, Alfie. Are you ready?'

I place the letter in my shoulder bag and together we start along the track. It isn't a typical trip to the shops. Walking across nearly two miles of stony track isn't exactly popping out for a loaf of bread.

I am a guest in a strange land and I am determined not to flout any customs, so this morning I've chosen to dress in an outfit not too dissimilar to those worn by the women in Rhodes and on the ferry across to the island: a floral-print shift dress, knee-length, buttoned from top to bottom with a neat leather belt at the waist. On my feet I'm wearing some quite heavy boots, the sort ramblers might wear for a walk in the countryside. In my canvas shoulder bag I've got a pair of low sling-back town shoes to wear for the last few hundred yards of the path and around the town.

Alfie is kitted out in standard shorts, vest and plimsolls. I worry about his fair, freckled skin; the first purchase on my language lesson will be a hat to protect him from the sun. It's only April and the air has a chill to it today, but the sun has a power unlike anything I have experienced at the height of summer at home. I remember poor Margot, Gerald Durrell's sister, whose encounter with the fierce Greek sun is so graphically and hilariously described in his book; I want no repetition of that with my precious boy.

On the way across the scrubland I outline to Alfie what I have learnt so far about the history of our new island home. As soon as the Germans are mentioned, Alfie's ears prick up. His granddad would have liked him to read only Bible texts, but Alfie loves his comics and those comics are full of stories of the Second World War with their pidgin German: '*Gotte und himmel*', '*Achtung Minen*' and '*Donner und Blitzen*! Look out, look out, Tommy iz coming'. Alfie was an early reader and he's devoured books and comics from a very young age. His teachers told me that I've got a gifted child with the vocabulary of a teenager, but his main gift is a mum who cares deeply about him and encourages his reading rather than dumping him outside the pub with all the other kids and going in for a Babycham or two.

As we pass the pillbox, Alfie's mind will be full of thoughts of the commandos or maybe the Royal Artillery who once manned it. It's a six-sided grey concrete slab construction about seven feet high, with long open slits two feet below the top and just above Alfie's head. There is a small door, now bricked up, on the sea-facing side of the building. This and that other reminder of the war – the empty houses on the Kali Strata; some destroyed, some seemingly intact, at least from the outside – are there for him to explore while I do my shopping.

I can trust this nine-year-old to disappear and be back when told to be. He has spent much of his nine years playing alone, despite the threat of bullies, on the streets in Kirkdale, in a city with a population of hundreds of thousands. An island of two thousand inhabitants poses no threat whatsoever.

'Let's find this famous Kali Strata, then.' We could see the higher steps from the track, and after walking around the harbour the entrance to the street is easy to find. I leave him at the foot of the wide stone steps and watch him skip away.

'See you later, sunshine.'

Chapter Twelve

Nico

When I see Maggie pat Alfie's shoulder and give him that run-along-and-play signal, my heart lifts. I had hoped that I would see them this morning. The welcoming provisions I left were deliberately light. I did not want her to be holed up at the cottage for days on end.

My 'surprise' bumping into her on the harbour – 'I've only been here five minutes' – may not be particularly convincing, especially in view of the three empty coffee cups and remnants of breakfast on the table. The taverna has the best view of every corner of the quayside and I have been sitting there for the best part of two hours.

'Maggie, hello. Sleep well?' I ask. I beckon her over to join me.

She must be very independent to travel all this way on her own with just a child for company, so maybe she'll want to keep to herself. Or perhaps she'll let me take her under my wing – a father figure to help her get used to our foreign life and customs. Hallelujah. She's happy to accept my invitation.

She tells me Alfie has gone to discover the empty buildings on the Kali Strata. She says that he's got a vivid imagination and assumes all sorts of characters in his games: the SS commandant (I'll have to steer him away from that one); the humble English soldier; the Greek resistance fighter (that's more like it); and the dashing army officer. She's clearly very proud of her little brother, but she soon moves away from the subject and starts to explain why she's here.

'My plan, Nico, is to bring tourists to Symos.'

I nod my approval. Anything that brings cash to the island would be welcome.

'Yes,' I say. 'How?'

'In English we call it self-catering, but I don't know

how to say that in Greek. No hotels.'

'No hotels?' I'm a little puzzled.

'No hotels. Rooms, houses, villas and cottages. Cottages like our cottage. I mean like your cottage.'

After the war, the English were here for some time and some of them were billeted on the island. A young man called Colin Jenkins, a scholar on National Service, lodged with us and he taught me the language over the winter of 1945. Years later, working on and off at Cosmo's taverna has helped me to keep using my English and I've got a good vocabulary, even if my grammar is not always perfect.

'Yes. I understand. Like my cottage. You want me help you find them?'

'No. I mean yes. I mean not yet. First I have to be able to speak Greek as well as you.'

I laugh. 'Momma says I speak very badly. You speak Greek already quite good.'

'But quite good is not good enough,' Maggie says. 'If I am to do well here, I need my Greek to be perfect. There are very few Greek women in business. Being a woman will make it even harder.'

I admire this young woman who is setting out to learn my language in the same way that I was once determined to learn hers.

'Why not I help you?' I suggest. 'I you help with Greek. You me help with English.'

'But your English is already very good, Nico.'

'Good is my English but better I want learn.'

I wonder if I am over-exaggerating the shortcomings of my grammar a little, but I want to buy as much time as possible with this lovely young woman.

'Okay. You've got a deal.'

And so, over a thick black coffee and a slice of baklava, a deal is struck and after these brief refreshments we set out together along our own yellow brick road.

Chapter Thirteen

Nico

I really like Colin Jenkins. He's middle-aged now and has a family. He teaches classics at Eton College. He says it's quite a well-known school in England. He comes to Symos when he can and always brings Momma a special gift. But however fine a man he is, it is so difficult not to link him to that terrible day when I sailed back to Symos on my own with the grimmest cargo ever to land at the Custom House.

I knew that Momma was expecting her boys home and would have brushed her black hair until it shone and, unusually for her, put on a smudge of lipstick. I remember seeing her watching me navigate carefully into the harbour. She was wearing her favourite dark-blue dress and waved happily to Papa Benediktos as she passed him on her way to welcome us. Gone were the days of dressing like a widow to watch the fleet return. How sad. Little did she know the major role the Papa would be playing in our lives over the next few days.

As our colourful skiff headed past the deserted London Sponge offices, where as a child she had danced to the music of the brass band, she must have thought it strange that her husband had entrusted this most difficult stage of the journey to sixteen-year-old me and hadn't even bothered to come on deck to supervise. But I was doing a fine job, keeping the boat in a straight line and heading perfectly for the Karteras family mooring, following the age-old instruction to keep the circular window of the Custom House in the dead centre of the prow.

She didn't need to see my face as I docked the boat to realise that something was amiss. However much Tata wanted to encourage me to learn, mooring was a two-man job and he would never leave a son to do it single-handed. My face only confirmed her worst fears and, seeing the outline of the forms beneath the tarpaulin on

Give Me Your Tomorrow

the deck, Momma sank to her knees on the jetty and let out a wailing scream that could have been heard on Rhodes.

'Oh, Nicos! Nicos! What have you done?'

Hearing her anguished cries, a small crowd gathered. The island was under British occupation and a couple of English military police started to take control. We had got to know some of them by name, but they couldn't speak Greek and we couldn't speak English. One held back the crowd while his colleague went to investigate.

The soldier headed along towards the boat and put his arm around my wailing Momma's shoulder. He spoke to her in a gentle voice.

Momma couldn't understand, but, swaying from side to side and moaning indecipherable words to herself, she simply pointed towards the tarpaulin on the deck with me kneeling alongside it in an equally wretched state. I looked at my mother, my eyes imploring her forgiveness.

The soldier left her side and jumped onto the skiff.

I too couldn't understand what he said as he pulled back the tarpaulin. He winced as he caught sight of the terrible gash in Yianni junior's leg, then he put the tarpaulin back in place and placed a hand on my shoulder. He said something that was clearly kind and sympathetic, helped me to my feet and gestured for me to come with him.

'Smith!' he shouted to his colleague. He said something else and repeated 'Jenkins' several times.

His assistant saluted 'Yes, sir!' I understood that.

As Smith left for assistance, the crowd headed along the jetty towards Momma, but the military policeman, David Stephenson, held a hand up to them and shouted, 'Stop!'

He stood between Momma and me and waited. I needed to hold her and beg her to forgive me, but Stephenson's presence prevented me from doing so. We didn't have to wait long, as the British had set up their headquarters in the Custom House, and in a few minutes Bill Smith returned with two colleagues.

Stephenson gestured to Bill and the other soldier to keep the crowd back and then beckoned Colin Jenkins to join him on the jetty.

Years later, Colin told me how he became involved and the then unintelligible words that passed between them. 'Okay, Jenkins. We've got a nasty situation here. This young lad has just moored up with two bodies on board. I guess they're his family and this is his mum. Can you help?'

Colin, an Oxford-educated private whose classics degree had resulted in him being hand-picked to become a translator in Greece, stepped forward. Fortunately he had soon turned his knowledge of ancient Greek into an understanding of the modern language, and he broke into fluent Greek immediately.

'I'm Colin Jenkins,' he said. 'I'm here to help you. Let's get you off the quayside and into the Custom House.'

He led the way past the small crowd of locals.

I spotted Papa Benediktos in the group and asked, 'Can the Papa come with us?'

'Sure,' said Jenkins after getting the okay from his superior.

Our group went into the Custom House and entered the white office that had once been the economic hub of the island. We took the seats we were offered. Behind the large desk, framed by a Union Jack and a regimental flag was a photograph of the King of England. Stephenson seated himself immediately beneath it.

Papa Benediktos, a grey-bearded old man who had been the family's priest for over twenty years, sat between us holding one of our hands in each of his. Momma was leaning towards him, resting her head on the black robes of his shoulder and sobbing constantly. I, my eyes sore from tears, sat upright looking into the middle distance.

Stephenson conducted the questioning through Jenkins. Before he started, he looked me up and down and said something quietly to Jenkins. Colin nodded and smiled at me. I suppose we must have looked decent enough. Perhaps they weren't going to give us the third degree? Everyone appeared to be very sympathetic. Jenkins started to translate Stephenson's interrogation.

'Okay, son. I can see that you've been through a terrible ordeal. Tell us what happened.'

I tried to start my story. As I did so, I squeezed the Papa's hand for support and got a firm grip of assurance in return.

'Yianni was diving for sponges. I was *Kolaouzieris*.'

That was as far as I got. I started to shiver uncontrollably and my chattering teeth prevented any more words. Sweat streamed down my face and I felt myself slipping into a trance. Stephenson stood up. He said something and then clicked his heels and saluted. Jenkins returned his salute. He then translated for the Papa's benefit. 'The boy's in shock. No more of this today. He told me to get the medics to check Nico over. Look after them, Father, and find out for me what happened.' That was his parting shot.

Within a few hours of docking, the funeral director had brought two caskets to the quayside together with Sunday clothes collected from our family home by a friend. Out of the glare of the crowd, the mortician took the bodies into the cabin, dressed them respectably and took them out to be placed gently into the coffins. There was no shortage of volunteers to carry them up the two hundred steps to number forty-five. Momma and the Papa, his arms around me, stumbling along wrapped in an army-issue blanket, followed the procession.

At the house the lids were propped against the outside wall, one on either side of the grand portico, while the open caskets were laid on the large table hurriedly placed at the foot of the ornate staircase.

Momma went upstairs to change for her forthcoming vigil. Benediktos took me into the small front room.

'Can you talk?'

No longer shivering, I caught sight of myself in a

mirror. My pallor matched the lifeless corpses in the adjacent hall. I nodded.

'So what do I tell them, Nico?'

'I saw something big go under the boat. Yianni was diving. I felt him give the alarm signal,' I yanked my right hand a couple of times to demonstrate, 'and I shouted to Tata to come. Tata was in the cabin and he came up on deck. I said there was a shark and he just picked up his knife, put it between his teeth and dived in.'

A frown came fleetingly to Papa Benediktos's forehead. He did not look convinced. As a priest on a sponge-diving island, the Papa was as well versed in marine life as any diver and it would be difficult for me to satisfy him with my story.

'Go on.'

'I pulled on the *skandalopetra* rope and I could feel Yianni heading up. I pulled for a few minutes and then suddenly the rope went slack, like when you go fishing and you lose a big fish. And I fell backwards onto the deck. I pulled the rope to the surface and it was chewed and frayed.'

I gulped nervously as I realised there was a hole in my story. What if he asked me to show him the chewed and frayed rope? Both bellstones and their ropes were fully intact. I could make up a third, but my mother knew that there were only two.

'I looked into the water and saw that Tata had got Yianni onto the surface and was lying back and holding him around his chest with his left arm. They had drifted away from the boat and the boat was firmly anchored. I couldn't move it towards them. Tata was stabbing at the shark with his knife in his right hand.' I again did the actions.

Papa Benediktos looked concerned, but held my hand firmly for comfort.

I continued. 'Dad killed the shark but then two more started to circle.'

Sweat built up on the priest's brow. 'I have known

just one shark attack in all my years on Symos. Are you saying that three were involved?"

I nodded.

'Carry on.'

'Tata fought them with just one hand while holding Yianni up. It seemed to go on for ages, but finally it stopped and there were no sharks. Tata had finished them both off.'

'He was a very brave man,' Benediktos interjected.

I nodded again.

'So what happened then, Nico?'

'Tata must have drifted about two hundred metres. He waved to me to bring the boat towards him but the anchor had snagged and I couldn't shift it. So he headed towards me, dragging Yianni. He reached the boat and told me to pull Yianni on board. But I could see that there was no hope for Yianni. "No, Tata," I said, "You first. Yianni's dead." But he insisted. So I took Yianni's arm and pulled. He was so heavy and I'm not that strong. I felt Tata pushing him to help me. I pulled for ages and ages and finally dragged Yianni on board and went to help Tata.'

'So. When you got your brother on board, he was already dead?'

'Yes. His leg was in tatters. I then looked for Tata. But he was not there. He'd gone.'

Papa Benediktos must have known why Tata would make such an effort to get his son's body on board. How long had he preached to the congregation the importance of a Christian burial? Perhaps he saw a little truth in my story.

I continued. 'After ten minutes Tata came back up to the surface. I managed to get a lifebelt over him and after a struggle I got him onto the deck.'

'And he was dead?'

'My father was the greatest diver in Greece, Papa, but even he could not have survived underwater for so long.'

Benediktos shook his head and looked at me. 'I'll report back to the Custom House and make sure that they grant permission for the funeral to go ahead. You go and prepare for the vigil, Nico.'

Before long the story was all around Yiossos. Benediktos reported to Jenkins and Colin had related it briefly to the harbour master while completing the formalities and preparing the necessary paperwork. And soon everyone knew that I, Nico (the tuberculosis-damaged weakling who would take for ever to haul a sponge on board, never mind lift a strapping Adonis like his brother), had taken an eternity to get the body onto the deck. They knew that if I had not pathetically taken so very, very long to carry out my father's wishes, my father would still be with us.

At least Yianni Karteras was still a hero. On Symos his wartime exploits were legends to rank beside Homer's Odysseus, so nobody was in the least surprised by his valour in trying to save his eldest son or his insistence that salvaging his son's body was more important than his own salvation.

Nobody disbelieved my story. I may have been an overweight momma's boy, but I was a totally honest overweight momma's boy.

~

Momma, dressed head to toe in black, came slowly, falteringly but regally down the stairs to take her place alongside me. I had positioned two hard wooden stools at the foot of the staircase, allowing us to sit with our heads within a breath of the faces of Momma's husband and son, my father and brother, lying sightlessly in the two open boxes as the long overnight vigil began. It was a vigil interrupted regularly by visitors calling to deposit a small keepsake in the coffins or to simply pay their respects to both of us.

Years earlier, when the sponge industry had effectively come to an end and twenty thousand residents had left the island, property in Yiossos had become almost worthless. The Symos branch of London Sponge closed and the keys to the grand palazzo belonging to the company were handed to the Karteras family, with instructions to live in the house and keep it safe until business picked up and the owners returned.

Our menfolk had been reliable divers and the women had been efficient workers both in the processing workshops and in the offices. Handing the keys to us had been a sensible choice. The Karteras were not alone. Other families were asked to 'house sit' several properties that over the years would start to crumble and decay from misuse, and would suffer at the hands of Italian and German occupiers.

It had been Momma's father-in-law who had taken control of those keys, and when she had married into the family she had loved living in one of the most spectacular residences on the island. But her connections with the house stretched farther back – back to the day that she was born.

But now, as she sat looking at the ghastly white faces of her beloved son and husband, Momma decided she had had enough. The residence would be locked up after the funeral and she and I would move farther up the hill to live with my grandmother in San Stefano in the little house where Colin Jenkins eventually became our lodger.

Symos only really had one town, but the three hundred steps of the Kali Strata split Yiossos into the decadent part with its classical buildings at the bottom and the working-class, small, whitewashed stone houses in San Stefano at the top. And it was up towards the church of San Stefano that the still open coffins were carried the next morning, followed by a procession led by Papa Benediktos to rival the crowds that had once cheered the divers down towards the Custom House when the sponge fleet left town. But there was no cheering in this slow crocodile of sadness as it plodded wearily up the steps towards the small church.

As the long and mournful service ended, the congregation filed past the open caskets to place a final parting kiss on Tata and Yianni. When Momma and I had given our gentle kisses and whispered our final messages, the lids were placed onto the coffins and nailed into place. Although it was merely light tapping through pre-prepared holes, for me the noise of the hammering on the nails echoed through the church like a death knell signifying the end of my youth.

The two coffins were carried from the church to the graveyard behind. The cemetery resembles a large village of miniature, narrow, dazzling white churches, each with a single white stone cross rising from the apex of its roof. Each building in this model village stands at the head of a concrete tomb large enough to take three or four caskets.

The mourners stopped at the only open tomb and, after the old priest made a final prayer, the wooden boxes were put in place and the concrete lid slid back into position. There the bodies would rest for several years before, due to limited room, the graves would be needed for new bodies. Then Momma and I would have to return and in another mournful ceremony anoint the bones with wine before placing them in the town's ossuary.

The crowd turned away from the grave, leaving Momma and me alone for a few final silent moments. I thought that my mother should be the last one to leave the grave and pulled back from her, allowing her a last lingering minute with her beloved. I hadn't noticed that Papa Benediktos had also stayed behind and, taking a couple of steps back, I bumped into the old man.

I knew immediately who I had backed into. There was no mistaking the scent of the incense. I froze slightly as two black-robed arms came over my shoulders and crossed at my chest.

'Now, young man. We need to talk. Soon ...'

Chapter Fourteen

Nico

I went to visit Papa Benediktos a few days after the funeral. I walked into the church and found the priest kneeling before the altar in silent prayer.

'I am glad you came, Nico,' said the Papa without looking up.

'How did you know it was me, Papa?'

'I get very few visitors nowadays, Nico, and even fewer male visitors. I can recognise a boy's footsteps. I've been expecting you.'

'Papa Detective,' I said, nervously realising that I could not fool this wise old man.

'I'm God's detective, Nico.' He smiled. 'Come and sit here.' He patted a pew at the front of the church.

We sat together – old man and boy – before the altar. There were still a few dying flowers left over from the funeral dotted around the little church, and looking at the dropping petals, I thought of my father and brother starting to shrivel in their graves.

'I know that you lied, Nico. I know that you didn't tell the truth.'

I flushed. There was no point arguing with Papa Detective. I looked down guiltily.

'And I know why you did it,' Benediktos continued. 'You did it to protect someone. I don't know if it was your brother or your father, but I know you well enough, Nicos Karteras. You did it to help someone, didn't you?'

'Yes, Papa,' I said sheepishly, eyes still firmly fixed on the floor.

'Well?' continued the Papa. 'Who were you protecting?'

'You won't tell anybody?'

'Only our Lord,' said Benediktos, looking at an icon depicting the crucified Christ.

'Okay, Papa. I did it to protect Momma, I did it to protect Tata and I did it to protect Yianni.'

'I didn't expect it to be all three. Explain.'

'Well, Yianni was stupid. I told him about the sharks but he had to go and attack one and ended up in the water. And I told Tata that Momma wouldn't want him using the *skafandro*.'

'The skafandro?'

'Yes, Tata captured one from the Germans and wanted to try it out going for some deep sponges.'

'I thought he would have known better after all the trouble those suits have caused.'

'So did I, but this was such a fantastic suit he just had to try it. I tried to tell him not to. He died because I thought he would have enough air to let me leave the compressor for a few moments and try to save Yianni. It's my fault that he's dead.'

'That's not the way I see it, Nico. And how have you protected Anna?'

'I've protected her by keeping Tata's *skafandro* secret. She wouldn't have been able to take the truth.'

'You're a kind boy, Nico. You always think about others. But by thinking of others you have damaged others' opinion of you.'

I knew that the rumours around Yiossos and San Stefano all cast me as the villain.

'How are you going to live with that?'

'Well, it *was* my fault, Papa. I'll have to live with it.'

'I will be here for you, Nico. What do you plan to do? Most young men and women have left Symos now.'

'I'll stay here and look after Momma and my grandmother.'

'Are you sure? It's going to be a very lonely life for you. There are very few young girls around for you to marry and soon there will be fewer. I hear that the Alexandris are heading for Florida.'

It was news to me. The four Alexandris sisters, who ranged in age from twelve to sixteen, had often been singled out by Momma.

'Momma always said that one of those girls would be a perfect bride for me, Papa.'

'Maybe there'll be another, Nico.'

Papa Benediktos said the words without conviction. He must have known how few wedding ceremonies he carried out now compared to twenty years earlier, when every month saw him help a score of couples to make their vows. I could tell that he held out little hope of me finding any woman – never mind the virgin bride that tradition demanded – among the dwindling population of Symos.

'Remember,' he said, 'I'll always be here for you. And as a penance for your confession and to earn your absolution ...'

I wrinkled my nose and frowned quizzically.

'Confession?' I said, then realised that of course I had made a confession to the Papa. He had kindly and gently coaxed the words from me without the usual formalities of confession.

'For your penance ... nothing. Because you, Nico, are guilty only of humility and kindness and there is no punishment in my book for that.'

'Bless you, Papa. And thank you.'

I rose and left the church. As I headed back towards home, an overwhelming sense of relief poured over me. The guilt that for days had weighed so heavily on me like a bellstone had been lightened. At least Papa Benediktos and God understood.

~

A few weeks later, we left the palatial building that had been our home. It was a magnificent structure, but apart from the wonderful white cast-iron table and chairs on the balcony that had been deemed too heavy to ship, the London Sponge Company had returned most of the expensive fixtures and fittings to England before handing over the keys and the house was as sparsely furnished as any fisherman's home in San Stefano.

My life on the island revolved around looking after Momma and my ageing grandmother. As I had explained to the Papa, I felt that this was my duty. I had been responsible for the upheaval that had condemned my mother to a lifetime dressed in black. The three of us had few needs other than food and water. The skiff had been sold and with the proceeds from that, along with the savings set aside by my sensible father and grandparents, we got by.

Momma and her own mother, Nana, were just two of the many black-clad women you saw around San Stefano. Both the high mortality rate in the sponge industry and the ravages of the war had taken a heavy toll on the adult male population of the island. It was normal for widows to sit outside their front doors watching life pass by and share gossip with fellow widows in neighbouring properties.

Girls didn't feature much in my life. I wasn't a spoiled child or a spoiled young man, but food was one of life's few pleasures and Momma was an excellent and prolific cook. Overweight, I never looked much of a catch to the scarce young members of the fairer sex, and as there were a number of older men on the island who had lived a bit, captained ships, made a few drachma and weren't averse to spending those drachma on a pretty face, I soon gave up all hope of finding a partner.

Work was hard to find, but in the summer I would sometimes help in the taverna of our family friend Cosmo, on the thriving harbour waterfront, and at the start of the sixties I began to notice more and more non-Greek customers. They mostly made a day visit on the Rhodes ferry, but some would sail into the harbour on beautiful white yachts and stay for a couple of days. As the visitor numbers grew, I made a resolution: to polish my English.

These days, when I am not looking after Momma or working at the quayside taverna, I spend my time with the island's pyrotechnicians. Fireworks are an old tradition on Symos and most of the group's work is geared towards the massive Easter shows. But as visitor numbers to the islands increased, local officials suggested that a few more displays throughout the summer might attract even more visitors to Symos.

Give Me Your Tomorrow

Before I took charge, any sensible new volunteers who entered the fireworks workshop would have shut the door nervously, turned and flown down the mountain back to safety. Gloves and goggles were non-existent. The lack of ventilation was bad enough, but the heavy-smoking firework team's practice of puffing away while packing rocket tubes with sulphurous concoctions would send the bravest newcomer fleeing for cover. I'm glad to say I changed all that.

For ten years I had been a willing helper before the elderly Dimitrios decided to retire in 1956. He recommended to the Pyrotechnic Society that Nicos Karteras would be his natural successor to take charge of all future displays. By then I was just twenty-six and I would put a bomb (figuratively speaking) under proceedings. I loved it. The prospects of planning spectacular explosions added a bit of excitement to my life and – apart from some of the motley crew having a few lost fingertips; a misfortune that went with the hobby – there hasn't been a significant accident for ages.

I proved Dimitrios right. He had made a wise choice, and on the night of the Apollo Extravaganza, when he was well into his eighties, his eyes filled with tears of pride. For me, the display had been exhilarating, exciting, electrifying – everything my ordinary life wasn't. And now, just days later, in the company of my beautiful new tenant Maggie, am I stupid to feel the stirrings of something else that I thought I had lost – hope?

Chapter Fifteen

Nico

Life on Symos revolves mostly around the town of Yiossos and its smaller sister, San Stefano, immediately above. There are a couple of tiny hamlets around the coast accessible by boat or on foot, but there are probably less than two miles of driveable road on the whole island. Cars are a rarity.

When an octogenarian sponge magnate who had left Symos to make his fortune in Tarpon Springs, Florida decided to return to spend the end of his days in his birthplace, he drove triumphantly off the ferry in a huge pale-green Cadillac, all chrome and enormous white walled tyres. He managed to drive about two hundred yards along the quay before realising that the car was wider than the space available to leave the harbour. This resulted in great amusement for the crowd of onlookers, but for the old entrepreneur and his entourage just a shrug of the shoulders followed by some refreshment in the nearest bar. The car had remained on the quayside for weeks and was being suggested by some as a tourist attraction before the ancient owner shipped it off to an eager buyer in Rhodes at a bargain-basement price.

The track up to the mountaintop above the harbour, which branches off to a remote monastery in the island's interior, is navigable by motorcycle and I can reach my small complex of church, firework factory and TV mast on my trusty machine. Carrying boxes of highly flammable and volatile ingredients up a bumpy potholed track on the back of a hot two-stroke powered bike is seen by even the most foolhardy of the pyrotechnic crowd as a risk too far, and these are transported to the mountaintop by that most reliable and underrated carrier – the donkey.

Everyone knows me for my pyrotechnics. I'm Nico Fireworks; always willing to lend a helping hand; always one to turn to when they need cheering up; always ready with a smile on my face and an ear to listen. If only they knew the real Nico.

About once a month I travel to the Rhodes harbourmaster's office to collect the exotic chemicals that I ship in from around the world. During these trips I have time to kill before my return to Symos and I sit in one of the harbour's bars watching the world pass by.

Rhodes harbour is in a working area on the city extremities. There are a lot of seamen around and it fascinates me to watch the women at the port plying their trade. They offer to buy a lone sailor ouzo or a glass of retsina; all gaiety and tossing of heads. I marvel at how they hang on their target's every word as if entranced by his tales of engine-room grime or his scent of fish guts. How I wish that I could have someone look at me with adoring eyes beneath fluttering eyelashes and be fascinated by my fireworks.

But on the occasions that I have turned on my bar stool to find such a companion alongside me, despite the hardening I feel from the frisson of excitement – the excitement of the unknown, of the lavender-scented woman with the crimson lips, immodest cleavage and welcome smile and the thought of my virgin body being caressed at last – I always spurn their advances. Not because I want to. I want nothing more than to see and to touch what is beneath that tight skirt and above those stocking tops. I am so tired of being reduced to what Benediktos refers to as 'spilling your seed', and the opportunity to spill it into a warm moist body, even if done so while covered in one of the foul-smelling johnnies that I bought out of curiosity, is temptation beyond compare.

The women, sensing my interest, brush my face or gently stroke my hand and I feel my shoulders tense, my hands shake and my voice quiver. I make my excuses and leave the bar, a hand in my pocket surreptitiously adjusting myself in an attempt to appear nonchalant and avoid the embarrassment of leaving the establishment with my excitement obvious to all.

The women smile but they do not laugh. They know the mysterious power they hold over me. They know only they could give me those few minutes of pleasure – those minutes that obsess us all, from simple fishermen to prime ministers.

Why do I fail to succumb to their charms? How do I suppress the desires I so visibly feel? Throughout my youth and my adult life I have listened to the teachings of Papa Benediktos, who persuaded me that my remarkable survival from deadly tuberculosis was God's very own work. And I listened to my mother and her constant lectures on the sanctity of marriage and the overriding importance of virginity.

It has been drummed into me that all men should marry a virgin, and it is customary on the island for a bloodied sheet to be triumphantly draped from a bedroom window following a wedding night for all to see. This is an island of real men – seafarers, boat builders, sponge divers. Most of them tell me, 'Who listens to that rubbish? A small glass of red wine is exactly the right colour for virgin blood. And anyway all *men* should marry a virgin – who said that all *women* should marry a virgin?'

But for me, if a woman (I have given up on the thought of a girl) is going to save herself for me, I am going to do the same for her. Christ resisted temptation. I am no Christ, but I want to do the same. Restless dreams of hippy summers of romance always conclude with the sound of church bells and the vision of a bloodied sheet.

And so I always leave Rhodes with my precious cargo of pyrotechnic combustibles and my virginity intact, but with such overwhelming and bursting frustration that, back at home, after wishing my mother goodnight and going upstairs, I think of what might have been. I feel the whore's thigh and nipples as I lie on the bed and stroke my own thigh and touch my own nipples. The scent of her lavender, *her* lavender on *my* clothes, fills my nostrils: fills my head; fills the room;

and then I spill my seed – from just the slightest touch.

Chapter Sixteen
Maggie

The deal is mornings for my Greek and afternoons for Nico's English, and Nico thinks that there's no better way to start than to throw me straight in at the deep end. So I am armed with a shopping list in a busy and bustling shopping area where nobody at all speaks English (except Nico, of course).

Lesson one is 'The Post Office'. Nico guides me in through the door and stands, hands on hips, watching my performance. He shouts something across to the cashier, but I don't catch it. Hopefully he's telling her to go easy on me. She's serving (and talking) at lightning speed. I've got a few butterflies but at least the queue has given me time to get my thoughts together. Okay: very best Greek.

'I want to post this letter to England.' I hand it to the cashier, who quotes me the price. I hand over five drachma and she gives me two back. I must look puzzled as the cashier says 'Okay?' I check my change.

'No,' I say and struggle to tell her I expected two drachma and fifty lepta. Her face breaks into a grin and I see she is looking over my shoulder towards Nico, who laughs and says, 'Thanks, Agatha. Give her the fifty.' She hands me the small coin and the stamp and we leave the post office.

'Well. Thank you for that, Nico,' I say, pausing to place the letter in the collection box. 'The clerk – Agatha, did you call her? She seems nice.' About the same age as Nico, she had looked at him adoringly. An old flame, perhaps?

'Yes, Agatha's my cousin. We grew up together. I am sorry for tricking you, but it shows me that your Greek is very good already. I worry that you will not need many lessons.' Nico looks glum. I touch his arm. 'Beginner's luck,' I say. 'Wait until you hear my conjugations.'

Nico hasn't a clue what I am talking about, but it feels good to have someone to share this experience with. 'I wonder how long the letter will take to get to Liverpool?' I say.

'Go back and ask Agatha – she's not busy now.' The queue has gone as I go back into the post office. Agatha says she is confident that it will be there within a week. 'Okay, Nico, I've drawn up a list of everything I need, so where next?'

Nico looks down the list. 'My reading is not too good, Maggie.'

'That's my writing, Nico. Mum always said I should be a doctor. Let's see: chicken, salad, fruit, water, a hat for Alfie, another for me, Nivea cream for our white English skin, a couple of swimming costumes ...'

He takes my arm and we move into the market. It's a riot of colour with piles of shiny black aubergines, tomatoes like red tennis balls and scrawny bunches of lettuce leaves that would go on Mum's compost heap rather than her plate. My confidence grows despite the incessant and unintelligible chatter and shouting all around me. God knows how I would be on my own, but everyone seems to know Nico and, importantly, they all seem to like him and I haven't had to pay for anything yet. They all slap him on the back and compliment him on his Apollo Extravaganza. He's quite a celebrity.

I put my salad in my basket and we move along to look for chicken. I can't see a butcher's stall. Nico directs me towards a pile of small cages and sure enough there's plenty of chickens. But they're very much alive and fluttering. Fresh, I suppose, but what am I supposed to do with them? I look at their beady eyes and feel like I'm watching a bunch of inmates on death row. It's a good job Alfie's not here or he'd be begging me to buy them. I can see Chicken Little and her friends at home at the cottage. A woman points at one of the cages. The chicken man opens it, there's a fluttering of wings and feathers for a second or two and the poor creature's days are numbered. Somehow poultry no longer appeals. 'I think we'll have some fish.'

We buy fresh sardines and then visit the chemist for

some Nivea. I get a lovely wide-brimmed straw hat from the little dress shop for me and for Alfie I choose a white peaked cap from the children's outfitters. That will shade his eyes, but it's his neck I'm worried about so we find a linen supplier and I buy some white cotton tea towels. I'll adapt the cap by sewing one of the tea towels inside to hang down around the side and back. That will protect his neck and ears. A lot of kids wouldn't be seen dead wearing it, but he'll be made up when I show him his very own French Foreign Legion hat. Next he'll be asking if we can find a camel to get us around.

I've done pretty well for my first morning.

'Everything on your list?' asks Nico.

'Not quite. There's still the swimwear' – I can feel myself blushing; I'm not sure that Nico and I are well enough acquainted for him to help me while I try on the bikini I fancy – 'but I think I'll leave that for now.' I look at my watch. 'I promised Alfie I wouldn't be too long. Thanks for everything, Nico. Do you want to start on your lessons this afternoon?'

We agree on a time to meet back at the cottage.

I join up with Alfie. He's had a brilliant time and talks non-stop about his morning's exploration. I pass the tavernas and fishing boats at double-quick time. It's the first time we've done this bit alone; I don't think Nico will be in a hurry to translate some of the remarks I'm getting from the waiters and fishermen. At least they seem to be saying them in good humour. I'll be looking the words up in the dictionary when we get back. It's a pity my workmate Sam from Liverpool Electrical isn't here. She could put down any of the lads' comments instantly. I wonder how 'In your wildest dreams' translates into Greek.

~

Nico turns up a few minutes late for his first English lesson.

Alfie's waiting in the garden behind the cottage in legionnaire mode, on the lookout to give Nico cover from potential Arab ambush when he eventually comes down the path. He doesn't see the small white motorboat put-putting along close to the shoreline and misses Nico mooring at the tiny beach behind the island, climbing the rock staircase, crossing the island and the bridge and arriving slightly breathless at the gate in the picket fence.

'Sorry, Maggie. I am always proud to be on time. Everyone says arrive a minute late for Nico's fireworks and you will miss the start.'

'It's not a problem, Nico. It's only three minutes.'

'I borrow Cosmo's boat so I get here fresh and not panting like a dog, but it is a long time ago I last sail here and I get the time wrong.'

'Nico, don't *worry*. You *mistimed* it. There you are. Every cloud has a silver lining. You've got a new word for your vocabulary.'

'Every cloud has a silver lining?'

I explain. 'And you've got a new phrase too.'

I've given these lessons a lot of thought. I'm going to be tutoring Alfie, so I've got plenty of pens, pencils and notebooks if we need them. Nico's English is already very good. There's only the odd wrong word and a bit of faulty grammar, but he's not too sure with his reading, so I decide that the best way to start is to sit on the terrace with one of Alfie's books and try to get Nico to read it to me. The large print will help him with the strange English alphabet.

Sitting beneath the canvas canopy's wonderful shade, protected from the fierce sun, my senses fill with the heady scent of wild lavender and rosemary that carries towards us on a gentle breeze. I settle down to listen to a chubby, middle-aged Greek man reading *Well Done, Secret Seven*. It's surreal: quite surreal.

After a few chapters of Peter and his crew and Scamper the dog's adventure, Nico is making good progress. He knows that this is a kids' book but finds its large print easy and its simple vocabulary useful. The second part of the lesson is for us to hold a conversation and for me to correct him where necessary.

'Well done with the reading, Nico,' I say. 'We'll finish that now and we'll do what we call "conversation". Do you understand?'

'Not sure. Conversation?'

'Yes. That's what we're having now.' I make an expansive gesture, close my hands and open them again. 'We are having a conversation.'

Nico twigs. 'Okay. Yes, I understand.'

'Good. Now, tell me about the cottage.'

'The cottage was built by not my father but by the father of my father.'

'Your grandfather.'

'Gran-father?'

'No. Grand-father. Gran-*d*.'

'Okay, grandfather. Thank you. And my gran-*d*-father,' he smiles, 'lived here with my gran-*d*-mudder and her six children. Six!' he exclaims, holding up six digits.

'Wow. Eight people living in here!'

Nico smiles. 'Quite usual. Big family. Small house. Quite usual.' He continues. 'When my grandfather die . . .'

I interrupt, 'Died.'

'Sorry, Maggie. When my gran-*d*-father die-*d*, my uncle Khristophoros live here with his family.'

I don't correct him again this time; I know that it will come good and I want to hear more.

'My family. Sponges, sponges, sponges. It is in our blood. Khristophoros? Fish, fish, fish. It is in his blood. Khristophoros, he has two boys and a girl.'

The photograph in Alfie's room now takes on a meaning.

Nico points to the cliff. 'No bridge then. Me and Yianni and little Khristophoros, Spiro and Agatha. There. We dive.'

I stand up and walk towards the gate.

Nico joins me. 'Dive here,' he says.

I can make out a well-worn rock just below the clifftop. It juts out from the cliff like a small diving board and I can imagine the children's screams of pleasure as they dived the thirty feet down to the water.

'Thirty metres deep.' Nico points it out again. 'Sometimes *skandalopetra*.' He mimes clutching the bellstone to his chest. 'And sometimes lose a tooth,' he adds, bringing the imaginary stone to his mouth with a thump. 'At the bottom, everything beautiful. Beautiful fish, beautiful big, how you say, *astakos* and *garida*?' He holds his hands out and moves his fingers as if he is playing a very fast tune on an invisible piano.

'Crabs?'

'No. No crabs. Lobsters and prawns. How can I forget these when I help in a taverna?'

He goes on to explain that it was here that they had practised their sponge divers' breathing, exploring the nooks and crannies in the submerged rock walls that house an amazing variety of life. It was the perfect spot: although the water is incredibly deep, the channel between the island and the cottage is normally calm, with the seaward side of the island taking the full force of any rougher seas, leaving this secret gulley peacefully quiet.

He leads me back to my seat on the terrace.

'Khristophoros. The Germans, they kill him. So his wife and the kids they come to live with us on Kali Strata.'

'I'm sorry.'

'No sorry, Maggie. Everyone on Symos lose someone in the war. After a short time they go to the USA to Florida to my aunt's family. Only Agatha stays on Symos.'

'So the cottage was empty?'

'Yes, the cottage empty since 1945. Before she leave, my aunt she says to me and Yianni, "Nico, Yianni, you look after my cottage and one day I come back to Symos and retire there." But my mother has plenty letters and photos from her. Big car. Big house. My aunty not come back to Symos. "You come to Florida, Anna," she says. But Momma, she says, "No, Penelope, I want to be bury with my Yianni." My mother, she never leave Symos. Never.'

I'm saddened by Nico's story; it makes me think of him as Caliban imprisoned on his barren remote island. But comparing him to the ugly Caliban is cruel. Perhaps he could be the more lyrical Ariel, and his mother, Anna, keeping him captive and at her beck and call, his Prospero.

Nico sees my pensive look. 'Sorry, Maggie. You, how you say, boring?'

'No, no, Nico, I'm not bored at all. Quite the opposite, in fact. Your story fascinates me. Go on.'

'In 1961 I looked and saw cottage is broken. The windows is smash and there's sheeps in the rooms.'

'How sad.'

'So I say to Momma, "I, Nico, will feex the villa." I see some tourists in Yiossos and I say to Momma. "We can rent out rooms to tourists like Mrs Constanides. But our rooms have a real sea view."' He laughs. 'The best in the Dodecanese.' He points at the vast expanse of water.

I share his laughter. 'Well, Nico. I have to say that you have made a very good job of "feexing" it. And finally, "at long last" as we say, you've got your very own "tourists" to rent it. And it really is beautiful.'

'Like you,' Nico says softly and then blushes and clumsily knocks the Blyton book off the table, as if to distract me from his comment.

How do I take that throwaway line? Is Nico going to be just another man in the world of men who are only interested in how a woman looks, or is he the sweet innocent who genuinely wants to help me with my Greek that he first seemed? We've been in each other's company for a fair few hours and the worst that has happened is this ham-fisted attempt at a compliment. He's hardly a womaniser. But however pleasant a person he is, Nico has none of the dashing looks of the man who left the harbour on the shiny new motorcycle. My first impression was of a father figure and I don't think that's likely to change.

Give Me Your Tomorrow

As Nico bends down to pick up the book, Alfie appears on the terrace and the awkward moment passes.

He says, 'So *there* you are Nico. I've been watching out for you from behind the cottage.'

'I come by boat today.'

'You've got a boat! Fab. Can I have a ride?'

'Another day, Alfie. Nico has to leave soon. What have you been up to?'

He tells us that he's been exploring behind the cottage. He's decided that the land leading down from the track is a pretty credible desert. There's no sand, but as the ground is treeless it makes a passable Sahara for him. 'I shot a few Arabs who broke for cover from behind the outhouse, but I got a bit tired of that so I tried to see what makes all this flipping noise.' For me the cicadas' constant chirps have blended into the background of our new life and I barely notice them.

'What noise?' I ask.

He takes a matchbox from his pocket and shakes it, provoking its occupant into overdrive. 'That noise,' he says. 'It's like a flipping ugly giant fly. Took me ages to find what was doing it.'

He returns the matchbox to his pocket. 'Is there any water, sis?' My public status of sister has sunk in completely and is now second nature.

'It might not be very cold but there's a bottle here,' I say, picking up the bottle I had placed in the shadiest part of the terrace.

Alfie goes to pick it up. 'Good lesson, Nico?' he asks.

'Beautiful,' says Nico.

'You're not doing too well,' says Alfie to me beneath his breath. 'I would never call a lesson "beautiful".'

Nico takes his leave and as his little white boat heads on its way back to Yiossos, we wave from the terrace.

'I really like Bobby,' says Alfie.

'Bobby?' I look at him quizzically.

'Yes: Bobby Charlton, Mum.'

I smile. Yes, Bobby Charlton with his famous comb-over hairstyle. And I think that perhaps I might prefer his team mate Georgie Best, all dark flowing locks, skinny frame and Irish charm. But that's the story of my life: I have always been more likely to meet a Bobby than a Georgie.

'Don't let me hear you calling him that again,' I say.

Chapter Seventeen

Liverpool

'Jesus saves, Johnson? Get him in goal tomorrow.'

The comment fell on stony ground. Fred, used to the mockery, focused on his audience and stood firm, his Bible in his left hand, his right holding his leaflet with the promise of salvation for anyone who might be prepared to stop and listen. What would Jesus have done? Turn the other cheek. That's what Fred would do. That's what Fred always did.

'God bless you and peace be with you.'

The joker, cap pulled down over his eyes, hands in pockets and collar turned up to keep out the biting wind blowing up from the Mersey, hurriedly turned away into the pub, keen to catch up with his mates in the warm snug. The single onlooker, a wad of leaflets in his hand, appeared to be concentrating intensely on something he had spotted on the pavement.

Fred paused in his sermon. He looked far away, his head filled with images of the fiends who had taunted him over the past ten years, looming into his mind like some foul creatures in a Hieronymous Bosch hell. Their ridicule and derision poured into his brain like waves on the sand, each pulling and goading him to break before breaking themselves and ebbing away.

Today's weak quip was nothing compared to when Maggie's condition became impossible to conceal and Gladstone Street had been awash with hilarity.

'Look at Mr and Mrs Holier Than Thou! Our daughter's not knocked up.'

Fred started, his trance interrupted by movement in front of him. He looked down at his grandson, who, teeth chattering, was now stepping from foot to foot.

'Come on, Alfie. Let's call it a day.'

~

Maggie: Liverpool

I hated the religious family life, but I was thankful for one decision – the decision to choose life that was made for me on Christian grounds – because for over nine years Alfie has been my life. But the impact that God had on my life and on Alfie's life became overbearing. The church had been founded in America and was led by laymen who had decided that they alone were holders of the Truth and they alone would be saved when Christ returned on Judgement Day.

Religious meetings were held in barely furnished, spartan rented meeting rooms; the church believed that all the signs of ostentation and wealth so flamboyantly visible in the traditional C of E and Roman Catholic cathedrals and churches were not part of Christ's teaching. Meetings among members of the church (brothers and sisters) were held three times a week: on Wednesday nights; on Saturdays, when congregations in other districts would hold an open house and welcome likeminded brothers from afar to brotherly fraternal gatherings (or 'church with egg sandwiches' as I called it); and on Sundays, when there was both a morning and evening service and a Sunday school in the afternoon for children. Both Alfie and I saw this as unfair, as at least the grown-ups had Sunday afternoons free. Not that there was much fun to be had during this free time. Dad was such a strict observer of the Sabbath that radio, television, music and any other signs of enjoyment were strictly banned in our house on Sundays. Gaiety was grudgingly accepted but not encouraged on the other six days of the week.

~

Alfie: Liverpool

Two o'clock every Sunday afternoon I was dressed in a flipping suit. I was the only kid in the street who had a suit. Apart from Granddad, I was probably the only *person* in the street to own a suit. It was dark green and checked. Granddad said I was too young for long trousers, so it had flipping *shorts*. I wore a white shirt and a green-and-silver striped tie, and Nana combed a parting then spat on my hair and slicked it down on one side and combed the other into a quiff. As I left the house my tummy was always full of flipping collywobbles.

I always hoped for rain so Hodge and his pals would be playing inside, but one dry Sunday, as I closed the front door and stepped onto the pavement, my collywobbles got worse and I wished the ground would open and swallow me up. A feeling of terror hung over me like the thunderclouds I had prayed for. No rain. Not a spot, despite the promise of a sunless grey sky. I saw the girls skipping – a few splashes of colour in the murky light. They went from five to about twelve and had their huge flipping skipping rope stretched right across the cobbles. Two girls were turning the rope and four more were jumping to the tune.

Lucy had a baby
And she named him Tiny Tim.
She put him in the bathtub
To see if he could swim.
He drank up all the water.
He ate up all the soap.
He tried to eat the bathtub
But it wouldn't go down his throat.
Lucy called the doctor,
Lucy called the nurse.
Lucy called the lady with the alligator purse.

When they spotted me, the words changed.

Maggie had a baby
And she named him Alfie. Ooh!
She put him in the bathtub
That's where he does his pooh.
He drinks up all the water.

*He never uses soap.
His green snot runs all down his face,
He really is a dope.
Maggie called the doctor,
Maggie called the nurse.
Maggie called the lady with the Alfie-gator purse.*

That was just the girls. I'd heard it a hundred times. Sticks and stones. I hurried on, eyes down – the bus stop was only a few hundred yards. Over and over in my head I said to myself: 'Sticks and stones may break my bones but words will never hurt me. Sticks ...' I felt there was someone behind me but I didn't want to look.

*Alfie's mum's a slut
Alfie's mum's a slut
Ee Aye Addio
Alfie's mum's a slut.*

I walked on without looking back. I knew that I hadn't heard the last of it.

'Who wears short shorts?' sang one voice.

'Alfie wears short shorts,' came the chorus. Those *flipping* shorts. Why did I have to wear them?

I guessed that there were maybe four boys following me.

'Nice quiff,' came next and a hand came from behind and ruffled my hair. I pulled my head away from the hand, pretended I hadn't heard anything and tried to hold back my tears. I held the Bible tightly. Granddad said it would protect me. I walked faster. Two more kids were ahead. One took aim and a rough leather football flew towards me. Slam. Smack. My cheek stung like mad and I felt my nose move sideways and back again.

'Can we have our ball back, please, Alfie?' I swallowed and felt a trickle of blood run down my throat. I took my white hankie from my breast pocket and held it to my nose. A kick to my shin followed. Six boys surrounded me. They were mostly bigger than me; between nine and twelve, I guessed. They weren't from my school. All six wore jeans and tops. Some wore the blue long-sleeved shirts of Everton, others the red of Liverpool. Their leader, Freddie Hodge, had cropped hair and wore a Ben Sherman shirt.

'Who said you could play with our ball? Who do you think you are, bloody Tony Hateley?' said one of the red tops.

'Not worth a ha'penny,' chimed in a blue top, ducking as the red aimed a swing.

'What's this?' Hodge said, snatching my Bible. 'The holly bibble. Do you want to read it, Terry?'

The Bible was thrown high over my head to one of the gang behind me, who caught it with a goalkeeper's leap.

'Well saved, Terry.'

'Turn the other cheek. That's what Jesus said.' Granddad's words echoed in my head. But I couldn't go to Sunday school without my flipping Bible, so I turned to face them.

'Give it here,' I said, grasping towards the book.

'Ooh. "Give it here",' the yob who Hodge called Terry mocked me.

'*Please.*' I was desperate.

'Say pretty please.'

'Pretty please.'

'Now pretty pretty please.'

I looked down and mumbled. 'Pretty pretty please.'

'Okay, you can have it.'

Terry held out the Bible towards me, but just as I was about to take it he looked down, laughed and dropped it. As I bent to pick it up, I felt a hard kick to my bum. I flew forward and fell head first with my nose right by the holy book. Although my nose was still bleeding, it was still working and I breathed in a stink that made me feel sick.

I picked the book up and, gagging from the stench, wiped away the horrible brown mess with my bloody hankie. Cheers rang all around me as I struggled back to my feet. A bloodied nose, grazed knees and probably a heavily bruised bum – this was the worst Sunday-school journey yet.

I saw the safety of the bus stop ahead. An old man and an old woman were standing waiting for the bus. I knew that my horrors would be over when I reached the stop, but I had a couple of hours ahead of me to worry about the journey back home.

'You all right, love?' the woman asked me. She seemed very nice.

'I'll be okay,' I said, holding back my tears and wondering what to do with my filthy hankie (a Christmas gift from my grandmother, neatly embroidered with the initials AJ). I decided to put it in the bin and face the music when I got home.

I caught the bus to the city centre. The bus conductor wrinkled his nose as he noticed my scent. 'Old Spice, son?' he asked.

I smiled. At least I could see the joke. I would have loved to come back with the quick-fire witty reply that one of Hodge's gang would have given – 'More like old flipping spaniel' they would have said – but it was Sunday and, as Granddad says, Sunday is not a day for jokes.

The bus conductor did it for me. 'Or maybe Old Yeller,' he said.

I smiled again.

I arrived in the city centre and found my way to the door next to a fish and chip shop that was the entrance to the meeting rooms. I climbed the stairs to the Sunday-school room. I opened the door and saw Miss Hargreaves and seven children sitting around a table, all neatly dressed like me in their Sunday clothes. I looked around the class and wondered if they too had run the gauntlet to reach the safety of this cold, bare room.

'Nice of you to join us,' said Miss Hargreaves, looking at her watch.

I didn't try to explain. 'Sorry I'm late, miss,' I said. I must have sounded feeble as, for once, she didn't start one of her lectures.

'I'll let you off this time.' Miss Hargreaves got up from the table. 'I've just got to go and prepare the hymn chart for this evening. While I am out please read Psalm 1 together.'

We began: 'Blessed is the man who walks not in the counsel of the wicked, nor stands in the way of sinners, nor sits in the seat of scoffers.'

But as the door shut behind Miss Hargreaves, our chant-like reading came to a quick stop. Johnny Smith leaned over to his satchel and picked out *Robinson Crusoe* – the illustrated school edition. He opened the dog-eared book at a turned-down page and handed it around the Sunday-school class like some of the boys in the top year at school did in the playground with a magazine called *Playboy*. I saw it once for a few seconds before someone snatched it away. What a weird name for a magazine. There were no boys and no playing in it.

'Look at that, Alfie,' he whispered when he was sure that Miss Hargreaves was out of the class. 'Man Friday's got a bare bum. You can't see his willy, though.'

I looked at the page with the white man dressed in furs and the naked savage kneeling in front of him and I felt a strange tingly feeling. I've never seen an adult undressed. As the book was passed around the table there were plenty of giggles and titters. Johnny reached again into the bag. He had a dictionary! He started to read.

'Fart: a small explosion between the legs.'

Everyone fell about laughing.

'Penis: the male organ of copulation. Vagina: the passage leading from the uterus to the vulva. Tit: related words bosom, breast, knocker.'

I laughed along with the others but I didn't really understand what Johnny was talking about.

When I made it home it was dark. I hoped that Mum wouldn't notice anything, but she was waiting and the first thing she said was, 'Alfie. Look at those knees. What's happened to you? Was it Freddie Hodge again?'

She took me upstairs and gave me a bath, and while

she was dabbing my sore legs I told her the whole story.

~

Maggie: Liverpool

When I saw Alfie's knees, it confirmed my worst suspicions and I realised the full extent of his unhappiness. On top of the stigma of his illegitimacy, my parents' zealous adherence to their religion was causing the poor kid to be severely bullied. He was totally repressed, and I knew only too well how that felt. It started the chain of thinking that made my decision to escape inevitable.

It had been similar for me when I was a child, although I at least enjoyed ten years of normal childhood before Mum and Dad got involved in religion – Alfie has known nothing else. But between the age of ten and Alfie's conception, I suffered from the same sheltered upbringing that was blighting his life.

Any conversation involving sex in our household had been couched in biblical language during daily Bible readings. The mention of 'laying with' a woman and the chapters in Genesis about Sodom and Gomorrah caused particular embarrassment to Mum and Dad, who would blush, get all flustered and quicken the pace of the readings.

Mum had just once attempted to explain the facts of life to me, shortly after my periods started. For weeks I had heard Dad whispering, 'You'd better tell her, Mother.' So one evening while Mum was ironing and we were alone together in the sitting room, she looked up from a shirt and said, 'You know what the girls talk about at school that's dirty?'

I gave her a questioning look.

'Well, it's not!' Mum continued triumphantly as if she had finally revealed some terrible secret that she'd been keeping for months. 'Do you understand?'

'Yes, Mum,' I said. But I had no idea at all what my mother was talking about. It was a complete riddle to me. Something that's dirty that's not. Maybe if I had spoken to any of the girls I might have known, but I had no friends and spent all my playtimes in the library swotting or alone by the gates in the playground feeding the pigeons, just wishing it was time to go home. I thought long and hard but eventually I gave up.

'Did you tell her, Mother?' I heard Dad ask Mum later.

'Yes,' Mum said.

'Everything?' asked Dad.

'Everything,' she replied.

So when I went to that party, I truly had no idea.

Parties were not at all popular within the church, but on the day that turned my life inside out my mum and dad were away at a fraternal gathering in Warrington. Having given a lift to a couple of potential converts, they had no room in the family car for me. A classmate, Sue, who had recently started to come over and talk to me in the playground, invited me around for a girls' night in. She was nice, Sue. She was my first and my only school friend, but just as I was getting to know her, she told me her dad was going to be moved away with his job and she was having a farewell get-together. She was amazed when I accepted the offer.

I had no idea what to wear, so I went in my school skirt. I did my best to improve an outfit with a short-sleeved fawn mohair jumper that had been Mum's until it shrunk in the wash. It clung tightly to my breasts and I suppose it emphasised my developing curves.

It wasn't really a party: just four girls dancing in the front room to Elvis, Bill Haley and Frankie Laine. Sue's older brother and a couple of his friends joined in later after a few brown ales at the pub. They were dressed in ridiculous outfits: knee-length jackets trimmed with velvet; bootlace ties; tight drainpipe trousers; suede shoes with crepe soles; hair slicked back with Brylcreem. They clearly thought themselves the bees' knees. They weren't old enough to be in a pub, but they were full of themselves and talked nineteen to the dozen, going on and on about 'the ale' as if it were some magical elixir.

Sue turned a couple of light switches off and the room went quite dim. We danced a bit and one of the boys tried to show off his jive.

Sue put on a slow record and we sat down. The jive boy sat next to me on the sofa and gave me a kiss. It tasted of what must have been beer – yuck! I could see Sue and another boy kissing on the armchair. She let the boy's hand move beneath her blouse and I watched, mesmerised as his hand moved down to her knee and then up her skirt. I didn't want to be different. I craved acceptance. I returned the boy's kiss despite the sickly-sweet taste. Following Sue for guidance, I let his hand undo my bra.

I looked across to Sue and saw her put her hand on her boy's crotch. I wasn't sure about copying her any longer, but she winked at me and like an idiot, a stupid sheep, I did the same and felt the curious stiffness inside his drainpipes. Before I knew it he was tugging at my knickers. He pulled them down and touched me intimately. He mumbled something about was I 'up for it'. I didn't know what I might be 'up for'; I said nothing. I didn't pull back at once; I should have done. I had given him a green light and he was in no mood to stop. He got on top of me and pushed inside me. I shoved him away in shock, but – as I now know – I didn't shove him quickly enough.

~

My parents were horrified on discovering my predicament. It was February and Mum and me were together in the sitting room.

'You're putting a bit of weight on,' Mum joked. 'Pull your jumper up and let me see.'

I lifted my school jumper. Mum gulped nervously. 'That's not puppy fat.' She sat down. She started sweating and looked anxious.

'And lift your blouse too.'

'Mum, what is it?' I asked.

'When did you last have your . . . you know what?' She couldn't say the word period to me.

Give Me Your Tomorrow

'My "you know what"?' I looked puzzled.

'You know, Maggie,' Mum whispered, 'you know, what happens every month ...'

I knew what Mum meant. After my periods started, my mum had told me where she kept her sanitary towels and what to do with them, but I had no idea what the periods were and why they happened. When they stopped just as suddenly as they had started, I had thought nothing of it and was pleased that they had passed.

'Oh, I haven't had that since before Christmas,' I replied.

Mum counted on her fingers. 'That would make it about sixteen weeks. You had better sit down, love.'

I sat.

'Maggie, you're pregnant!'

'Pregnant? How can I be pregnant?'

'There's only one way, Maggie. You've been with a boy.'

'Been with?'

'You know – been with!'

I thought back to the party. The only time I had ever been in contact with any boy. Was that it? Those few uncomfortable and messy seconds? It couldn't possibly have been anything else. I looked at the floor and then rushed from the room and up to my bedroom. I slammed the door and threw myself onto the bed and wept.

Mum followed. She knocked gently on the door. 'Can I come in?'

I couldn't answer through my sobbing. I sensed the door opening.

'Oh, Maggie, darling. What have they done to you?' She put her arm around me and joined me in my weeping.

'Something happened with Sue's brother's friend at Sue's house one night. Is that what made me pregnant, Mum? Just that?'

'I'm afraid so, Maggie. I'm afraid so.'

'What am I going to do, Mum? What will Dad say?'

'He'll say that the Lord will guide us.'

The Lord did guide us. Dad prayed nightly and decreed that there was just one option; abortion was the devil's work and he was not letting any grandchild of his be put up for adoption.

'Mother and I will help you, Maggie. You did a wicked thing, but if you pray for salvation the Lord will forgive you.'

~

Mum and Dad wanted as quiet a life as possible, away from the limelight. This was a problem of the Johnsons' making and with Christ's help they would overcome it. They did not want to become involved with any family in the neighbourhood – the neighbourhood in which they were already pariahs. Leaving school as soon as it became impossible to hide my pregnancy any longer, I went on to bring Alfred Johnson into the world on 21 July 1959.

For the next nine years I worked on the record counter in Liverpool Electrical, a small city-centre store while Mum looked after Alfie for me. I witnessed the excitement of the Mersey sound, Beatlemania, sixties fashion and everything that went with it. Although their regime was cold and strict, my mum and dad were supportive in their way, taking only a nominal sum from my wages for housekeeping and leaving me to squirrel away a good chunk of my weekly income.

The whole family continued with the routine of regular weekly religious meetings and daily prayers and Bible readings, but I knew that with a social group that revolved solely around the church I was not leading a normal existence. And while I was grateful for the support that we got from my parents, I was unhappy with being an isolated outsider at work who was never able to join her colleagues even for a coffee after the shop shut at six. In addition, following Alfie's recounting of his harrowing day, I could no longer pretend that our lifestyle was not affecting my son. I hated Alfie being the subject of regular and serious bullying and abuse in the local streets and at school – me, his mother, called a 'slag' or a 'slut' and his grandparents 'nutters'.

So the plan was hatched. The mouse went to evening classes, gained some confidence and decided to go it alone. I had seen the seeds of the holiday industry sprouting in the sprinkling of travel agents opening in the city and I decided that it had an exciting and very positive future. My big idea was to learn to speak a Mediterranean language fluently as a precursor to starting a holiday business. By the time I had plucked up the courage to enrol, the Italian and Spanish classes were already full; the Greek course became my salvation.

How could I take a nine-year-old boy away from Liverpool to a strange and hostile land? How could I leave a nine-year-old boy in a hostile Liverpool was more to the point.

Chapter Eighteen

Maggie

Life continued with lesson two, 'The Butcher', lesson three, 'The Market' and lesson four, 'The Fish Market', where I didn't even know the English names of the huge, exotic and colourful array of fish and other marine creatures, never mind their Greek equivalents. Today it's time for lesson five, the one that Nico tells me is the most important yet – the most important by far.

He looks into my eyes. We are sitting at a harbourside table after enjoying a post-lunch coffee.

'Try holding your breath for one minute. Just sixty seconds.'

I laugh. 'Easy.' I take a deep breath as Nico looks at his watch.

Lips pursed, I concentrate. I count in my head: one Mississippi, two Mississippi. When I get to twenty, I smile thinly through tightened lips; at forty I start to struggle, puff out my cheeks and wave my hands in circles. Nico starts to count out loud: 'Forty-five, forty-six, forty-seven ...' I gasp and gulp greedily to replenish my lungs. I roll my eyes in surprise.

'Now, think about trying to hold it for five minutes – three hundred seconds.'

I'm staggered. I offer an appreciative 'wow'.

'And over thirty metres' – Nico points towards St Spiridion's lofty tower – 'down.'

I shake my head in disbelief. Hardly any light, a footstep away from a brush with a sea urchin, surrounded by inquisitive fish (sometimes sharks) and all the time concentrating on cutting sponges, placing them in a net and returning to the surface before running out of air. Those men were pretty brave, I think.

'But it brought us all of this,' Nico says, gesturing expansively around the imposing architecture. 'Imagine when twenty-two thousand people lived here in 1912, and just think of what it was like when the diving fleet left the harbour.'

The oblong harbour is well over a third of a mile long and two hundred and fifty yards across at the widest point. As Nico spins his tale, my mind floods with pictures. I see every square inch of water covered by craft in all shapes and sizes, ranging from the tiniest dinghy to a small steamer. Nico tells me that on the sponge fleet's annual sailing, the water's surface was so packed that the local boys would attempt to cross the harbour (but rarely succeed in doing so) by leaping from deck to deck; I imagine that boisterous, adrenaline-filled, euphoric chase.

The departing crews would attend their local churches in their Sunday best and then march ceremoniously down to the harbour in processions of colour beneath showers of petals, between rows of cheering wives, sisters and girlfriends in traditional costume and not so exuberant parents and grandparents, whose experience generated a more subdued adieu born of sorrow. The parties from each church would converge at the Custom House at the head of the harbour, where final farewells were made, babies were kissed and the harbourmaster would shake each man firmly by the hand, slap him on the shoulders and wish him a safe and bountiful voyage.

And one by one the vessels were boarded and rigged. The local priests would pass from boat to boat, anointing their bows with holy water. Floral crosses were thrown overboard to pacify the waves, and slowly, in an orderly fashion, the captains would weigh anchor and head out to sea, a flotilla of kids in dinghies following each boat to the breakwater and then turning back to track the departure of the next leaver.

Every bell on the island would peal; every musician would be on the quayside to play for each vessel as it chugged slowly past under a blazing sun in a perfect blue sky. Outside the London Sponge offices a small brass ensemble in bandsman uniforms playing a triumphant 'Land of Hope and Glory' added an unlikely and eccentric touch of England to the spectacle.

I am totally captivated by the scene in my mind. I had read a little about the island's colourful history, but Nico has brought it to life; he plays out in turn the actions of diver, priest, bandsman and harbourmaster as the ceremony unfolds in front of me.

As the huge sponge fleet noisily departs over the horizon I come out of my reverie and ask Nico what would come next.

'They reached Rhodes before night, so the captains would buy some final provisions. And the crew' – Nico shrugs – 'all dressed up ... would ...' – he struggles for the right word – 'entertain, the ladies.' He blushes.

Each crew included three or perhaps four divers. These were the cream of Symos' manhood – heroes who were so much in demand that ship owners and sponge merchants would haggle over fees for the best of their number and pay them in full before they set sail. These prima donnas stood out among the groups of Symiots. Usually taller, slightly better dressed as a result of their cash advances and unquestionably more confident than the rest as they took their seats in the quayside tavernas, they would attract crowds of small and not so small boys who would clamour around in awe of their heroes. The divers thrived upon the attention of the kids and regaled them with stories of killer sharks, giant squid and ghastly man-eating sea monsters as they feasted on their last decent meal before autumn. And the crowds invariably caught the eyes of young women, some of whom gave the most handsome divers plenty of material for more salacious tales to share with shipmates over the forthcoming long, hot and celibate summer.

I smile as Nico finally finishes his description. 'Time for *you* to come up for air now Nico.'

Nico looks apologetic. 'Sorry, Maggie. I bore you again?'

'No. No. Not at all, Nico. Not at all. That was wonderful. Tell me more about those divers. What made them so special?'

Give Me Your Tomorrow

'It was just about here,' he begins, pointing to the edge of the quay. 'Yes, here one day in 1865.' Nico speaks as if he had been there. 'A young salesman set up a show ...'

'A demonstration, we call it.' I think of the smart young man who arrived on our ferry and imagine him standing in the spot Nico is pointing to.

'He set up a *skafandro*.'

I am puzzled. It's a new word for me.

'Sorry, Maggie. A *skafandro* is a diving suit. You know?'

'With a big round helmet?'

'Yes, that's right. A big crowd of naked divers gathered.'

I raise an eyebrow.

'No, Maggie, they weren't naked at the time.' Nico smiles. 'A big crowd gathered, and do you know who he put in the *skafandro*?'

I make a guess. 'The smallest?'

'No. He put his *wife* in it.'

Knowing how keen Greek men are on preserving their masculinity, I realise what a bold step the salesman had made.

Nico continues, 'And even worse ...'

'Go on.'

'She was *pregnant*!'

I imagine the faces of the bold and brave Greek divers, men who had prided themselves on the skills that they and their families had developed over centuries, as they watched the salesman lower his wife into the deep harbour.

'And as he lowered her into the water he asked the crowd, "What's the longest dive you have heard of?" and he got the answer "Seven minutes" from some joker. So the salesman, he got out his watch and he showed it to the crowd. And after ten minutes he brought his wife back up.'

I have to say I admire the salesman's showmanship and chutzpah, but I pity the poor divers for their complete emasculation. 'Ouch,' I say. 'That must have hurt.'

'It did, Maggie. Everything went down after that. Two thousand years of history. Pfff!' He clicks his fingers. 'Just like that. Not long after the suit came the *gagava*. That's another new word for you. It was a machine that was dragged along the seabed.'

'Yes, I've heard of that.' I've done my homework and remember reading how this terrible machine indiscriminately ripped up and collected sponges and anything else that happened to be there, including the next year's still undersized crop. As the clouds of silt produced by these monsters settled, their particles clogged the sponges' pores and started to kill the golden goose that was already reeling from over-exploitation.

I nod sympathetically as Nico goes on to describe how massive demand for sponges had led to both the development of synthetic alternatives and to the search for new sponge fields in the New World and Australasia. The warm waters of Florida and Australia were found to have huge, as yet unexploited reserves of the Greeks' golden fleeces.

'Yes, Maggie. It was not long before the island emptied.'

I already knew *why* the Venetian-style palazzos had fallen silent and empty on the island's streets, but now I really *understand*.

'Well, Nico.' I lean over and squeeze his hand. 'At least you are still here.'

Nico nods and smiles. 'Yes, at least I am still here.' And I get the feeling that he's glad that he is.

'Tell me more about the sponges.' I love to see the passion that the subject brings to Nico's face. Apart from when he's enthusing over his fireworks, I haven't seen him so animated.

He tells me how, before the *skafandro*, the young men of the Dodecanese had honed their skills as sponge divers – diving naked into the seas around their islands. Their only equipment a knife to cut the sponges, a net to hold them in and one of my teardrops to weigh them down.

As well as helping to speed him to the depths (the sooner the diver reached the sea bed, the sooner his valuable harvest could commence), Nico explains how the *skandalopetra* acted as a lifeline, an umbilical cord between the diver and his boat. It was the job of the *Kolaouzieris* to keep in touch with his naked companion and to act as his guardian angel, playing out the rope attached to the bellstone. To enable the harvester to move freely along the sponge fields without the encumbrance of the heavy weight, he would leave it on the sea bed but remain linked to it by a second, finer rope. At the end of the dive, as he sensed his supply of air running dangerously low, he could stand on the stone, tug the rope to give the signal to the *Kolaouzieris* and be hauled up to reach the surface with minimum effort. Alternatively, he might disconnect the rope to surface under his own steam and let his colleagues haul the stone aboard unhindered.

Nico proudly relates how the Greeks of the Dodecanese became the greatest gatherers of this wonderful gift of nature. Symiots and other Dodecanese men developed the ability to breathe underwater for periods that are, after my brief experiment, hard to imagine, and evolved into a super race able to harvest the sponges found in abundance anchored to rocks near to and on the seabed.

'Anything else, sir?' Nico turns to see the waiter, whose hope of an early-afternoon break evaporated when our lesson began.

We both laugh as I look at my watch and show it to Nico. 'We're so sorry' comes from each of us almost in unison, raising more laughter as we both stand as if synchronised. Our eyes meet in a glance that gives me a fleeting feeling of togetherness, a feeling that I haven't encountered before but one that I hope I might encounter again.

Nico ensures that a decent tip gives the poor boy a

little compensation for his marathon shift.

~

And so the lessons continue day after day (except weekends) until I feel that my goal of fluency is rapidly approaching. For some of the later lessons I return to the places where I made my first steps and Nico arranges for the shop owners and stallholders to allow me to man their counters for an hour or two under strict supervision – and with the caveat that Nico makes good any losses caused by my errors. Fortunately for Nico, he has been a good teacher. His wallet remains safely in his pocket and the owner of the tiny music shop even reports record takings.

Chapter Nineteen

Alfie

I love the mornings. Every day except weekends Mum leaves me to play at the bottom of the Kali Strata steps and I fly up them two at a time – sometimes three if I feel lively. I've explored most of the ruins up there now. I never got back inside number forty-five. Last time I looked someone had put a flipping padlock on it, so I'll never know who was hiding upstairs. I've made a few friends. There's always a group of old ladies sitting in the shady part of the street where it widens out into a square and they always wave and seem to like it when I shout '*Kalimera* old ladies!' to them. Mum says I'm doing well with my Greek, but I don't know what 'old ladies' is yet. They seem to understand anyway. There's a few old men too; they sit drinking coffee and playing a game that looks like draughts but Mum says it's called backgammon, which is a bit funny naming a game after a slice of posh bacon. Perhaps the counters are supposed to be fried eggs. I shout and wave to them too, '*Kalimera* old men!', but they usually seem too busy to notice me.

Sometimes, if I reach the right steps at the right time, I can hear the children playing in the school playground and I hide behind a plane tree (I'm learning all the local plants and trees too). I peep down and watch. It's no different to Liverpool; there's some kids running around, some throwing balls, some skipping, some fighting and there's always one alone in a corner. He always looks a bit lost and I feel sorry for him because that's exactly like I was at playtime and I know what it feels like. If he spots me peeping he waves to me, but I always dodge back behind the tree. I'm not a very good soldier if I get spotted by the flipping natives.

It's Friday afternoon in late April. We're heading back along the path to the cottage; Mum's ahead, and I'm behind. I'm in a fierce dogfight with a Messerschmitt. I'm dead surprised when another Spitfire hurtles past me with arms out wide. The Spitfire circles me but he can't see the Messerschmitt and flies off along the path, leaving me to finish the skirmish alone and watch as the German plane hits the water with a huge splash. I watch the other Spitfire disappear just below the water tower down towards one of the cottages that we spotted puffing smoke on our very first day on the island.

The boy is small and can't be very old but he keeps turning up on the path and flying past. He doesn't make a lot of noise but I once heard a couple of booms and bangs. I know who he is; he's the kid from the corner of the playground. I wonder why he never plays with the others. He seems okay. He looks quite normal. I wonder if he's got a funny religion too and gets teased all the time. Or perhaps he talks funny or maybe he's a bit smelly.

The little Greek boy is about four foot six and has curly black hair. Mum says he's got olive skin. She buys olives in the market. Some are black, most are green (and all taste flipping awful – yuck), so I don't get how his skin is olive. If it was the Mekon or a couple of flipping Martians zooming past in a flying saucer then I'd get it. But he just looks a bit brown like all the others round here. He wears grey flannel shorts like me. Instead of an ace snake-head belt, his shorts are tied up with flipping string. He's got big thick leather sandals and a white shirt: well, it was probably white when he put it on. He's like most of the kids who filled our streets: 'ragamuffins', Granddad called them. I like that word.

There's quite a few more flights past me and Mum and away into the distance and I've spotted an invader as well. Quite a few times I've seen somebody darting between boulders behind the cottage like a Red Indian scout – not a very good one or I wouldn't have spotted him.

~

It's afternoon and we're on our regular trek back to the cottage. I'm wondering if the Mekon will show up today.

Give Me Your Tomorrow

Maybe he'll help me out while I try to dodge heavy anti-aircraft fire. 'Neeeeeaaaaw.' Oh no. I've been hit. I need to make an emergency landing. Too late, the joystick has jammed. 'Mayday, Mayday!' I bail out just in time as my Spitfire goes up in flames. I float down to earth and make a perfect landing. I roll over and kneel to gather up my parachute. As I kneel I see another plane circling, arms stretched wide. Friend or enemy? I don't recognise the markings. I hope it's a flipping friend or I'm a sitting duck. The pilot lands and walks towards me. He stretches out his hand to me. I grab it and he pulls me to my feet.

We look at each other and we both smile. He has to look up to me as he's not very big. 'Me Alfie,' I say, pointing to my chest. 'You?'

The boy points to his own chest. 'Milos.'

I'm chuckling inside. I wonder if Milos too has been reminded of 'Me Tarzan, you Jane' from *Tarzan of the Apes*.

'Alfie. Nine,' I say in my very best Greek, holding up nine fingers.

'Milos. Eight,' comes the reply, together with the correct number of fingers.

I'm so happy. Milos looks smaller than eight, but eight is perfect for a friend.

I can't speak a lot of Greek but we chat away together as we follow Mum along. I've no idea what he's saying and I guess that he's the same, but at least here's another boy about my age, who isn't laughing at my freckles or trying to trip me up. My very own friend at last.

As we walk together towards the water tower we catch up with Mum just as the path branches off down towards Milos's home.

'Milos, this is my sister, Maggie,' I say.

Mum holds out her hand to Milos and he shakes it. She says something to him in what I bet is perfect Greek. Whatever she says, it seems to please Milos. A big grin comes across his face and he says, '*Efharisto poli*,' which even I know is 'Thank you very much'.

He smiles at me, waves and flies away homewards down the path. He turns just once to fire a couple of rounds towards the crest of the hill.

'What did you say to him, Mum?'

Mum says, 'I said, at least I hope I said, "Very pleased to meet you, Master Milos. Would you like to come to the cottage and play one day? With your mother's" – I got stuck for the word "permission", so I said "if your mother will allow" instead.'

'I don't know what it is, Mum, but Milos seems so nice.'

'Yes he does, sunshine. He seems like a lovely kid.'

'He talked to me like an ordinary boy. He didn't laugh and point at my freckles. He didn't look down his nose at my clothes. He treated me like just another boy.'

'You *are* an ordinary boy, sunshine. You're as normal as everyone else'.

The next morning is a Saturday and there are no plans at all for the day. So when I spot Milos heading towards the cottage early in the morning, I am excited thinking about all the games we can play.

I show my new friend around the place, but it is clear that Milos knows the flipping cottage better than us. Mum says she'll be an interpreter and it will be an extra lesson for her – she never stops! Milos tells us that his father helped Nico with a few of the big jobs when Nico was doing up the place. The bridge was the biggest job; Mum says it would have been impossible for Nico to do that on his own.

Milos loves the same things as me: cowboys and Indians, pirates, spies, Zulus, and anything to do with the war. I read all about these things, but Milos is lucky – he's allowed to go to the pictures. He says that the Odeon shows plenty of cowboy and war films and, like me, Milos loved watching the Zulus at Rorke's Drift, even if I only saw the photos outside the Fleapit. I saw the kids at Southport sand dunes playing Zulus and some of the boys at school told Miss Higgins that their dads took them to see the film.

'Can I go with Milos to the Odeon, Mum?' I ask.

'We'll see, sunshine. I think you need to wait until you can speak more of the language.'

'I don't mind. I can watch the pictures.'

I really hope she lets me.

In Liverpool, all the kids had dens. I never had one, but Freddie Hodge and his gang had one in a big tree in the park. Sally Thompson and her lot built one on the rec from corrugated iron propped together like a tent. Even Johnny Smith had one, though I think it was just his dad's flipping outhouse. But at least he had one, his own *private* den. I always wanted one but I had no friends to help me build it.

I don't know what the Greek is for 'den' and neither does Mum, but Milos seems to understand when Mum explains in Greek that I want us to make our own special hideout.

The island is the best place for it. It's far enough away from the cottage for us to be secret, but it's near enough to get provisions and, as Mum says, if there's an emergency. The cliffs make it like a fortress and the bridge could be a drawbridge over a moat. It's a pity that there's no flipping caves, but there is one place that stands out – the old olive tree. The highest spot on the island can be our den and our lookout post.

We head across the bridge to the centre of the bare little isle. Even my four foot six skinny 'ragamuffin' finds it dead easy to climb the thick trunk. It's only about ten feet wide once we climb to the top of the short trunk. Standing at the top of the trunk where the branches point out, both our heads are well above the leaves. There's just enough room for both of us to sit with our legs on either side of a thick branch and let them dangle down. It's not the most perfect HQ, but it's my very first den and it's going to be flipping great.

We have to have a sign. 'KEEP OUT' is what Freddie Hodge and Sally Thompson had on theirs, so we'll do the same but ours will be much better. There are some flipping big pieces of driftwood in the cottage. Nico piled them up for us to use as fuel for the wood burner, but it's not very cold and we don't use much other than for cooking, so Mum won't mind if we take one. I find a brilliant piece. It's about two feet by two feet and looks as if it might have been a hatch cover on a small boat – perfect.

One at a time, we carve into the soft wood. I carve in English and, after Mum says what I've carved, Milos does it in Greek: 'KEEP OUT'. Now I'm going to add a name and I've got a flipping fab one. Beneath 'KEEP OUT' I carve 'ALAMO HQ'. It's a bit complicated for me to explain to Milos, so I ask Mum to translate for me.

'Alfie says your new den is called the Alamo. Have you heard of it?'

Milos nods. 'John Wayne,' he says. He's lucky. He's seen that film as well.

Yes, 'The Alamo', the place where Davy Crockett and Jim Bowie held out against thousands of Mexicans. I can be Davy Crockett and Milos can be Jim Bowie.

I ask Mum to explain the rest of the name for me. Mum speaks very slowly.

'Al for Alfie,' she says, 'and Mo for you – Milo.'

I think Milos gets it. I'm dead chuffed.

Mum helps us to make a hole in the sign and we use some thick cord from the cottage to hang it from a broken branch on the trunk. I tie the arms of an old red jumper of mine (I'm not going to need it here) to a broom handle as our own standard for the Alamo.

I can't wait for the adventures to begin.

Chapter Twenty

Liverpool

Frederick (Fred) Johnson was almost beside himself with anger as he read and reread Maggie's letter. The third commandment, 'Thou shalt not take the name of the Lord thy God in vain', came to mind.

The phrase Maggie had used, 'And God am I sick of it', had been chosen for maximum effect. She would have known that despite the 'sorry' in parentheses it would hit home with far more impact than any shocking oath, curse or swearword and might, just might, cause her father to take a step back and look at what he had done to himself and his family.

As an only child, Fred's own childhood had been blighted by the health of his infirm mother. Her frailty, which left her wheelchair-bound from Fred's infancy, had prevented his father, Harold, fulfilling his burning ambition to join the thriving family business in Canada. The business, a chain of grocery stores, was hugely successful and had become a household name across all the provinces. Every time a new store was opened, Fred's grandfather, Arthur, had written asking Harold to come and be its manager, offering a salary beyond his wildest dreams. Every time Harold had excitedly looked at the map to find the new location and then looked pityingly at the frail Edna and realised that even if she survived the crossing, the winter climate would kill her. This left him with only poorly paid clerical work and the heavy, frustrating weight of disappointment.

When Edna eventually died after holding on until almost forty, she left the coast clear for Harold to finally set out on his Canadian adventure. But tragedy hit again when a heart attack struck the poor frustrated man stone dead as he ran for the bus on his way to the P&O ticket office. Fred blamed himself for being an orphan at just eighteen. He was convinced that if he had not foolishly used the petrol ration on taking his sweetheart

Mary to the seaside while on weekend leave, his dad could have driven to get the tickets and would still be alive and finally enjoying some well-deserved success in life.

Alone in his parents' marital home, a place where both he and Harold had drawn their first breaths, he saw the abject insularity of his position and marriage to Mary, a teenage orphan like him, seemed an escape route from loneliness.

With the war over and the infant Maggie growing up, Fred started life in Civvy Street. He was an intelligent man but had deliberately flunked his grammar-school entry after overhearing his mum and dad agonising over how they could afford the uniform. (Arthur's wealth in Canada came from the belief that you stood on your own feet. He might offer his son a job. But charity? Never.)

This left Fred with a determination to succeed against the odds, but he struggled to get on with his fellow schoolmates, whose failure in the exams was unintended and whose arrival at the secondary-modern school had been expected. They loved football, cricket, smoking and girls but were completely out of touch with Fred's interests in reading and music. This made him come across as having a superior view of himself, whereas, in reality, he was wracked with loneliness and low self-esteem and craved acceptance, which never came, sending him into a vicious circle of self-loathing and rejection.

He was a handsome man: tall and well-built, not athletic and with no interest in sport – more bookish. His army career was spent as a bandsman and he saw very little action during the war. Without a grammar-school education, he was expected to follow in his father's footsteps as a humble clerk in the Docks and Harbour Board, but Fred wanted more than that. Being presentable, well-spoken and intelligent, he managed to get a junior position in sales.

Like all salesmen he was always striving for more, and after spells selling typewriters and domestic appliances, he landed a good job as area representative for a major book and news wholesaler. He was totally committed to making something of himself. And he was very good at his new job: well-liked by customers for his politeness and courtesy (a different class from the typical spivvy reps they were used to). Sales in his area soared.

One evening, Fred was sitting alone after work in the pub near his office, waiting for Mary to join him for a rare night out.

'Would you like to find Jesus?' A short skinny woman in thick-rimmed glasses and wearing a small beret on her permed brown hair was quizzing a group of his co-workers at the next table.

Quick as a flash the response came back: 'Why, love? Have you lost him?' An exaggerated search under the tables and chairs followed.

'No. He's definitely not here.'

Fred was embarrassed by his colleagues' cretinous behaviour. He had no interest in religion but invited the woman to join him and to make amends agreed that he and Mary would come along to one of her services. After a few months of attending meetings, Fred became a convert and was baptised into the church in a ceremony of full immersion and officially became 'Brother Fred'.

He continued to do well with his job, but he became distant and distracted and his manager started to notice unusual trends in his sales. None of the saucy men's magazines that were still in their infancy but selling well nationwide could be found in any of the local newsagents in Fred's patch, and none of the more risqué paperback titles were anywhere to be found in his sales reports. His sales were otherwise outstanding, but when he was overlooked at the annual national sales awards ceremony despite his certainty that he had won, he felt that his time was up and, with that typical salesman's swagger, that he was good enough to go it alone.

Once he had embarked on a new project, Fred's determination to succeed was such that he never did anything by halves. He threw himself totally into his new role as a self-employed sales rep by day and his religion by night. Normally, he would have just one overriding obsession in life, but now that he had two, Maggie and Mary were ignored. But Mary's unquestioning love for her husband led to her acceptance of his devotion to his work and an acceptance of the brethren, which in turn resulted in her own full involvement and eventual baptism into the church. Maggie's relationship with the church was simply taken as read. She had no choice.

When he was not working or at the church meeting rooms, Fred would hide himself away and try to solve the riddles of the book of Revelation. He was convinced that the brethren were right and he became a fire and brimstone preacher for their cause. He visited other congregations to present their weekly lectures and was soon the brightest star in the church constellation, guaranteeing packed rooms whenever and wherever he spoke.

When other speakers visited the Liverpool congregation and were invited back to lunch at Fred and Mary's, he would encourage them to join him on a soapbox at the Pier Head in the afternoon to preach the message and spread the Truth, an offer that was always rejected on the grounds of a need to prepare for the evening lecture or something similar and patently untrue; 'hypocrites', he called them. So Maggie would stand at the foot of the soapbox handing out the leaflets in support of her dad.

Alfie's arrival was an event that could have destroyed Fred. Having finally found in the church the acceptance that he had craved for so long, this bundle of innocence could ruin him. How could such a zealot hold his head high and continue to preach his message of abstinence and the sanctity of holy wedlock? And it did cause embarrassment and not a few sniggers among the brothers, who thought that he had grown just a bit too big for his boots.

Give Me Your Tomorrow

But Fred grasped the nettle that his daughter had handed him. He used the parable of Maggie and Alfie to bring a modern touch to his teachings and as background for talks on themes such as 'Let him that is without sin cast the first stone' and a tortuous take on Samson's 'out of strength came forth sweetness', with the rotten flesh of the lion representing corruption and Alfie (of course) the sweetness. And he pulled it off and his star in the congregation continued to rise.

All of this did not mean that Maggie did not love her dad. After all, one of his favourite sayings was 'God is love' and he did try to love everyone – sinner or saint; but being utterly absorbed in his faith, he had great difficulty in expressing it. She just thought that the life he had chosen was totally wrong. Or even if it was right, it was totally selfish and wrong for her, wrong for her mum and wrong for Alfie.

Chapter Twenty-one

Maggie

Dionisios Rodopoulos is very proud of the Odeon cinema. It isn't part of the famous cinema chain created in England by Oscar Deutsch, but when Nico took me to look around, Dionisios told me that he had seen lots of Odeons during a trip to England and was happy to borrow the name – a name that is, after all, ultimately derived from ancient Greek.

Behind the neo-classical façade on the harbour front is the small theatre accommodating about eighty red plush seats. Dionisios and his wife, Elena, have run the cinema for over thirty years. Nicos tells me that in its heyday the Symos Odeon had two tiers, a lot more seats and was packed every night. The circle is now in need of repair and no longer in use. Since the erection of what Dionisios refers to as 'that damned television mast', business has started to decline, but there are still enough families on the island without TV for the Rodopoulos to make a living. If Dionisios shows a western or a war film for his Saturday matinee, he can guarantee a full house of local children and, if the Liverpool fleapit is anything to go by, I imagine poor Elena has all her time taken up in guarding the exit to repel gatecrashers.

I've started to let Alfie go to the Saturday matinees with Milos. They love it.

~

Alfie

As usual, me and Milos are first in the queue. It gets us our favourite seats: dead centre two rows from the back. We always start here but it isn't long before the usual nonsense starts.

'Ow!' I put my hand to my stinging ear. Someone in the row behind did the springy ruler trick and boy was it painful – the flipping stingy ruler trick! Milos joins me as we climb over into the next row.

Soon there's sniggering behind us. It happens every flipping time. This week it's Milos's turn to put his hand to his head and feel the sticky lump in his hair.

'I needed a haircut,' he says, trying to make a joke of it as we climb another row forward. He looks back. 'Thanks for the gum.' He ducks.

'Here we flipping go again,' I say as all sorts of stuff that you could find in boys' pockets rains down on us. They're using the back of our heads for target practice. It's not long before we're in the front row and having to crane our necks up to see the screen.

'We might as well start here next week,' I say to Milos, but he's not having that. He's quite tough, my little ragamuffin friend.

A big tomato whistles past my ear. It bounces off the screen and rolls under Milos's seat. Milo bends, picks it up and in one action stands up and flings it back to where it has come from. Splat. A direct hit.

'You little—' The teenage voice goes quiet.

That can only mean one thing. The box office has closed and Dionisios is on his way down to join us. His moustache seems to bristle as he watches us all like a hawk. Mum says Nico told her he was once a military man and his commissionaire's outfit is his old army uniform. There's so much flipping scrambled egg on his cap that he must have been a blinking general or something.

The house lights are still on. Dionisios stands at the front with his back to the screen peering at us all from under the cap. You can hear a pin drop. I hear a murmur from somewhere in the middle. Dionisios's head juts forward. His eyebrows and forehead make a fierce frown and his eyes are on stalks. He is flipping terrifying. He holds his chin forward and clenches his teeth. The whole lot of us shut up. I swear I can hear the knees of the kids behind us knocking. It might even be mine. I've nicknamed him the Gorgon. And thanks to the Gorgon we enjoy the films without further attack.

Mum says that Dionisios could never be accused of giving poor value for money. There are always two feature films and a Greek newsreel or report from somewhere far away squeezed in between. We love all of it. We can act out everything we see on our own private island.

After *Fun in Acapulco* we scrambled down towards the sea and dived into the channel below the bridge. We were not brave enough to copy the champion Mexican high divers in the film (but Milos reckons neither was Elvis, who used a stuntman), so our diving spot was only a few feet from the waves.

Today's matinee newsreel is all about the 'adolescent initiation and fertility rites' (whatever they are) for the teenage boys on an island. At least that's what the posh bloke who is in it says. It's in English with Greek writing underneath, so I find out that it's the Pacific island of Vanuatu. For these celebrations, the boys climb the highest trees on the island and, with a rope woven from lianas (like Tarzan's) tied to a treetop at one end and to their ankles at the other, they jump headfirst towards the ground. Of course the ropes are short enough to make sure that the poor native boys have no more than a flipping big fright and a very exciting couple of seconds as they see the ground flying towards them. The ropes go tight and jerk them back in the air just before their heads end up like that tomato Milos threw. They must be flipping brave. If a branch snapped or someone tied a bad knot, there'd be more than flipping tomato juice everywhere.

Milos nudges me. I know what he's thinking but he's got another think coming. It's a good job there are no big trees near our cottage.

I know why the kids here throw stuff at me. I'm not daft – I'm not Greek, I've got pale skin. And *freckles*. A skinny foreigner who doesn't go to school? I stick out like a sore thumb. I might as well carry a sign that says 'KICK ME'. But why do they pick on Milos? He's a funny kid, he's dead brave, he's always laughing and Mum says he could charm the birds from the trees with his smile.

I ask Milos as the lights come back up.

'Why do they pick on me?' he says. 'My mum is Turkish – she's a Turk.'

I don't really understand the answer.

'So what?' I say. Turkey is a mysterious place. We can see it shimmering like an oasis in the view from the north side of the Alamo.

Milos doesn't say any more; he just shrugs and looks at me as if I should understand.

The matinee finishes and we head back together along the coast. It's the last Saturday in May. The second film was cowboys and Indians; we plan to use the Alamo as a cavalry fort and Milos is going to be Sitting Bull. We look around for feathers left behind by the market's chicken sellers so Milos can make a headdress. It won't be much of a flipping headdress with the few scruffy brown ones we pick up. He'll have to be Sitting Hamster.

Suddenly there's a bang. It's a real one this time, not the pretend sort that we usually make up when we pass the pillbox. We jump together like a couple of Mexican beans – and then there's another bang and another. It sounds like gunfire but we see small squibs or bangers being thrown from behind the building. They land just ahead of our feet.

We look at each other.

'I don't like the look of this, Milos. What should we do?'

'There's only one thing we can do,' says my friend. 'Run!'

I grab Milos's hand and we flipping scarper. We fly along the track with a big cloud of dust behind us. But we aren't winning this race and I can see that the flipping firework throwers are right behind us. For a minute I'm back in Liverpool. I know what's coming next. But I know that Milos won't have heard of 'turning the other cheek' and Mum keeps telling me I've got to try to stand up for myself.

'Okay, Milos, stop.'

I pull Milos towards me and dig my heels into the path. We turn together to face our attackers; a gang of five teenage boys, one with a flipping big red stain down the front of his dazzling white shirt. It's not so dazzling now. We both raise our fists and put on our most fearsome faces. 'Think Zulus!' I whisper to Milos.

For a moment the teenage boys seem surprised.

'You want a fight, do you, little Turk and stupid English?'

We are outnumbered and surrounded.

'Only if you want a kicking,' says Milos bravely.

The teenagers look at each other.

'Listen to the Turk,' says the oldest. 'He's going to give us a kicking.' As he says it he lands a punch in Milos's tummy, leaving my poor ragamuffin friend doubled up in pain.

That's the signal for a full-on attack. Blows and kicks come at us from all sides. For our size, I think we put up quite a fight and I land a couple of well-aimed kicks and punches. For a few seconds I think I'm Cassius Clay. I *am* the greatest. I drop my fists, skip a couple of steps and wave the teenager towards me. I float like a butterfly, I'll sting like a ... But then – ow. Ow. Ow and ow again. Cassius Clay? Little Weed more like. One of the yobs is laughing and puts his hand on Milos's head and stands back at arm's length. The boy's blinking strong and poor Milos can't move. His flipping arms are whirling like a dervish but they are so short that he's punching into thin air.

The teenagers are starting to lose interest. I can see two of them with their hands in their pockets just watching now that both me and Milos have bloody noses. Perhaps they'll leave us alone now. I stumble from a punch. I hope it's the last one. I grab at the puncher's sleeve. Oh no. I've made a big mistake. I feel sick as the sleeve tears away in my hand.

'Look what he's done! Look at my shirt!' shouts the teen.

'Look at yours? Look at mine,' says another, pointing

Give Me Your Tomorrow

at his chest.

'Shit, Costas. You're in trouble,' adds a third.

Costas looks at the torn sleeve. I bet it's the only shirt he's got and he's going to get a good hiding for ruining it when he gets home. Someone's going to pay for it and that someone's me. I crumple as punch after punch takes away my breath and I fall. Poor Milos is paying for it too and he's on the ground with me. Even he's given up the fight now and we're both curled up into balls with our hands over our heads. Kicks keep on coming. I'm doing my best to be brave but I can feel my lips quivering and I can't help letting out a couple of sobs. Milos grabs my hand and gives it a squeeze. He doesn't make a sound. The kicks die down. I can't breathe properly. My ribs. Are they broken?

I look up and see the bullies heading back towards town. They're laughing.

We dust ourselves down and limp off in the opposite direction. My nose is bloody, my knuckles are grazed and my ribs are bruised, but at least I am not on my own. As we pause to catch our breath, I put my bleeding fist against Milos's torn and bloody knuckles and say, 'Blood brothers.'

'Blood brothers,' says Milos.

We scramble homewards along the track. Above us we see clouds. Not the fluffy white clouds we usually see here; these are flipping huge black ones like on the day me and Mum landed on Symos. I remember what happened then and it's going to happen again. We go from day to night in seconds. There's no shelter. We're going to get wet. Wet? We're going to get flipping soaked.

Chapter Twenty-two

Maggie

The last day in May, the day that I set as my target for fluency, is a Saturday. This is usually a day off, but I am within a whisker of reaching my goal and with a final push I can do it. Nico's doing brilliantly too. I'm not sure if his English was ever really that bad. I think he may have struggled a bit on purpose. He's gone well beyond the Secret Seven and the Famous Five and can tackle far more difficult titles and speak fluently on whatever subject I choose for our conversation. I sometimes buy an English newspaper and let him read about cricket, which he finds extremely confusing but I bet it's a welcome break from posh English children with their gung-ho, jolly-hockey-sticks lifestyle.

He's agreed to come this afternoon despite it being Saturday. He didn't take much persuasion. Perhaps both of us will be ready to end our lessons today. Perhaps neither of us really wants to. I've had more than a few feelings of affection for Nico. He's so kind. Nothing is too much trouble.

I really want to tell him about Alfie. It was so easy to just latch onto his mistake when we arrived. I was tired. I should have explained; but things aren't so Swinging Sixties here in Greece, and I know from the way Nico talks about some of the sailors and their adventures in Rhodes that he's not big on promiscuity. I've read all about the virgin-bride traditions on these islands and I bet Nico wouldn't settle for anything less. Not that he has a lot of choice here; otherwise he probably would have been snapped up a long time ago.

If he'd known about Alfie from the start, he might not have rented the cottage to us. It was hard enough in Liverpool. It's all about the pill now and free love, but that didn't stop Elsie Gordon across the road disappearing to her family in Wales for four months and coming back as soon as her *mum* had a baby.

I'm going to tell him at the end of today's lesson. If he takes it badly, at least I've achieved the first part of my plan and we can go to another island to do the rest. Though I'm not sure that's the best idea. Alfie's so settled here and where else would we find somewhere like this?

Alfie and Milos are on their regular matinee outing to the Odeon. Nico and I sit at the antique table on the terrace, shaded from the day's dazzling light.

'It feels different today,' I say, wiping a bead of sweat from my brow.

Nico nods. 'It's like M Day.'

'M Day?'

'Yes: Maggie Day – the day that you arrived. Remember the heat before the huge rainstorm?'

'Of course I remember. "Maggie Day" ... I like that. Whoever thought I'd get my own day? Put it in your diary and we'll celebrate it every year.'

Nico looks pleased by my words. '*Every* year?' he says. 'With fireworks?'

'I still haven't seen any of these wonderful fireworks I keep hearing about.'

'You will, Maggie. I promise. You will soon.'

'So does it mean that we're heading for another storm?' There has been almost no rain since we arrived and I am quite looking forward to a short break from the incessant heat.

'I think so. In one, maybe two hours' time.'

'We'd better get cracking then.'

'Cracking?'

'Sorry, Nico. Cracking means to get started. We'd better get cracking with our lessons. We'd better get started with the lessons.'

'Okay, I get it. You want me to test your latest words?'

'Yep.' We spent our last lesson in one of the sponge emporia and I was fascinated by more tales of naked divers and their history.

'Diving suit?'

'*Skandalopetra.*'

'No, Maggie.' Nico is surprised. I rarely get the words wrong. 'No, those are the *skandalopetra* – the bellstones. You know that.' Nico points to the stones beside the door.

'Stupid me. Of course I meant *skafandro*. It's just that I always think of the stones as my teardrops – my *klamata*.'

Nico laughs at my description of the stones as tears. Perhaps he can see the likeness. It is my only mistake and I manage to translate the rest of Nico's words perfectly.

'Very good, Maggie. Very, very good. You speak Greek better than some Symiots now.'

I am pleased with the compliment. I've hit my target right on time.

'Okay, Nico, your turn now,' I say.

I shake the collar of my blouse to waft some air around my clammy body, but it feels as much use as blowing a hairdryer on full power down my back.

Nico's almost daily hikes to the headland have had quite a dramatic effect on his physique. Instead of the podgy, double-chinned specimen, the fatherly figure who led us to our Shangri-La two months earlier, I am now sitting on the terrace with a man who could almost be described as slim and who looks closer to forty than the fifty-year-old I had taken him for on arrival. Nico has been my near constant companion for almost two months. He's not quite *handsome*, especially with that daft hairstyle, but, as they say, beauty is only skin-deep.

Nico isn't unaware of the changes that have come over him. He jokes that the little tailor's shop in San Stefano has done a very good trade in new shirts and trousers and says he's tired of his mother's fuss about him not eating enough and looking like a skeleton.

I've thought very carefully about what book to ask him to read from for this final lesson.

I had contemplated a scene from Thomas Hardy. There are some parallels between me and Bathsheba Everdene, and more than once I've wondered if Nico might become my own Gabriel Oak – sturdy and reliable but not very exciting; yes, more Bobby Charlton than Georgie Best. But unlike Gabriel Oak, Nico will never accept a fallen woman – an unmarried mother. His views remind me of my father, who would rail at any women or girls who heckled him on his soapbox – 'jezebels' or 'harlots', he would call them.

I've never had a boyfriend. My knowledge of love and romance has come mostly from my books and just a little from my records, but I've really started to feel happy when Nico is around. My hand shakes slightly as I hand him the book. Nobody has ever spoken words like these to me, and if Nico has not noticed my growing attraction to him then these lines should leave him in no doubt. I know that he is going to struggle with this and he won't understand all the words, but I close my eyes to listen.

Shall I compare thee to a summer's day?
Thou are more lovely and more temperate:
Rough winds do shake the darling buds of May,
And summer's lease hath all too short a date:
Sometime too hot the eye of heaven shines,
And often is his gold complexion dimm'd;
And every fair from fair sometime declines,
By chance or nature's changing course untrimm'd:

But thy eternal summer shall not fade
Nor lose possession of that fair thou ow'st;
Nor shall Death brag thou wander'st in his shade,
When in eternal lines to time thou grow'st:
So long as men can breathe, or eyes can see,
So long lives this, and this gives life to thee.

As he finishes (it was a very brave attempt and I hung on every word), I open my eyes to see Nico's puzzled look.

'All these new words. I don't understand.'

'They're old words, Nico. William Shakespeare. I just

wanted you to read something very different for your final lesson.'

An explanation of the sonnet's lines and their marvellous creator might save us both our embarrassment, but God steps in for us: as the landscape around us blackens, the first heavy drops land on the canvas.

'It's here.' I say. 'A bit sooner than you said.'

A slow drip, drip, drip turns into a deluge. We sit close together watching as bolts of lightning play all along the horizon and thunder crashes and rolls around the mountain behind the harbour.

'Wow. This is spectacular.'

'Almost as good as the Apollo Extravaganza,' jokes Nico.

I smile and look at my watch. 'The film will have finished. I hope the boys have found some shelter.'

'They are good boys. They will be okay,' says Nico reassuringly, although I bet he knows that the storm has arrived at a time when they will be well along the track. 'You want me to go and look?' he asks.

'No. Like you said, they're good, sensible boys.'

A drip comes from a patch that Nico has so beautifully stitched in the canvas – and then another and another in close succession.

'We've got a leak,' I say. I look up to see the awning transformed into a great pregnant swollen belly, filled to bursting by the deluge. Before I have time for another word, it splits and spills its contents like a huge trawler's net releasing its slippery catch into the hold. And Nico and I are in the centre of that hold.

We both instinctively leap to our feet, screaming more in amusement than in shock as gallons of water fall on our heads and flood the terrace.

I rush inside, laughing. I throw off my soaking blouse and jeans and wrap myself in a large bath towel before bringing another to the terrace. I come to the terrace naked but for the towel and, still laughing, throw the other towel to Nico. He catches it gratefully and goes inside to remove his saturated clothes.

He returns sheepishly.

Everything seems so perfect but at the same time so wrong. What would Dad say? How would Nico's mother react if she could see him and a woman who isn't his wife both wearing nothing but towels?

He wrings out both sets of clothing and lays them across the picket fence. The storm is passing and the sun is already starting to reheat the soaking landscape. Within half an hour wisps of steam will be rising from the clothes.

As we sit in the full glare of the sun between the split halves of the canvas awning, I lean across to tenderly brush back the bedraggled long thin strands of hair dangling around the side of Nico's face into his favoured comb-over.

Although they are starting to blur, the words on the soaking book that lies open on the table are still legible. Nico reads them out loud while I am still brushing the thin strands. 'So long lives this, and this gives life to thee.' He looks into my eyes and repeats the line as if the meaning has suddenly become much clearer: 'So long lives *this*, and *this* gives life to *thee*.'

My choice of book has worked; I feel an overwhelming feeling of affection for Nico as he speaks the words so gently. He leans forward to touch my arm and moves his head towards mine. I close my eyes, waiting for the very first meaningful kiss of my life. But just as our lips meet, the sound of footsteps and exhausted breathing breaks the spell. We open our eyes and move quickly apart as a bedraggled Alfie staggers into view.

What on earth will he think, seeing Nico and his mother wrapped in nothing but towels? He looks a bit shocked at first, but hopefully the soaked clothes and split awning will tell the story and no explanation will be called for. We've only got eyes for each other and Alfie's intrusion has broken one of the most magical moments of my life. I wonder if he notices the starry-eyed state we're both in. For a moment I fail to notice the bloody state that *he* is in. Poor Alfie. If ever a kid needed his mum it's now, but the poor angel has to make do with his sister. If Nico was not here he'd be sobbing on my shoulder and I'd be Mum or even Mummy, but he's still playing along with the charade and, no doubt to impress Nico with his bravery, he's not even crying – although the streaks down his face show the torment he's been through.

When Nico sees his cuts and bruises, he knows straight away who is responsible.

'You don't need to tell me who you met on the way back from the Odeon, Alfie.'

'No?' says Alfie.

'It was the Dave Clarke Five. Yes?'

Alfie nods.

Nico's not suggesting that a famous London pop group has flown over to Greece to assault my little boy; he's told me about the tearaway children of the Ioannidis family. Nico saw a newsreel about the Dave Clarke Five (and their unusual bow-legged stamping dance that is imitated on dance floors throughout Britain) when he went to see a James Bond film at the Odeon. Late one evening, as Nico was making his way up the deserted steps of the Kali Strata, a few paces before he reached the dogleg that leads up to the whitewashed houses of San Stefano, he spotted small flames and heard a commotion. On investigation he found a group of five teenagers frantically stamping on the ground in an attempt to extinguish a box of smouldering fireworks that had been dropped following the careless disposal of a cigarette. Nico immediately recognised the Ioannidis boys. Their dad is away at sea for months on end and their mum, who has an unhappy dependence on Metaxa, struggles to control the five tearaways.

'Who do you think you are? The Dave Clarke Five?' Nico had said as he reached the stamping quintet.

And the name stuck. From that night onwards the

Give Me Your Tomorrow

Ioannidis brothers were the Dave Clarke Five. Nico went home pleased with his wit; his only regret is that he had not found an excuse to christen them Dave Dee, Dozy, Beaky, Mick and Tich.

The eldest Ioannidis boy, Costas, now known to Nico as Dave Clarke, was once a member of Nico's firework crew. But after finding one too many shortages in the chemical stock, Nico increased the minimum age for membership to twenty-one.

'It is time for us to teach that gang a lesson.'

Alfie and I nod in agreement.

Nico takes his clothes inside and returns fully dressed a few minutes later. He ruffles Alfie's hair.

'Don't worry, Alfie. We will teach Dave Clarke a lesson that he won't forget.'

He looks at me. It's a mixture of tenderness and longing. He looks exactly how I feel.

'When will I see you, now that our lessons are over?'

I am lost for words. Are our lessons really over? Should I have fluffed my lines to squeeze out just a few more precious moments like today?

'I'll be shopping on Monday. We could meet for a coffee.'

Nico almost snaps my hand off at the invitation.

'What time?'

'Ten okay?' I can tell that if I'd said 6 a.m. the answer would be the same.

'Ten is perfect.'

He pats Alfie on the back. 'Remember Alfie. A lesson he won't forget. Goodbye ... Achilles.' Alfie swells with pride.

Nico turns to leave. 'Monday. Ten o'clock. Don't forget.'

As if I would.

As I bathe Alfie's scrapes and grazes with a mild antiseptic and he winces in self-pitying pain, I reflect on the afternoon. It had been just about perfect, even the soaking – especially the soaking! The choice of the sonnet had been embarrassingly saccharine to say the least, but it had had the desired effect, and as Nico had reached out to touch my arm (just before Alfie's abrupt interruption), I felt something that I have never felt before.

When Alfie has been consoled (it wasn't the first beating in his life and he will cope) and his wounds have been suitably treated, I say, 'You'll live,' and then I pick up my diary. I tick across every page in April and May and then write on each page in June in bold capitals 'RESEARCH ISLAND'. I haven't mentioned stage two of my plan to Nico yet, but it's a perfect excuse for us to continue working together – I am going to need a guide.

Chapter Twenty-three

Nico

I am still glowing with the warmth of the afternoon as I turn up at Cosmo's taverna for my evening shift. Cosmo and his wife Karena's excellent cooking, the fine position right on the harbour and, just maybe, the friendly waiter who can speak a few languages, make the taverna the first to fill and the last to empty every night.

At around eight thirty there's quite a fuss in Yiossos as a beautiful private yacht motors quietly into the harbour. It's so big that it has to drop anchor in the middle of the harbour instead of mooring right on the quayside. A small motor launch manned by a sailor in a smart white uniform brings the very important-looking passengers to the shore. A glamorous group of men and women disembark to be met by a crowd of excited children.

There are six men and six women. Their ages range from early twenties to maybe sixty, with all of the women looking a few years younger than their partners. The men are dressed very smartly in navy-blue or black jackets and tailored white trousers. Some wear sandals; others wear deck shoes. Everything they wear is like something from a glossy magazine. The women are all beautifully dressed. Their clothes, a mixture of trousers and flashy dresses, are probably from fashion houses in Paris or Milan.

Yiossos has seen nothing quite like this since the glorious days of the London Sponge parties. Word of the yacht's spectacular visitors quickly reaches every corner of the town and is soon exaggerated to incredible levels. Within fifteen minutes of their landing, the new arrivals are Richard Burton and Elizabeth Taylor and their friends, but by 9 p.m. the Queen of England, no less, is walking around Yiossos with Prince Philip, Prince Charles and Princess Anne.

I bide my time. I know the routine; every group of

visitors to Yiossos strolls from the landing jetty and heads around the harbour, taking in the beauty of the view and the delicious smells and lively music from all of the tavernas. As they pass each one, the owners proudly try to get them inside and tempt them with the marvellous food that they have on offer. As they reach the pillbox, the visitors will perhaps take a refreshing drink at the bar at the headland and watch the sun dip below the mountainside before returning along the waterfront on the same route.

It is only on this second walk-past that I approach. The customers will have noticed Cosmo's almost full taverna as they first went by. They will be interested in the only place where nobody harassed them by trying to sell them dinner. While my competitors are busy pestering them and noisily touting their establishments, I prepare a table of just the right size in the best spot available. The most polite 'Good evening, I've got the perfect table for you just here', accompanied by a genuine smile, works every time.

And this time is no exception. The glamorous twelve take their places and, as he takes his seat, the head of the party, an Englishman in navy-blue blazer, red cravat and white slacks, calls me across.

'Great table, young man ...' He pauses.

'Nico, sir.'

'Thank you, Nico. Great table. Now, we would like a traditional Symos menu. I'll leave it entirely to you. But try to give us something to remember. Something memorable. Cost no problem.'

'Certainly.'

I have never been given a free rein with an important party like this before, so it is with some worry that the meal begins with a simple salad of feta cheese, olives and tomatoes sprinkled with olive oil.

'You're doing just fine.' The man in the cravat is very reassuring.

Baskets of pitta bread follow, accompanied by a variety of wonderful Greek staples – tzatziki,

Give Me Your Tomorrow

taramosalata and dolmas. I offer suitable wines to complement each taste – a robolla, a dry muscat and a beautiful red xynomavro.

'Everything good?' I ask nervously.

'Everything perfect,' more than one of the guests echoes in approval.

Although moussaka is probably the most famous of all Greek dishes and Cosmo's moussaka is widely seen as the best on the island, I am sure that they will have sampled poor versions while on their cruise, and, however delicious Cosmo's cooking might be, they might be disappointed to see this as my choice of main course. So I bring them styphado, a superb veal stew slow-cooked with onion, garlic, tomato, olive oil and a little red wine.

'Ladies and gentlemen, this is the speciality of my boss, Cosmo, and his wife, Karena. I hope that it will give you the good memories you asked for.'

And, washed down with a heavy dry red mavrodaphne, it receives a great reception.

I have no hesitation in bringing out that other popular Greek dish, baklava, to end the meal. Cosmo's baklava is baked daily in San Stefano and its layers of syrup, almonds and filo pastry is honestly the best baklava in the Dodecanese.

It appears that the cruise party has just completed filming a major new movie on location in the Greek Islands. With filming over, the Englishman in the blazer (apparently a famous director; Milos would know) had agreed to take some of his team of actors and their partners on a short island cruise in his private yacht. The yacht is a spectacular vessel. The director tells me that there are six luxury passenger cabins as well as accommodation for another seven crew. With the yacht moored in the middle of Yiossos harbour like a small cruise liner, it is no surprise that he and his glamorous guests have caused such a stir.

The VIP guests enjoy their feast to the background music of Cosmo's sad tunes played mournfully on his accordion. As the meal ends and the tables are cleared of dirty plates, some furniture is moved aside to create space.

There is a buzz around the taverna.

'Are they going to do Zorba?' asks one of the women from the yacht.

'I think so, darling. Pity Quinn's not with us to judge the standard,' says the director.

'I liked Alan better.'

'You must be the only woman who did.' He laughs.

The group settles back as the taverna's stereo bursts into life and, though scratchy, the unmistakeable two opening chords on the mandolin ring out.

Cosmo and I become Basil and Zorba and begin to dance the *syrtaki*. The dance, though it appears to be traditional, is new. But in the five years since the film's success both of us have learned each step to perfection.

Very slowly at first, side by side with arms across each other's shoulders, left leg kicked across to the right, right leg kicked to the left, a bend of the knee, a touch of the ground, a snap of the fingers – all in perfect unison. Then faster, moving apart and facing each other with arms held aloft. Then moving together and then apart, faster and faster as Theodorakis's music increases in tempo. The guests seem to adore it. They clap with great enthusiasm.

'Bravo! Bravo! More! More!'

The film group rise together to applaud us with a standing ovation. We take our bows but the noise continues, so we perform the last few steps again without music by way of an encore.

The taverna starts to empty, but the table of twelve remains, enjoying coffees, brandies and a smoke. They seem to have enjoyed a special evening, but when I present their bill they seem surprised. 'This can't be right, Nico.' I worry that I have added it wrongly. I blush and, taking it back, find myself stammering, 'S-s-sorry.' I look at the bill. I can't see anything wrong. It is a very big bill. Probably the biggest since the old captain's wedding. What do I do now? 'I'll ask the boss,' I say. 'A discount, perhaps?'

The director bursts out laughing. 'A *discount*, Nico? At these prices we'll sail here from Athens every night. No need for any discount.' He pays in full and hands me more than a day's pay extra. 'Share that with Costas and the rest of the staff. I asked you for something to remember and the meal has certainly been that. Thank you very much. We will be back.'

With just that one table still occupied outside, I start to tidy the tables in the inside seating area. I enjoy this nightly wind-down, and, after an evening of traditional music, part of my regular routine is to put some pop records on and hum or sing along to myself. This evening I am so full of joy that I have been waiting to burst into song all night and my voice is more than just a little louder than usual.

I put on one of the Monkees' biggest hits. As the catchy tune begins with Micky Dolenz singing a line about true love being the stuff of fairy tales, I join in. Suddenly I have found myself in the middle of my very own fairy tale. Until now love has always been for others – never for me. The song speaks my emotions so perfectly that Neil Diamond could have written the words just for me. On reaching 'I'm in love', I lose all my control and sing at the top of my voice.

And, as I sing of my love, I turn to see my remaining guests rising again from their seats, they sway to the Monkees' beat – they're cheering, clicking fingers, loudly joining in the chorus – all eyes are fixed on me. It must be clear to them all that this is more than just a song. I sing with a passion that comes from my heart. I really am a believer.

The song finishes to even more applause than we got for Zorba. The guests leave to return to their floating palace. They wave and shout their thanks. One of them says the evening will leave them with 'golden memories'; another says it was 'an enchanted evening' – it sounds

like something from Maggie's Shakespeare book.
　'She must be some girl,' shouts one of the women.
I nod. 'More lovely than a summer's day.'

Chapter Twenty-four

Maggie

Although I have allocated a whole month to research the island, my work will be complete in a few weeks. The island is small and I have had already learnt almost everything about Yiossos from my morning language lessons. I aim to prepare a comprehensive dossier on Symos with a view to promoting it as a holiday destination. The island's tourism committee has made very few efforts to date and its outstanding beauty together with the warmth of the residents has been greatly underexploited.

Nico's doing his best to stretch the research out for as long as he can, but investigating an island with just one major settlement (well, two if you differentiate between the neoclassical buildings of Yiossos and the whitewashed stone dwellings of San Stefano) and two or three seaside hamlets was never going to take us a month.

As a thank-you for his contribution to the taverna's success, Cosmo's been letting Nico use his boat, and for the past few weeks we have been hugging the coastline and exploring the island's bays and inlets. Apart from just a couple of times when he went to visit Milos, Alfie's been with us – the gooseberry in the back of the boat.

I think that it is clear to the islanders that Nico and I have become an 'item'. Once or twice we've got tongues wagging by holding hands in public and Nico's mum has even invited me to their house for a meal. Well, I'm not sure if it was his mother who invited me, but that's what Nico said.

~

I look around nervously. There's not a soul within sight in this street of whitewashed cottages; it's so narrow that residents leaning from upstairs windows can touch their neighbours opposite. I glance upwards. Shutters close silently as if untouched by human hand. I turn and think

I see a small tousled head pull back from the corner. I sense a hundred pairs of eyes weighing me up like a tiny fly in a very big web. I walk backwards and forwards past the door a few times. I can hear talking through the partly open shutters.

'Sit down, Nico. It hasn't stopped. She isn't due for at least another ten minutes.'

I imagine Nico nervously worrying if I'll turn up.

'Where *did* you get this from, Momma?'

'It belonged to Helena's husband.'

'The undertaker?'

'Yes.'

'He's certainly not Hercules, is he?'

What *are* they talking about?

'You want to look smart for your lady friend, don't you? And that shirt was Tata's best.'

'Yes, Momma, I'm sure she'll be very impressed when she sees the two of us dressed for a funeral.'

It sounds like I've been invited to dine with Morticia Addams and a reluctant Pugsley. I need to put him out of his misery. I give a sharp rap on the door and turn back towards the silent street while I wait. I hear activity behind the door. I put on my best smile as it opens. This is going to be my biggest test yet. I don't expect a word of English will be spoken.

It's Anna who opens the door. 'Sit down, Nico,' she says over her shoulder. The door opens into the cottage's living area. Nico sits at the immaculately laid table; starched white linen looks strangely out of place within the gloom of the stone walls lit by a single small window. Sure enough, he is dressed in a black suit. His mum is in the customary widow's weeds. I had expected Nico to welcome me, but it's clear who will be running tonight's proceedings.

'Welcome, Miss Johnson.'

Nico stands. He interjects: 'It's Maggie, Mum.'

Anna nods. 'Welcome, Miss Johnson.'

'How do you do, Mrs Karteras?' I offer my hand.

Anna turns aside into the room, leaving my hand for

Nico who stretches from behind her to clasp it. 'Come in.' He takes my cotton shawl and hangs it from a peg by the door.

I blink to adjust my eyes to the lack of light in the room and sit where Nico indicates. He looks uncomfortable in his mortician's suit. His smart white shirt cuffs leave his hands hiding like rabbits in a burrow; his jacket buttons strain like dogs on a leash and his trousers reveal more calf than modesty should permit.

'We need some candles, Momma. The sun will be down soon.'

He catches a glimpse of his reflection in one of the family portraits that cover the walls and stops to straighten his tie. 'Sorry, Maggie.' He's speaking in English. He inspects the ridiculous sober suit. 'I'm sorry if I look like we're holding a vigil.' He clutches a jacket lapel and rolls his eyes: 'Hand-picked by my mother.'

Feeling Mrs Karteras' displeasure, I respond in Greek. 'You said we would speak only Greek tonight, Nicos.'

Anna nods. She looks appreciative. I hope my accent was good. Perhaps I'll be a hit. Nico gets the message and reverts to his native tongue.

Anna is already silently ladling soup into three bowls on the table. She sits down opposite me and looks me up and down. Wearing a white smock and trousers, I think I have dressed modestly for the evening. I hope that I am meeting with her approval. Anna repeats her scrutiny and stops as our eyes meet. I smile and hope for a glimmer of response but the older woman turns away towards her son. 'Give thanks,' she says.

Nico and his mother close their eyes and he quickly says a brief grace. Opening and closing his eyes firmly in my direction together with a gentle inclination of his head, he gives me the message to follow. I close my eyes and repeat Nico's words in perfect Greek. Anna follows suit.

We eat the cold soup.

Nico ventures to break the silence. 'Mum's really been looking forward to you coming. It's been years since we used these.' He unfolds the crisp serviette and dabs his lips.

I nervously offer a smile. 'Wonderful soup, Mrs Karteras.'

'Avgolemono.' Any pleasure at my compliment does not reflect in her face or in the monotonous tone of her response. She collects the empty bowls and takes them to the sink.

Nico looks at me. 'Sorry,' he whispers.

He holds his hand out to me across the table and I squeeze it gently. 'It's okay.'

Anna carries the next course to the table – a bubbling octopus stew in a steaming cauldron. She smiles for the first time as she carefully piles her son's plate high with the aromatic concoction. I am convinced that if she had a free hand, Anna would pinch Nico's cheek in delight. The smile fades as Anna takes my plate and serves a portion that might starve a sparrow.

'Wouldn't you like a little more than that?' Nico asks.

'Oh no, Nico. I'm sure your mother knows how much we girls need to watch our figures. Don't we, Mrs Karteras?'

Anna snatches my plate back, quadruples the size of my helping and puts it back in front of me with a resounding thud. I know it's Greek tradition to smash plates, but don't they normally wait until they're empty?

Nico's mum offers him a glass of retsina. He holds out his glass and she fills it. She points the bottle in my direction and nods towards my glass. 'Miss Johnson?'

'Me? Retsina? No really, Mrs Karteras,' Anna gestures again with the bottle. 'No, Mrs Karteras, I shouldn't. It's a man's drink.' Another insistent prod of the bottle. 'All right. If you insist.' I hold out my glass and Nico's mother fills it triumphantly. As she pointedly and noisily pours herself water, she looks at her son without a word but with eyebrows raised and a face that says: 'Slut!'

The octopus course is eaten in silence as Nico's attempts to involve his mother in conversation fall upon stony ground. The dinner plates have barely left the table when the galaktoboureko arrives.

'I've eaten this so many times, Mrs Karteras, but Nico was right when he said that nobody makes it like you. It's simply fabulous.' Again the compliment passes without comment, although Anna looks proudly and lovingly at her son.

As I finish the final crumbs of delicious filo pastry, I sense Anna, who has left the table after eating very little, hovering behind me. She is holding my shawl outstretched.

'Oh. Is it that time already?' I am tempted to add 'how time flies when you are enjoying yourself', but instead I find myself saying, 'Thank you for a marvellous dinner, Mrs Karteras. Your cooking was wonderful and every bit as good as Nico told me it would be. You must both come and join me and Alfie at the cottage very soon and I will cook you an English dinner.'

I find myself manoeuvred the short distance to the front door by Anna, using the shawl like a matador's cape directing a submissive bull. Poor Nico, his route to me blocked by the bullfighter, can only utter a brief and exasperated: 'I'll see you tomorrow.'

I take my shawl and drape it around my shoulders as Anna opens the door. 'I probably don't need this,' I say as the warm air rises from the cobbles. 'But then again ...' I think of the myriad unseen eyes and raise the shawl over my head and around my face. Before I have stepped right into the street, Anna closes the door. I can still hear through the shutters.

'Happy?' she says. 'I did what you asked.'

'Very happy. Did you like her?'

'What do you think?'

I reflect on the evening as I head back home. For now, Anna still has Nico and she's clearly not in any hurry to lose him. He must be everything to her. I know what Alfie is to me. Nico told me how she pulled him through his tuberculosis, leaving his bedside for only minutes at a time. The loving ordeal of his convalescence must have completely occupied her for that twelve months of their lives and forged an unbreakable bond between her and her son.

Nico doesn't know much about my background. I tend to steer him away from my past, but he's happy to talk about his. He's told me his big secret. He says I'm the only one who knows the truth apart from the priest. I feel very honoured. He's sure that the island's gossips blame him for the terrible accident, but I bet Anna knows her son better than she knows anyone in the world and I also bet that Anna knows that whatever happened on that boat it wouldn't have been Nico's fault. Having devoted herself to her son, she'll think none of the girls on Symos is good enough for him. None of them will be able to cook for him as well as she can; none will keep his clothes in such good order or make sure that he is in good health. Why on earth would he need a woman while he has her? And as for a foreigner? It doesn't bear thinking about.

~

Nico is undeterred by his mother's negativity; he even jokes about the evening – whenever we are in a taverna he suggests that I might like some retsina or asks if I would like a bigger portion. He continues to show me his island.

Yiossos is in the north of the island and farther north out of the harbour there is just one small hamlet, Agios Giorgios. Travelling there one morning by boat, we moor at the taverna-come-general store and walk past the three or four fishermen's houses and along the stony beach in the wide bay surrounded by imposing white barren hills.

The water is warm, clear, calm and shallow for a hundred yards.

'Perfect for children here,' I say, rolling up my white cotton trousers and paddling into the sea.

'Yes, but they must be aware of these,' says Nico,

joining me in the clear water and bending to prise a sea urchin bristling with a thousand tiny spikes from its home on a rock. I look down into the crystal shallows and see that the bay houses a large colony of these spiny creatures. If I fulfil my plan, it is this sort of attention to detail that will make my visitors to Symos feel well informed.

Continuing along the beach, Nico stops as we reach a dusty track running inland.

'Come down here,' he says, taking my hand.

After walking for a few hundred yards, completely hidden from the beach by a group of tall cypress trees, we come upon a small, whitewashed stone chapel.

'This is beautiful,' I say as we reach the tiny building. 'I could never have found this without you.' I squeeze his hand.

'Come inside. You will see some very special relics here.'

And inside the chapel we find, adorning the walls, the most intricate and delicate icons (so much finer than the cottage's gaudy modern versions) depicting a very Greek Christ. With its ancient stone pews and an ornate altar, this is truly one of the island's hidden gems. Despite my rejection of most things religious, this building is a real treasure.

'I can't believe that something so beautiful could be hidden so well.'

'Something so beautiful and hidden so well.' Nico repeats my words and smiles. I wonder what he's thinking. I feel the urge to try and kiss him again, but we're in God's house. It wouldn't be right.

We walk back towards tiny Agios Giorgios holding hands.

'Thank you so much, Nico. I couldn't have done any of this without you.'

We sample the food in the taverna. Like most Greek taverna food, it's good solid home cooking, with not much choice: lamb, chicken, moussaka, salad and plenty of extremely fresh fish.

I have tried the food in every eatery on the island and have made comprehensive notes on them all. When Nico, Alfie and I were all smitten by the most violent stomach upset not long after eating at one taverna, I didn't just write it off. We singled it out for future investigation. I want to be totally thorough and also totally fair. It turned out to have been a horrible virus brought into the restaurant by a visitor and not a matter of poor hygiene. It had laid low all of the customers and staff and, it seems, most of the passengers on a cruise ship.

Nico has shown me around most of the island's sixty plus churches. Each has its own character and distinctive charm. He took me to the ancient, but still operational, pharmacy in San Stefano, with its huge wooden counter, antique medicine cabinets and row upon row of eighteenth-century pottery drug jars colourfully decorated with painted flowers and bearing the name of the contents boldly in black – unchanged in a century.

The only other inhabited spots are a near mirror image of Agios Giorgios called Kalamos to the south of Yiossos (but with two tavernas, not one), and a bay with a steeply shelving beach on which an enterprising shepherd has installed umbrellas and sun beds and built a small restaurant serving delicious grilled fish caught just a few hours earlier.

There is a still inhabited ancient monastery that welcomes visitors and has an excellent assortment of original icons and frescos to admire, as well as a thriving shop selling copies of the icons, books about the island and a unique lavender honey made by the monks. Transport wise, a boat followed by a short walk inland is by far the best way to reach this peaceful place as the one road (in the loosest sense of the word) running along the spine of the island is potholed and has numerous blind bends, steep gradients and sheer unfenced drops to inaccessible arid gorges. However welcoming the monks might be, I feel that the risk of losing a visitor en route makes the road a definite no.

That is about it by way of habitation on Symos.

~

Boat and foot are the only means of reaching most of the remote beaches. It's a hot day and Alfie is visiting Milos. Nico and I pass Kalamos in the boat and sail on beyond the sun-bed beach. Here cliffs rise spectacularly above us and – away from the shelter of the coast – the sea has quite a swell. The water is gin clear and Nico, keeping close to the shoreline to avoid the rougher water, cuts the motor.

'Here, Maggie. You want to try and be *Kolaouzieris*?' He hands me the glass-bottomed bucket that he had used all those years ago. It's ancient but still in one piece.

'Okay. What do I do?'

'Put the bucket with the glass just under the surface and then just look.'

I am spellbound. I have read about the sponge divers and imagined what it was like for them, but there is nothing like experiencing exactly what their young *Kolaouzieris* had seen. I concentrate on the marine life below. My bottom is sticking in the air in what I imagine is a very unladylike pose.

'Wow, Nico! There's so much life down there. It's so colourful.' My voice echoes around the bucket, giving it an unexpectedly loud trumpeting quality. 'What a view!'

With my head in the bucket I can't see his face, but his tone as he replies suggests that there's a broad smile on it. 'Yes, it's a fabulous view.'

The boat drifts away from the shore and the seabed becomes more and more distant. The depth of the water scares me slightly and I don't like the squid and octopus that I see alongside the multitude of colourful fish. The combination of looking over the side of the boat into the deep and the movement of the growing swell starts to make me feel sick.

I hand the bucket back to Nico. 'Can we drop anchor, Nico? I feel queasy.'

'Queasy?' This is not a word in Nico's vocabulary.

'Sorry, Nico. Sick. I feel a little sick.'

Nico puts a comforting arm around my shoulder. 'Okay, Maggie, but I will not anchor. I will get you to calm water. Then maybe we will stop.'

Nico manoeuvres the boat towards the coast, carefully avoiding the jagged rocks clearly visible just below the surface.

'Feel better?' he asks with genuine concern.

I nod. 'Much better.' I can smile again. The nausea has gone.

It looks as if Nico is heading the boat straight into the cliff when a near invisible opening appears behind a steep boulder. He cuts the motor and allows the boat to float without power through the narrow entrance to a cave.

'This is a very special place,' he says.

He takes a torch from beneath his seat and shines it around the grotto. It is just large enough to hold the boat. He shines the flashlight down into the water and I can see that it is deep.

'So cold. So deep.'

I am amazed at how cold the air is in the cave and I shiver slightly. Nico shines the light upwards again and I can make out the blue and white of the Greek flag painted high on the roof of the cave, together with writing that has faded and the date 1943.

'My father does this,' says Nico, shining the torch across the writing. 'It says: "The bravest fighters Stavros Mitsotakis and Georgiou Levendakis. They died for Symos. Never forget them."'

I realise that this was the grotto Yianni and his comrades had used to hide their boat before setting out on their dangerous resistance missions.

'How beautiful. Thank you so much for showing this to me, Nico.'

Nico smiles. 'You are the first. For me this place is very special.'

'I know it is.'

Give Me Your Tomorrow

I feel a tear of gratitude for being allowed to share this very private place. However exciting and evocative it might be, this is somewhere that will never appear in my holiday information dossier.

I blink as Nico punts the boat back out of the cave, using the wall to propel us into the brilliant sunshine once more. I am amazed at the transition from cold to hot and dark to light that hits me so suddenly. Nico starts the motor back up and continues to steer the boat along a few feet from the base of the cliff wall. What surprise will come next? Another cave?

I have to crane my neck to look up at the sheer cliffs. I see them open up and move back into a sheltered crescent no more than fifty yards wide where instead of dropping steeply into the sea they give way to a narrow strip of white shingle. This is the most secluded spot that I have ever seen. With a gap of just twenty yards between the horns of the crescent, the cove's shelter from the elements is total.

Nico drops anchor a few yards from the shingle. He jumps overboard, pulls the boat closer to land and ties its rope firmly around a boulder.

'Welcome to my private beach, Maggie.'

He holds out his hand to help me step out into the shallow water. He places a picnic rug in the shadiest spot on the beach and sits down. He pats the rug beside him.

'Come and sit.' He beckons.

I sit alongside him and look up, wondering which one of us might be brave enough to make an affectionate move. But Nico stands and says, 'Now wait here. I will not be a long time.'

He pushes the boat back into the water. I lie back on the rug and close my eyes. Bliss. I'm in heaven. I'm glowing all over and it's not sunburn. It's only a few minutes before Nico returns holding aloft a brace of fresh mackerel.

This is the first time since our soaking that we have been really alone. We have been in the boat so many times during the past two weeks but almost always accompanied by Alfie. Even when we have left him playing near a shore or at the headland with Milos, we have always been under a watchful gaze: the priests in the chapels; the fishermen mending their nets; the taverna owners on their terraces. But here we are truly together: no passing boats, no chance of a walker or goatherd reaching this spot on foot; we are very much on our own.

Nico builds a small fire on the beach using driftwood and he grills the fish to perfection, flavouring it with just a lemon that he has brought with him from the market.

We're both fully dressed; he's in white trousers (a change from his usual black) and a black T-shirt; I'm in a yellow sundress and I've got my trusty straw hat. I've got a bikini in my basket on the boat and I've seen that Nico's got his trunks with him, but which of us is going to pluck up the nerve to suggest getting undressed and putting them on? Not me.

We sit closely together on the rug and enjoy a simple meal of grilled mackerel, olives, feta cheese and dolmas. Nico has placed four or five bottles in a rock pool in an attempt to chill them.

'Beer or lemonade?' he asks.

'Lemonade, please.'

He opens one of the bottles and hands it to me. 'Here, Maggie. I hope it is cold enough for you.'

He opens another bottle and takes a swig. 'Perfect,' he says.

I agree. My lemonade is a perfect refreshment to finish the snack. 'Perfect.' I smile and clink my bottle against his.

I left Liverpool with no intention of looking for love. My purpose was to give Alfie a fresh start in life, to escape the claustrophobia of the brethren and to make myself a career. When I met Nico he had been simply a father figure, a good man to have around, someone who knew the island like the back of his hand and someone that I could rely upon in case of need. In those first days at the cottage when Alfie had referred to our landlord as 'Bobby', I had laughed at the comparison. I thought of him as likeable, but there were no romantic feelings whatsoever.

Since the night of Alfie's conception, my contact with men has been strictly platonic, confined to my father, the brethren, work colleagues, customers and fellow night-school students. I loved the music that I sold and I had a few juvenile crushes on some of the stars whose photos were on display all around our department. The store had private booths to let customers sample songs before buying and a fair number of young men had asked me if I wanted to join them inside to share 'Love Me Do' or 'I Want to Hold Your Hand', but, though flattered by the thought, I was firmly under the discipline of the Truth (and my bosses) and all requests were politely declined.

Being in Nico's near constant company since first setting foot on the island might naturally have led to friendship. Or if things had gone badly on either side, the relationship could have broken down quickly. But the relationship has not broken down and both of us, both we students, have eagerly anticipated every lesson. Well, at least I know that *I* have and I feel pretty sure that Nico has too. Our youth was so similar – a heavy influence of religion, limited opportunities to meet the opposite sex, shy inhibited natures – that the growth of our affection has perhaps been inevitable, fated even (if I believed in fate). I knew from the first lesson when Nico paid me a clumsy compliment that he was attracted to me, but he's told me plenty of times since that he's too old for me. He thinks I'm about twenty – that's another lie I've not put him right about. Every time I see him he looks better than the last and I no longer think that the age barrier is insurmountable. He's just a really, really nice person.

I don't want to ruin something special – a relationship that has become so important. I know that Nico wants me, but he seems just as scared as I am of saying so. Neither of us has tried to make a move since my attempt at Shakespearean romance that turned into a Shakespearean comedy. That run-up to our very own tempest was the most blatant attempt at courtship during our two-month companionship. Perhaps *The Tempest* would have been a more appropriate choice, because my experience of men is hardly greater than Miranda's: 'O brave new world/That has such people in't!'

One of us has to make a move now. This is just so romantic. Waves lapping, sun shining. What could be better? I rub my nose against Nico's and move my lips towards his to steal a kiss. Nico's relief is palpable. He wants this just as much as I do. He mirrors my movement and lowers his lips towards mine, at the same time stretching out a hand to gently stroke my arm in the same way that he did on the day of the deluge (before Alfie's bloodied and battered interruption). As our mouths move closer I feel a surge of excitement. I close my eyes as our lips meet.

I was hoping so much for pleasure, but the sweet taste of beer instantly reminds me of the breath of Alfie's young father on that fateful night; a vision of the slobbering youth pawing and pushing against me comes vividly into my head. I shudder at the memory. I tense and pull away.

'Maggie, what is it? I'm sorry, I ... I thought ...'

'Nothing, Nico, nothing. It's not your fault. It's me. I'm sorry. I'm so, so sorry.'

I start to cry.

Why am I doing this? I can't understand my body's response; but the beer on Nico's breath reinforces the involuntary tenseness and again my thoughts are in the dim Liverpool front room with Frankie Laine singing and the teenage boy pushing inside me. I wanted this kiss so much. I wanted to tell Nico how I felt and to say 'I love you, Nico', but the moment has passed.

I know that Nico's life has been full of disappointment and he's used to rejection; the overweight kid who hangs around with his mum – that's what he says they called him. He thought I had feelings for him. I've held his hand and even visited his mother. He'll never guess that his only mistake was to bring that beer.

We return to Yiossos in silence. I can't understand what happened. I wish so much that it hadn't.

Chapter Twenty-five

Nico

Maggie has written up lots of notes on everything we have seen. Her research has been thorough. She has said nothing about our lunch on my private beach and we still seem to be the best of friends. Maybe that's all that she thinks we are – friends. With my limited experience of love I am frightened of doing anything to risk losing the friendship, so holding hands and one or two goodbye kisses on the cheek has been the closest we have been.

I feel part of the Johnson family. The best way to a man's heart is through his stomach, or so Momma says. Perhaps the best way to a woman's heart will be through her little brother. Seeing Milos's and Alfie's skinny legs hanging down below the olive branches and their heads just peeking above the tree they call the Alamo has given me an idea. I really like those kids.

I arrive at the island early in the morning. The boat is piled high with planks and a bag full of tools.

The boys look down from their perch.

'Hi, Nico.' Alfie waves.

'Good morning, boys.' I return the greeting. 'Where's Maggie?'

'Shopping in Yiossos. You going to build an ark?' asks Alfie, seeing the pile of planks that I've brought to the top of the island.

'An ark?'

'You know, like Noah.'

'Of course. Yes, we'll start by filling it with a pair of boys.' I smile. 'No, I'm building something better than an ark.'

'What?'

'A surprise.'

'Can we help?'

'Sure.'

The boys look on as I cut down the planks and make them all the same size. I lay them together side by side.

'You're building us a raft. That's really fab, Nico,' says Alfie. He looks very pleased.

'And you think Maggie will say it's safe to sail a raft here?' I point to the waves crashing against the island's base.

'Perhaps not.'

'Here, Milos, take this rope.' I hand the end of a strong nylon rope to Milos and start to lash the planks together.

'You *are* making a raft,' says Alfie.

'Just wait and see.'

I finish my rope work and study the results. Yes. It's worked just as I wanted so far. 'Okay. I have to go back to Yiossos. I will return soon.'

Alfie and Milos wave me off. They still don't know what I have planned for them.

It is not long before I am back. This time I have two aluminium yacht masts balanced across the bows. They are not very well fastened and I worry that they will end up on the seabed.

The boys climb down to the cove to meet me.

'You're building a raft with a mast,' says Milos.

'Wrong again. Help me get these to the top.'

The boys help me to carry the poles to the island top and across to the Alamo.

'Now I need to cut these to size.'

I take one of the masts and push it up through the branches of the tree. I rest the bottom on the ground at an angle of about seventy-five degrees.

'That's lucky. They are just long enough.'

The boys remained puzzled. The mast has just over half its length above the branches and the rest below.

I hand Alfie a strip of black insulating tape.

'Climb to the top and put this around the mast when I tell you.'

Alfie climbs and I tell him exactly where he should tape the mast.

'Okay. Good.'

I take the mast down and, using a hacksaw, cut the

mast neatly at the taped point.

'Now we make the rest the same.'

I let Alfie and Milos take turns with the hacksaw. It is hot, hard work, but we are finally rewarded with four aluminium poles of equal length. I take these and wedge each one firmly into the rocks around the base of the tree on the four corners of a square. Each is tilted slightly inwards so that it goes in between and through the branches and its top finishes level with the others, just about where the boys' heads reach as they sit in the tree.

The boys finally understand.

'You're doing up the Alamo,' says Alfie.

'Doing up?' My English is good, but I don't know this phrase.

'Making it better,' says Alfie.

'Correct. I'm "doing up" the Alamo.'

'Adults are not supposed to mess with dens, Nico, but ... you're one of us. Isn't he, Milo?'

'He's *almost* one of us. He's not a blood brother,' says Milos.

'Well, think of me as a big brother instead. Okay, now you two go to the top and pull.'

Alfie and Milos climb the tree and stand together while I lift the 'raft' upwards. It is heavy, but the boys manage to heave it above the branches. I climb up to join them and together we place it on top of the mast sections and fix it firmly to make a sturdy platform above the branches. I saw a slot into one edge of the platform and make a ladder from the wood left over from the planks. Once on top, the boys can pull up the ladder behind them and rule over their kingdom from their very own fortress. The broom handle with the red jersey is brought to the top and placed in the centre of the deck. The ALAMO sign is nailed permanently into place.

'Thank you, Nico.'

The boys are so pleased with my gift. They stand together peering across the landscape as I gather together my tools.

'Maggie ahoy!' cries Alfie, pointing towards the track.

'Where? Where?' I say, eagerly jumping to my feet.

Milos points to the small figure quickly coming closer along the track and we all wave.

She reaches the gate in the picket fence and looks across to the brand-new Alamo.

'Wow, Alfie, that looks fab,' she shouts.

Just like you, I think.

Chapter Twenty-six

Alfie

Mum and me are walking back to the cottage with Nico. It's just a few days since Nico did up the Alamo and it's been flipping great. I keep telling mum how great Nico is, but I don't think she needs me to tell her – she looks at him all soppy like in one of those films they show in the trailers at the Odeon. My head feels funny. It's felt like it all morning. I thought it would go away but it's getting much worse. 'Maggie, my head's all itchy.' I scratch my scalp. It's itching like flipping mad.

We stop. 'Let's have a look, sunshine. Don't scratch it. It usually makes things worse.'

Mum looks at Nico. 'He's caught something at the Odeon, you think?'

'Possibly a parasite.' Nico nods.

Mum says, 'Maybe the Odeon's a bit like the Fleapit.'

We called the cinema in Kirkdale 'The Fleapit'. I never caught anything myself as I was never flipping allowed to go, but the kids at school were always catching stuff there so I suppose 'Fleapit' was a good name for it.

Mum starts to look through my hair. 'Nico's right,' she says. 'Looks like you've got a nasty case of ringworm, sunshine.'

Ringworm! Flipping heck, that sounds nasty. I don't like the idea of flipping worms in my head. It was bad enough when I had them in my flipping bottom.

Mum wipes her hands on her hankie. 'We'll have a proper look when we get back to the cottage.'

Mum asks Nico to check my head as soon as we get back. 'There's a scaly red ring on his scalp.'

Nico looks at it very closely. He's like Sherlock flipping Holmes. I think he's going to say 'Elementary my dear Maggie', but he says, 'There's only one thing to do. We need to shave his head and treat it with ointment.'

Give Me Your Tomorrow

Shave my head! Flipping heck. I don't like the sound of that. What will Dave Clarke and his brothers think? What's Greek for 'baldy'? I'll soon find out. Mum goes into the cottage to see if there's any hair clippers or ointment, but I think she knows she won't find any. Phew.

Nico says, 'Don't worry, Maggie, we've got some at home. I'll bring them tomorrow.'

Flipping heck. I've been telling Mum how flipping great Nico is and now he's going to help her to flipping scalp me.

'Thanks, Nico,' says Mum. 'What do you say to Nico, Alfie?'

I know what I want to say to Nico, but I say what Mum wants to hear instead. 'Thanks, Nico.'

He stays with us for a while. I play outside on the terrace and can hear them inside. They're laughing a lot and I hear them talking about me as Nico's about to leave.

'No. Alfie's a good boy,' says Mum. 'He's never been any trouble. Never any tantrums – do you know what they are?' I hear her explain a tantrum to Nico. It's quite funny. I bet she's stamping her feet and doing all the actions. 'I'm sure he'll be fine when we do his hair.'

~

'Sit down and do as you are told,' says Mum. We're on the terrace. Mum has set up a chair for me to sit in and Nico has brought his ointment and clippers. They look like something a farmer would use in the Middle Ages.

I've got my arms folded in front of me. 'No. I don't want to be bald. Leave me alone.'

'Alfie. You want to stop the itch? Sit down and let Maggie do it,' Nico says in his flipping calm voice.

'No! No! No!' I struggle as Mum tries to grip my arm. I pull away, go into the cottage and slam the door. I don't want to be bald. It's bad enough having flipping freckles.

I can hear them talking on the terrace.

'Let me try,' says Nico.

I hear him come into the cottage. He'll never find me. I'm dead quiet.

'Alfie? Come on, Alfie. Maggie is only trying to help you.'

'She's not.' Damn. I shouldn't have said that.

Nico hears and heads into my room. He won't find me. Nobody except Harry Houdini could squeeze under here. Harry Houdini and Alfie Johnson. I'm nowhere to be seen. I see Nico's feet. He walks around the room. He hasn't gone. Go away. I'm calling on all my Houdini magic powers for him to go away but they don't flipping work. He gets onto his knees and put his head to the floor. He can see me. I hope he can't see I've been crying.

'I'll make a deal with you, Alfie.' His voice is kind.

'What deal?'

'We'll both do it.'

'Both of us?'

'Yes. I can be Yul Brynner and you can be Telly Savalas.'

Telly Savalas. Wow! Me and Milos saw *The Dirty Dozen*. He was dead tough. Even flipping Dave Clarke wouldn't mess with Telly. Me and Milos can sneak into the Alamo and it can be a German castle.

He's not going to flipping catch me out though. 'Okay, Nico. Only if you go first.'

I reach out a hand from under the bed. Nico takes it and he's dead gentle. He pulls me out.

'Here. Wipe your eyes. You don't want your sister to think Telly Savalas has gone soft.' He gives me a handkerchief.

'I'm not Telly yet.'

We go out to the terrace together.

Mum looks surprised at the change in me and gives Nico that soppy look again with her gooey eyes.

'Changed your mind, then?' she says.

'Yep. But Nico's going first, aren't you, Nico?'

Mum looks even more surprised when Nico nods and sits in her barber's chair.

Give Me Your Tomorrow

'A little off the top, sir?' She smiles.

'All off. Everything off,' I say. 'He's going to be Yul Brynner.'

'And who are you going to be?'

'Telly Savalas,'

Ever since we met him, I've laughed at Nico's daft flipping hairstyle. I can't think of seeing him without it. Mum says I mustn't call him 'Bobby'. When I say anything about it she just says, 'If that's how he likes it, that's how he likes it. Remember the brother at the meeting room with the toupee?' Do I remember? He must have been flipping mad to pay for that. Johnny Smith once said, 'Has anyone lost a guinea pig?' as he walked past and brother Paul said, 'A guinea pig? Who has lost a guinea pig?' and went and told Miss Hargreaves and we spent the rest of Sunday school on our flipping knees trying to find one.

'You absolutely sure about this?' says Mum. Nico nods, and then she says, 'Okay. Let battle commence.'

Nico sits dead quietly as the remains of his Bobby Charlton fall around his feet.

When *The King and I* was on at the Odeon, Mum was always looking at the poster and saying how handsome Yul Brynner is. And now she's finished Nico's hair, she looks at him and does that whistle like the flipping builders always used to do. 'We've got our very own film star here,' she says.

Nico closes his eyes as she hands him a mirror, but when he opens them he looks quite pleased.

'Yul Brynner, eh Alfie?' he says. 'I'll be fighting the women off.'

Why would they want to fight him? 'Don't worry, Nico. You'll have Telly Savalas to help you.' I hold up my fists in front of my face.

Mum shakes her head and laughs. And five minutes later I'm Telly and I'm sitting on the terrace with Yul.

Chapter Twenty-seven

Maggie

Nico has saved the firework factory visit to last.

The cluster of buildings is a speck on the mountaintop above the harbour, and it is a tortuous journey of over a mile to reach it. It's not that the mountain is a mile high, but it is very steep. After a short level start through a flat plain, the track zigzags backwards and forwards for almost a mile as it winds its way to the summit.

There could never have been a more ideal location for a TV mast. There could never have been a better location for an army lookout, and there could never have been a better location for a church. I've read up about it. In the Middle Ages the church was the site of a Knights Templar fortress, but only a few stone ramparts remain today. After the fortress came the church. At some time in the eighteenth century the stovepipe-hatted priests decided that they would be at their closest to their God on the top of Mount Agios. It was a labour to build at that height and distance from the town, but the church was completed along with a small house for the priest. Nobody lived nearby, but the islanders made the exhausting trip to the top of the mountain by donkey or on foot on feast days and holidays as penance for their sins.

When the Germans overran the island in 1943, the priest's house was commandeered as an ammunition dump and the church was used as a lookout. I can't wait to see the view.

Television started to expand in the sixties, and the huge TV mast, which was criticised by many as an eyesore, was erected after much public debate. It acts to pick up and boost the signals for the national TV service. Seeing the future of his beloved Odeon in jeopardy, Dionisios Rodopoulos was at the forefront of the protest. But there was no halting progress and the building of the mast went ahead.

When the British wrested control of Symos in 1945, the townspeople of Yiossos, knowing all the shortcuts, beat the soldiers to the top of Mount Agios and the Germans' supply of dynamite found its way into all sorts of secret caches throughout the island. But when peace set in and the need for such dangerous material started to recede, there was a sort of amnesty and the people of Yiossos began to use the explosives in their Easter celebrations. This led to the formation of an official fireworks society, and, for reasons of both safety and commitment (only the keenest were going to trek the mile to the top of Mount Agios), the old priest's house was chosen for the fireworks factory.

Nico offers me a choice: donkey or motorcycle. Having only experienced a brief and distinctly unpleasant donkey ride on Llandudno beach during my childhood, I opt for the latter. I'm quite excited at the thought of riding pillion with my film-star boyfriend. I'm glad that Alfie's not with us, or I'd hear about nothing but Triumphs, Nortons and Steve McQueen and *The Great Escape*.

I wait on the quayside outside Cosmo's. Nico disappears briefly and returns a few minutes later. It's not quite what I had in mind. Perhaps we didn't do the word for moped when we were doing our lessons. I'm not going to be riding pillion. He's brought two very unglamorous machines to the harbour side. More Keystone Kops than Steve McQueen, but never mind; it's still an adventure. Nico gives me a two-minute lesson on how to ride the moped after I've given him tuition on the difference between mopeds and motorbikes.

I follow him as he sets off into the harbour's hinterland. The thing that concerns me most about the journey up to the summit is the dust. There's been no rain again for weeks and the stone track is dust-dry. I'm wearing neither goggles nor helmet and if Nico goes ahead I have to steer to the edge of the track to avoid his vapour trail – a cloud of thick brown-red dust. So I try my best to ride two abreast.

The day is stiflingly hot, but even the drone of the mopeds can't drown out the constant singing of the cicadas that seem to inhabit every inch of the way.

We arrive at the summit and park the mopeds in the shade of a tall cypress. What a lookout point! The terrace that surrounds the church has panoramic three-hundred-and-sixty-degree views of the whole island and miles beyond. I can just make out our little island shimmering like a diamond in a sea of sapphires. Unless they came by submarine or under the cover of darkness, there would have been no possibility of enemy troops making a surprise attack.

Nico shows me inside the ancient church. It has fallen into disuse and disrepair since the invasion.

'I do not think that many of our visitors will make it up here,' says Nico.

I'm pleased to hear him say 'our visitors' rather than 'your visitors'. My behaviour on the beach doesn't seem to have put him off; he seems as keen on me as ever.

There is not much to see of the TV mast. It is a tall silver mast anchored by steel guy ropes and situated within a compound surrounded by a ten-feet-high wire-mesh fence, alongside a small hut that houses its controlling equipment.

And so on to the fireworks factory, Nico's pride and joy.

He's already told me that until the formation of the firework society in the 1950s, pyrotechnics on the island had consisted of groups of the bravest or most foolhardy residents (usually teenage boys) creating huge explosions using munitions left over from the Second World War. As this had been viewed as both extremely dangerous and not particularly interesting, the powers that be in Yiossos had asked for volunteers to do the job properly.

Dimitrios Papadopoulos had been chosen to be in charge. A respected senior citizen, he could be trusted to come up with a sensible display. Nico was among the first to volunteer. Since he had lost his brother and father, his life had been devoid of purpose. His contemporaries who had survived the war had left to find fortune overseas, and he was left isolated, looking after his widowed mother whose widowhood he blamed upon himself. There was little opportunity for Nico to work and there were no potential wives for him. But he was fascinated by the spectacle of fireworks.

In those days anybody could join the fireworks team, and the first meeting in the priest's house had been packed to the rafters. But the weekly journeys up the mountain soon sorted the wheat from the chaff, and after six months the group had dwindled to a mere half a dozen devotees.

Nico says that the displays had been a bit dull when Dimitrios was in charge, but when Nico took over he changed things and carried out lots of experiments here on the mountaintop. He judged his success on the size of the cheers drifting through the still nights from the harbour down below. They usually told him when things were going right.

Nico shows me around. It is only one room but it is divided into distinct segments. There is a cage along the back wall, firmly padlocked and packed full of boxes, tins and canisters with a huge variety of labels: aluminium, ammonium chloride, ammonium dichromate, antimony trisulphide and so on through to xylene with scores more and a dozen varieties of sulphur in between. Some containers with 'DANGER' or skull-and-crossbones symbols are quarantined within cages within cages. I am surprised by the neat organisation of it all, having heard Nico's tales of gory accidents in the past.

A long table runs down the centre of the room on which stand measuring cylinders, mortars and pestles, weighing scales and a number of riddles for sizing the black powder that forms the underlying propellant behind the multicoloured displays. On shelves on the rear wall are piles of cardboard and paper in various thicknesses and reels of fuse material. On the walls are printed charts covering the various chemicals, together with a number of sketches drawn by Nico to try to explain the effects he is aiming for. Among the charts and sketches is a poster of a group of USA Apollo astronauts.

'Ah,' I say. 'The inspiration for your Apollo Extravaganza?'

'Yes and no,' explains Nico. 'Yes, they were the inspiration. But they are also the theme of our next display.'

'Right. So when's that going to be?'

'Not long. You know that the Americans are going to put a man on the moon?'

'Of course.'

'Well, at the very moment when they land on the moon, we will celebrate with my biggest-ever display.'

'But you don't know exactly when that will be.'

'It does not matter. We'll be ready. Everyone will be watching it on television.'

'What – even in Symos?'

'Yes, even in Symos. The Greek TV service has agreed a deal with Eurovision and we are going to see the pictures live.'

'Wow. I didn't know that. But what if it happens in the daytime? Your fireworks won't show up very well then.'

'It won't be daytime. The Americans will plan it for the best time for their TV viewers. I'm sure it will be very late at night here.'

'Past Alfie's bedtime.'

'Does it matter? You have to let him watch. I have planned it especially for you and him.'

'Oh, Nico, that's so exciting. I can't wait.' I give him a playful hug.

The journey down from the mountain is more hair-raising than the ascent. Nico accidentally slips ahead and a cloud of dust flies straight into my face. I instinctively brake and that instinct probably saves my life, as when my moped hits a pothole and slips from under me it is travelling at just a few miles an hour.

Nico said that he would stay alongside me, but the track is so narrow and there are so many bad ruts he really had no alternative but to pull ahead. My wheels are still spinning as he brings his machine to a halt, lets it fall and runs back to me. I'm covered in a thick layer of dust. My moped hangs precariously close to a sheer drop. Ignoring my bike, Nico kneels beside me and puts his hands gently beneath my back.

Although the day is stiflingly hot, Nico told me to wear my jeans and I am so glad that I did. They seem to have taken the worst of the fall. The jeans are in tatters but my legs have suffered only minor scrapes and grazes.

My eyes are closed. Nico takes a handkerchief and bathes my face with water from his moped's pannier. The water is hot but I open my eyes and look up. He looks distraught. Poor Nico.

'Nico. Don't worry. I'm okay. Honestly. I'm okay.'

He lifts me across his arms and carries me in the way of movie husbands taking their new brides across the threshold. He emerges from the settling dust cloud: the bald monster from the blue lagoon holding the screaming starlet. One hand grips just beneath my breast, the other supports my thigh. Here is Nico the saviour, Nico the hero, not Nico the boy who let his family drown. What a pity there is nobody around to see him. My saviour. No longer the podgy father figure with the dodgy hairstyle, but the trim man in his prime who looks just a little like Yul Brynner.

This certainly beats Liverpool Electrical and fraternal gatherings.

Chapter Twenty-eight

Liverpool

Maggie religiously continued to write home every week. But after that first letter offloading of all her deepest thoughts, religion got no further mention. Her letters were bland, the sort of thing found in any postcard home: great weather, beautiful scenery, sun-kissed beaches, friendly people, recent snap enclosed.

Maggie was very proud that Alfie had found a friend and Milos was often mentioned in her letters, as if to say: 'See, Mum. See, Dad. Alfie is normal. He has a friend now, like any boy.' And in a similar vein, and making a similar point, her landlord gradually seemed to figure more frequently than her mum and dad might have expected.

After the blasphemous tract had arrived, Maggie and Alfie had been excommunicated from Fred's world and Mary, or 'Mother' as he called her, was told firmly, 'Don't reply to her. She's made her choice.' And mother Mary, meek and mild, obeyed.

Everyone has at least one Damascene moment in his or her life. It might be the time that they first realise that they are in love, or maybe the time that they realise that they are not. Fred Johnson's came on Sunday 25 May 1969.

Liverpool is a city built on shipping and (whisper it) slavery. The elders, who developed it into a majestic monument to trade, were philanthropic in their town planning and presented their citizens with a surfeit of parks and green spaces in which to spend their scarce leisure time. One such park was a mile from the Johnsons' terraced home.

For the Whitsun holiday a travelling fair was given permission to ply its trade and the park was full: a waltzer, dodgems, sideshows, goldfish in bags for prizes, candy floss, a boxing booth, a helter-skelter slide, hot dogs, a merry-go-round.

The bus jerked to a halt at Fred and Mary's stop. Fred wondered if the heavy braking was done intentionally to make the Bible-carrying couple in their Sunday best stagger forwards and backwards as it lurched to a halt.

'The bus was busy today, Mother,' Fred said as he watched the double-decker head up the hill towards the park.

'It's the fair. They're all off to the fair.'

Fred saw the bus stop again and watched as its passengers emptied out into the sunshine in the distance.

'But it's Sunday. It's not open on Sunday.'

'Have you not seen the posters? They got permission to open on Sunday this year.'

Fred was disgusted. As he and Mary walked home the few hundred yards from the bus stop, the sounds of all the fun of the fair drifted down from the park.

'They're defiling the Sabbath. Can our Lord not have just one day any more?'

'They're just having a nice time, Fred.' But Mary knew that he would not understand.

'Well, they're going to hear about it from me.'

He decided to make his views heard. As soon as he got home he filled his soapbox with leaflets and donned a canvas tabard emblazoned with the words 'I AM THE WAY, THE TRUTH AND THE LIFE' over his smart dark-grey suit and tie.

'Are you coming with me, Mother?' he asked.

'Sorry, Fred, but I've got a terrible headache. You go without me.'

Fred walked up the hill towards the park alone. Since Maggie left, Mary had started to suffer her headaches on a regular basis.

Usually when Fred gave his soapbox oratories they would be planned well in advance and a few of the newest recruits to the congregation would be rounded up to support him. And they would stand in a small huddle around the soapbox, nodding appreciatively and hanging on to the orator's every word with rapt attention. Their presence would attract a small crowd of listeners and sometimes a new convert would join the flock. Hallelujah.

But today's impulsive oratory was unplanned. The sun shone brightly and the crowds were continuing to head towards the park. The park was near to the city's famous football stadia and the crowds flocking up the hill reminded Fred of winter Saturdays when he could be seen in his tabard handing out leaflets to the throng at the turnstiles.

As he headed up the hill, a couple of the kids who had tormented Alfie mercilessly came beside him. They had to run to keep up with Fred's pace.

'My old feller says that's a soapbox.'

Fred ignored the comments, looking straight ahead in the same way that Alfie had done.

'What's in it, mate?'

No respect for their elders, Fred thought, seething at their cheek. Again he ignored them.

'Soap,' said the other kid.

'You going to the park to sell soap then, mate?'

Fred was determined not to snap but turned and glared at the boys. 'No, but I hope to cleanse some sinners.'

'You what?'

The boys gave up and ran ahead into the park.

As he entered the park Fred was uplifted to hear the strains of 'Nearer My God to Thee' being performed by the band of the Royal Marines at the bandstand. He smiled at the bandsmen as he passed. The bandstand was surrounded by deckchairs filled with an appreciative audience. But when the melody of his favourite hymn died away, Fred's heart sank as the Marines ended their recital with a medley of Beatles songs.

'Bigger than Jesus,' Fred muttered beneath his breath. He would never forgive John Lennon for his blasphemous comment.

He set up the soapbox just beside the path on the

crest of a small rise. The fair covered a huge grassy area below and visitors were converging on it through the many ornate stone entrances throughout the park. He thought the spot perfect. Near enough to see the fair and to hear the sounds, but not near enough for the noise to drown out his words.

He chose for his text a lecture that he had presented many times before, on the subject of Sodom and Gomorrah. As the fun-seekers passed him, Fred would use his Bible to point in the direction of the fair. 'Yes. That's the right way. That way to Sodom and Gomorrah, that way to sin! This way to salvation.' He would point to his Bible.

His mind, filled with images of Lot's wife turning to a pillar of salt, spurred him on to deliver his lecture with passionate conviction. Most fairgoers simply ignored him, but now and then a couple might stop and listen to a few words and take one of his leaflets.

'Thank you,' he would say. 'Repent and the Lord will forgive you.'

Plenty more would mock. But he didn't mind the mockery. He was brave. He could turn the other cheek. He was destined to a future of eternal life. They were sinners destined to rot in their graves. And he really was brave.

He needed to be brave when a gang of skinheads approached the park. Unfortunately for Fred, they chose the entrance nearest to his soapbox, and instead of simply walking past they also chose to provide Fred with an audience, knowing he would offer them with some entertainment.

Dressed in their black high-laced Dr Martens boots, turned-up jeans, braces and colourful Ben Sherman shirts, these boys and young men with close-cropped or shaved heads caused havoc wherever they went. After hearing the distant chanting of some football related song followed by 'Zigger zagger, zigger zagger, oi oi oi', Fred's heart sank as he saw them approach.

There were about twenty of them – a small gang as

skinhead gangs went. They stopped as Fred was pointing towards the fair.

'That way to sinfulness. This way to redemption and the light.' He held his Bible aloft. 'That way to Sodom.' He pointed again to the fair.

'What's he talking about?'

'I'll be *buggered* if I know!' They broke into fits of laughter at such wit.

But Fred was confident in his God, a God who would look after him, and he managed to preach above the clamour.

'Jesus is love. God is love.' Fred's voice was strained.

The insults continued to come.

'It's that feller who put his daughter up the duff.'

'Maggie may?'

'Nah, Maggie *will*.'

'She did for me.'

'And me.'

'And she'll never walk down Lime Street any more.'

'Here's the way, the truth and the life, pal.'

Fred didn't have time to duck.

When he came round, he was lying on the grass and could feel the trickle of warm blood running down from the gash below his closed eye. An inch higher and he might have lost his sight. As he focused with his good eye, he saw a young man's face close to his.

'You all right, mate?'

A small crowd had gathered, but the temptation of the fair was greater than seeing a feller with a gashed head. But the young man stayed. He lifted Fred's head.

'You're in a bad way, mate. You're going to have to have that seen to.'

He pulled Fred to his feet and put Fred's arm over his shoulder to support him. Fred was grateful to his young Good Samaritan. Dressed in smart, tight black trousers, shiny pointy winkle-picker shoes, a white shirt with round buttoned-down collar and bootlace tie beneath a long green cardigan, the young man was about twenty-one.

Give Me Your Tomorrow

Leaving the soapbox and leaflets strewn across the grass, he led Fred through the park gate and across the road. A row of neat Victorian red-brick terraces fronted the park and the young man opened the door to one and took Fred through the hallway and into a small kitchen at the back of the house.

'We've got a visitor, Archie,' he shouted.

After sitting the casualty down at the kitchen table, he shook Fred's hand firmly.

'Tommy,' he said.

'Fred,' was the response.

Tommy put a kettle on and boiled some water. He reached up to a small array of first-aid bits and pieces in a cabinet: lint, a few aspirins, cotton wool, Germolene. He filled a bowl with the boiled water and gently bathed poor Fred's cut and then applied the antiseptic. Fred winced at the sharpness of the pain.

'You'll get away without stitches,' said Tommy with an authority born of experience. 'But you're going to have one hell of a shiner.'

'What happened?' asked Archie as he came into the room.

'A bottle – skinheads,' Tommy responded with knowing raised eyebrows and a nod in the direction of the park, as if to say 'again'. Archie was an older man, perhaps thirty, thought Fred, who by now was sipping a very welcome cup of tea.

Archie placed a gentle hand on Tommy's and gave a sympathetic squeeze. Archie and Tommy knew all about skinheads. And that squeeze told Fred everything he needed to know about Archie and Tommy.

Chapter Twenty-nine

Maggie

The final part of my project involves checking out property suitable for self-catering holidays on the island. I am not interested in hotels or B&Bs, although I have researched these thoroughly for the sake of completeness. Most of the hotels are small affairs with no more than a dozen bedrooms; the B&Bs have only one or two beds; some are just a couple of rooms above a taverna. All are invariably clean and tidy and offer an extremely warm welcome.

But my only really happy holiday memories are of childhood experiences sharing cottages with Mum and Dad. We tried a static caravan once but didn't enjoy the close proximity of strangers, the bonhomie of the communal showers and the paucity of decent cooking facilities. Cottages offer a rural retreat with room to move, all mod cons (except the one with the thunder box, but that compensated by being totally away from it all) and, above all else, a feeling of freedom and the ability to do exactly as you choose. It is this feeling that I want to replicate.

Our white cottage is exactly the sort of thing that I am looking for. It has all the right features. Even a two-mile trek to town won't deter the sort of visitors I hope to cater for. I anticipate a middle-class British clientele that enjoys walking, bird-watching, fishing maybe, painting, hearty food, bargain prices, swimming, snorkelling, boating, ouzo, retsina and perhaps a bit of history. They will definitely want clear blue skies and clear blue seas and spectacular views. They will not want noise, tattoos, tea like mum makes or loud music (apart from traditional Greek). More Mozart than Monkees, more Beethoven than Beatles, they won't need coach trips (no chance of those on Symos) or wish to visit famous historic sites in a guided group (although discovering an ancient hidden church on their own will make their day and fill their postcards home).

Since the mass migration away from Symos there has been no shortage of empty property. The Italian and German military had done their utmost to redress this balance with their sometimes wanton destruction, but the hearts of both Yiossos and San Stefano remain and there are plenty of empty residences to investigate.

With Nico's help, I've built up a substantial list of potential lets. Some, like the cottage, are remote and have spectacular views. Others are in the heart of Yiossos and San Stefano; some are at the edge, but all offer the space and freedom that I am searching for. Some are rundown, but I can see how wonderful they might be given some attention. Others are already wonderful properties but lack a view or simply that 'something' that I know when I see it but can't find words to explain.

It's Sunday evening and, after an exhausting walk around Yiossos viewing properties, I sit with Nico outside a small café right on the harbour's edge.

'I love this time of the week,' I say, 'and the sexy swimming.'

'Sexy swimming?' Nico makes a quizzical face.

It is customary for the townsfolk of Symos, their ranks swelled by Greek visitors, all dressed up in their finest clothes, to walk from the landing jetty to the pillbox on a Sunday evening (and sometimes on other evenings too) and then walk back again. They repeat the process over and over until the crowds start to thin as the less agile among them make their excuses and fill the tavernas to watch until their younger counterparts too have tired of their promenading. This ritual constitutional is called the Volta. The people of Yiossos might tread the same path a dozen times or more in an evening. And as they stroll, pleasantries are made to fellow strollers, gossip is exchanged and more than a few sideways glances are snatched.

'The Volta, Nico.' I point at the promenaders. 'You know how if you go swimming in a swimming pool you swim up and down, up and down?' I move my arms towards me and away again to indicate swimming lengths.

'Yes.' Nico nods.

'Well, that's what the Volta's like. Up to the pillbox, back to here. Up to the pillbox again.'

'I see. Yes, like swimming. But *sexy* swimming?'

'Nico! Are you blind? Have you not seen the girls looking at the boys and the way that the boys look at the girls?'

Nico smiles. 'I suppose,' he says.

Many of the strollers are young people. Some might be with their parents, but they only have eyes for their counterparts of the opposite sex and many an eyelash flutters and, I suspect, many a heart skips a beat. I love to guess which girls will attract the most glances and which boys the most blushes. And I am usually right.

'Well, there you are – sexy swimming.'

'Yes. Sexy swimming.'

This ritual walking has no British equivalent. I love it.

'So, Nico, a new phrase for your vocabulary.'

Nico looks on and agrees what a good phrase it is.

'How about us? Shall we go sexy swimming?' He smiles.

'Why not?' I say.

So, happy and contented, I join Nico in the Volta. Not just a few women cast an envious eye at me as we hold hands and share a smile; and perhaps I'm mistaken but maybe a few men cast an envious eye at Nico too as we turn back from the pillbox just one more time.

As we are finishing our wonderful stroll beneath a full moon, Nico tells me that he has one more property to suggest for my portfolio.

'How about taking a look at forty-five Kali Strata?'

Chapter Thirty

Maggie

Nico has told me very little about number forty-five. I know that it had been his childhood home and that his mother moved out after the tragic accident, but until I see inside for myself I will have no idea what treasures lie behind the flaking green front door set in its neo-classical portico.

Nico unlocks the heavy padlock and removes the chain. Pushing the door open, he remarks that we should not expect 'too much'. Alfie's with us and looks a bit guilty as Nico shows us the damaged stair rail.

'Dave Clarke, I think,' says Nico, shaking a fist at the imaginary Dave.

'Sorry, Nico. Not Dave Clarke – Alfie Johnson,' says my son. I am shocked and embarrassed, but when we hear his explanation we understand. He told us how his flushing-out-snipers game only ever involved deserted property, and with no padlock in place and door ajar he had simply seen number forty-five as yet another enemy hiding place to explore. It was a genuine mistake. All those years of churchgoing have instilled an innate sense of honesty into him and, like George Washington, he cannot tell a lie. I'm proud of him.

'Ahhh. Now I understand,' says Nico. He makes a noise like Alfie's machine-gun impression.

'Not bad,' says Alfie, holding out an imaginary Tommy gun and returning fire.

Nico says we are not to worry as it will be an easy repair. I pause to marvel at the cool hallway from which the stairs rise. It gives Nico a chance to explain how number forty-five escaped German occupation and was not ransacked by storm troopers.

'There were a couple of reasons: although it is one of the most special residences on the island, it is two hundred steps up the Kali Strata and that did not make it the best building for the German officers in our temperatures. We saw what was happening in town. The Germans were wrecking house after house down by the harbour. It was Momma's idea. She called the family together and they wrecked the place themselves before the Germans got the chance. So when a gang of Nazis reached number forty-five, they saw a lot of smashed glass, some swastikas daubed on the walls and a pile of overturned furniture. She hoped that they would look inside, think that some of their comrades had arrived before them and move on to another house. And that's what happened. Momma was very careful about how they "wrecked" it and there was only a little amount of damage.

'And when the Germans had all found places to stay and it was clear that they needed no more properties, Momma locked up this great house and moved us in with my grandmother until the SS finally left. After the war we came back, but it was a very short time before the accident and we left here for good.'

'Accident? What accident?' says Alfie.

Nico seems pleased that I have not repeated his story to Alfie. He gives a very short outline of what happened.

'Sharks!' Alfie is excited, but I want to spare Nico having to retell his ordeal.

'Let Nico tell you about the sharks another time, Alfie. We're here on business.'

We stand at the foot of the stairs and I imagine his father and brother's coffins lying open and how he had joined his mother for that mournful night. I want to move Nico away from painful memories.

'What's through here?'

Off the hall, the kitchen, though layered in dust, has a huge cast-iron cooking range and an enormous thick oak table filling the centre of the room, a table that had doubled for servants' mealtimes as well as fulfilling its primary role as butcher's block and cook's work surface. Hooks line the walls and I see them full of gleaming brass pots, cured meats and all manner of kitchen utensils. This kitchen could cater for a huge family and plenty of guests.

The rooms to either side of the hall could be for listening to music or for simply sitting and relaxing with a drink after a long day on the beach. I think that it would make sense to convert one to a bedroom, as little time will be spent indoors on the holidays I envisage.

I already realise that the house at forty-five Kali Strata is one of the grandest on the island. What an asset it would be to my business. We've only explored the large marble-floored hallway and had a quick inspection of the kitchen and two side rooms and it's like nothing else that we've seen. I want to know more about it. A place like this must have so many stories to tell.

Nico is happy to answer all my questions. The chairman of London Sponge had once used the room on the left as his private office, he tells me. The one on the right was the family parlour, the setting for most of their living, including dining.

We start up the stairs. They split after a small rise and curve upwards, one flight left and one right, to join an ornate landing with an elaborate stucco ceiling. The landing has two double doors that open into the grand salon. Nico stops outside one of the double doors. He wants to tell us more before he opens them.

He says that this room was once the social hub of Symos, used by the rich English owners to entertain clients and potential clients, bankers and civic dignitaries with dancing, banquets and general merriment. It was once lavishly styled with ornate crystal chandeliers, a grand piano, a French marble fireplace and comfortable seating around the walls. Four ceiling-high windows draped with the finest floor-length silk curtains completed the design. The shuttered windows open onto a raised stone balcony, which runs the width of the building and looks out onto magnificent views down to the harbour and to the Aegean Sea beyond.

To the rear of this floor is the sleeping accommodation: relatively small and simple rooms in relation to the grandeur of the salon, but plenty of them. In an attic above the salon is a dormitory that in 1905 had housed no fewer than ten domestic servants.

This was the splendour that had been left in the care of the Karteras family – except that by the time of London Sponge's decline, the soirees that had enlivened the place were a distant memory, the silks faded and the grand piano no longer in tune. It was only a shell. Nico, his mother and the multitude of aunts, uncles and cousins who had from time to time inhabited the place had many good memories of living in the abundant space, with such a fine kitchen and more than enough bedrooms for the hugest family.

Before Nico completed the sale of his dead father's skiff, he removed all of Yianni senior's belongings from the boat and stored them carefully in the attic dormitory. And when his mother had made the decision to leave the place forever, Nico had stored all her clothes (which, apart from her widows' weeds, she had vowed never to wear again), alongside them.

Once or twice every month, Nico returns to the house, removes the great chain and padlock and faithfully checks everywhere over in case London Sponge ever return. The Karteras are men of their word and I'm sure that the house will be looked after for as long as there's a Karteras on Symos.

Anna was born in 1904 in those servants' quarters at the top of the house. Her father was an experienced and accomplished naked sponge diver and her mother, Nana, was the cook for the house. The young Anna grew up in the happy and prosperous household and learned her cooking skills in the magnificent well-equipped kitchen.

The proprietors of London Sponge, the Mason family, were modern and enlightened and Anna and the other servant children were offered the best in education, health care and living conditions. They were always allowed a peek into the grand salon on party evenings. How Anna and her mother must have marvelled at the finery and tapped their feet in time with the music – music so different to the traditional island music.

London Sponge under the Masons was a good company to work for. It was probably the best on the island in terms of pay and conditions and their record on safety was second to none. Nana had lost two brothers (who worked for another sponge merchant) to the *skafandro*, but her husband Panagioti, Anna's father, and all his London Sponge colleagues dived using only the traditional skin-diving methods.

But one day, shortly before the 1911 sponge fleet set sail, proprietor Paul Mason had called together his entire workforce and told them that the company could no longer compete using naked divers alone. The sponge beds within skin-diving reach were becoming depleted and the fleets using the *skafandro* and *gagava* were leaving London Sponge behind. Unless London Sponge started to use the diving suits, the company would fail. Paul asked for volunteers, giving his assurances that only the safest practices would be used. Panagioti was the first to rally to the call. He trusted his boss and he knew that, used correctly, the *skafandro* would guarantee their futures.

But disaster had struck on their very first dives. The Masons had bought ten of the finest diving suits from London and the company's divers were the envy of the fleet as they set out to the roar of the crowd from the carnival atmosphere of the harbour. Once out into open waters, the sponge diving was a matter of every boat for itself and the competition for success was immense. Some said it was an accident. Others made dark references to sabotage. It was certainly difficult to explain how three brand-new air valves in three brand-new helmets could seize up. Nobody was able to identify the greasy substance that caused the failures, but everyone was able to identify the bodies of poor Panagioti and his two colleagues as the London Sponge vessels abandoned the harvest and returned forlornly to Yiossos just two days after they had set out.

Following the death of her husband, Nana had left number forty-five. The Masons did their utmost to persuade her to stay and they paid her an extremely generous settlement, but like Anna thirty years later, the heartbroken Nana simply wanted nothing more to do with sponges.

I can see Alfie starting to shuffle his feet. He's been good, listening to Nico's history lesson, but he'd rather see for himself.

'Can we see this grand salon now, Nico?'

'One moment, Alfie. I came yesterday and swept away the cobwebs and opened the shutters so you can see it at its best.'

He ceremoniously opens one of the double doors. Great shafts of sunlight stream into the room and dazzle us. Alfie runs through the salon, pushes open a tall window, climbs a couple of steps and marches onto the balcony. I follow and look out to the incredible sea views.

'It's like Buckingham Palace, Maggie.' His distinctive royal wave to the throng below is Prince Charles to a tee; I am relieved that he has not chosen to be Hitler or Mussolini giving stiff-armed salutes from the balcony.

Nico shows me around the fabulous room.

'These are the windows that were draped with blue silk curtains.'

I look at the height. 'They must have been enormous.'

'The English left them here. They took everything back to England except those curtains and your iron table. Momma once said that she was going to use that silk to make a ball gown for my bride when I get married. It is locked away in a trunk in the attic. I think she will be happy if it stays there.'

Nico looks around the room and continues, 'I never saw the parties. I was too young; but Momma and Nana told me how the salon floor bounced' – he holds his hands apart and moves them up and down – 'with all the dancing.'

I stand opposite him; the light is in my eyes and Nico

Give Me Your Tomorrow

is silhouetted against the tall window frames. I raise my arms from my sides and hold them high like a criminal cornered by armed police. And, head to one side, I slowly click my fingers and attempt Zorba's tune: 'Da dum' – pause – 'dum' – pause – 'dum' – pause – 'dum' – pause – 'da dum.'

Nico moves towards me. 'No, not like that,' he says.

Placing his right hand in my left and the other in the small of my back, he pulls me towards him in the style of the waltz and says, 'Like this.'

And from his position high on his royal balcony, Prince Charles looks into the salon and sees us dancing; spinning and reeling around the floor, locked in a silent embrace.

'Grown-ups!' he says.

Chapter Thirty-one

Alfie

Mum says revenge is a dish best served cold. She and Nico have spent a week or two planning what they're going to do to the Dave Clarke Five. I told her to forget it as it will only make things flipping worse, but Nico's got a plan and this Saturday afternoon we're going to put it into action.

The Saturday matinee at the Odeon is Elvis Presley's *Viva Las Vegas* and the Symos Fleapit is packed full as usual. Boys with their hair slicked back like the King fill the back rows. No chance of slicking *my* hair back; I'll be glad when it grows a bit and Mum stops asking me where my bovver boots are. The Dave Clarke Five are, of course, right in the middle of the Teds.

As the film ends and the crowd drifts away, the trap is going to be sprung. We're right at the flipping front again, but for once it's a good place to be as it means that Milos and me are the first to go through the exit near the screen. The Gorgon's sending everyone through this exit today as he'll have a flipping big queue in the foyer outside waiting to come in at the back for the next show.

I'm wearing my French Foreign Legion hat and it shades my head from the strong sun as we blink to get our eyes used to the light again. We've got a head start. We run along the harbour towards the Kali Strata and look over our shoulders and see the teenagers slouch out of the exit.

Milo stops, turns and shouts towards the Five, 'Your mother's in love with Metaxa!'

They hear his tease. They know that it's aimed at them and they do just what we thought they would.

'Get the little bastards.'

The chase is on. Like a pack of flipping hounds on the scent of a fox, the Dave Clarke Five fly along the quayside after us. They leap over fishing nets and dodge bollards. They kick boxes of sardines aside and the air turns blue as cursing fishermen stand up from their nets shaking their fists. One even starts to chase them. I hope he isn't going to ruin things – but the boys are running so fast that he soon gives up.

They're running so flipping fast that I am worried Milo timed his Metaxa insult wrong and we could be in for another beating in a few minutes. But perhaps he's timed it perfectly – just.

We reach the foot of the Kali Strata and we are maybe fifty yards ahead of the gang. I'm gasping for air in this heat but we jump the steps two at a flipping time. As we reach the open door of number forty-five I'm sure I can feel the breath of our enemies. The sound of their shoes clattering on the steps is booming in our ears like ... like – like the flipping Dave Clarke Five.

We head through the door and straight up the staircase and round towards the grand salon. I hope that Nico's done everything as planned. It looks like he has. The right-hand pair of doors to the salon are wide open; the left-hand doors just slightly ajar. We hurtle into the salon as the DCF are rounding the staircase.

There's loud music coming from the big room. The room is flipping dark, with all the shutters closed, but the doors let some light into the room and at the far end the bullies spot our two small figures: one wearing the 'stupid' white hat, the other crouching by him. The yobs rush towards the windows. They don't seem to notice the loud music, and as they reach their targets the doors to the salon slam firmly shut behind them. The room is pitch black.

'Shit!'

'Bits and Pieces', the Dave Clarke Five's hit, booms out from the record player, set up by Nico to play the song on repeat.

The two figures that lured the gang to the far end of the room were Nico's masterstroke. After years of running his shop, Mr Constantinides, the owner of the little tailor's in San Stefano, closed down. He couldn't sell the business, so he decided to sell his furniture and whatever else he could. Nico spotted two child dummies in the shop window and thought that if it was dark enough they could be taken for Milos and me. As the teenagers hurtled into the salon, Milos and me tiptoed onto the landing through the other door and helped Nico to bolt both double doors shut. We jump up and down to celebrate.

'It worked, Nico. It really worked!'

'What did you expect?' says Nico.

Okay, so now they are trapped and listening to blinking deafening music. What next? Milos and I watch through the keyholes. Nico goes upstairs. From what we can see of them the teenage boys don't appear bothered.

'What's going on?' one shouts.

Another of the brothers gets out a cigarette lighter and lights the room enough for us to see them properly. They hear a noise from above and their heads jerk up. Where Nico said there was once a fabulous crystal chandelier, a new fitting has been installed. Hanging from the ceiling are six of what Nico calls 'fifteen-centimetre pyrotechnic mortar bombs' – or flipping big fireworks to me and Milos. Each of the mortars is pointing outwards and down towards the floor, so that every corner of the room is covered.

Dave Clarke used to work as a helper in the firework crew, so he knows what they are and what sort of flipping bang they will make. It won't be a few squibs and bangers. Nico's torchlight shines down through the hole in the ceiling. The music plays on.

Nico has chosen his fuse very carefully: too short and it will all be over too quickly; too long and he says it would be 'unreasonable torture' (though Milos says we should make it even longer than that). We watch and see that Nico has lit the fuse. It starts to burn down towards the mortars.

Nico comes down from the attic to join us. We all put our ears to one of the doors. 'Fuck! Shit! Shit! We're trapped!'

Give Me Your Tomorrow

The boys rattle at the shutters to no avail and then hurl themselves at the double doors to the room.

'Let us out! Let us out!' Their screams of panic drown out the music. 'Please! Nico, please!'

They hammer on the door frantically. A yellow trickle seeps out from under it.

As the seconds tick away, Nico studies his watch. He is the greatest fireworks maker on Symos, maybe in Greece even, and he knows exactly when the fuse will reach its target. Finally, he says to his prisoners, 'So you'll leave Alfie and Milos alone?'

'Yes, yes, yes!'

Nico takes another glance at his watch.

'And you will never, ever bother them again?'

Another 'Yes, yes, yes!' and then: 'Never, ever, ever, Nico!'

Nico gives us the signal and together we release the bolts at exactly the right time. The scruffy ragamuffins spill out into the light and run away down the stairs, yelping like flipping puppies.

The mortars ignite and a single puff of white sparkles briefly lights up the room.

We get our first glimpse of our dummy doubles: two little Greek boys with wide round eyes and plaster hair painted black. And we decide to take them back with us to the Alamo, where they can stand as lookouts when we are not around.

'What do we call them?'

So many possible names, but our favourites are 'Zorba' and 'Basil'. So Zorba and Basil they are.

Chapter Thirty-two

Maggie

Milos's dad, Spiro, is from the oldest boat-building family on the island. Nico has told me how Spiro incurred the wrath of Yiossos when he returned home from the war with a Turkish bride. There has never been much love lost between the Greeks and the Turks, and although Spiro's family forgave him and grew to love this Turkish beauty – a striking woman who excelled as a swimmer – there was always a sizeable element in the town who continued to give Spiro a hard time. Moving the family to the cottage below the water tower had provided respite from the cruel and snide remarks. Trouble has been brewing on and off between the two countries throughout Milos's short life and the family has been an easy target for tormentors.

I've grown to really like Milos's mum, Hanife. She sometimes joins me on the terrace and impresses me with her spectacular dives from Nico's childhood diving spot. She's good company. I suspect she may have guessed that Alfie is not my little brother; but she knows what it's like to be an outsider and she hasn't said anything about it, playing along with my story. She was overjoyed when Milos told her how the Dave Clark Five got their comeuppance at number forty-five. Hanife wonders if perhaps she and her family might one day be accepted by the townspeople.

Alfie has persuaded Milos to get his family to join us this evening on our Sunday-night promenade. Milos says his father was not keen, but Hanife has persuaded him. It will be nice for Alfie to have company on our stroll. Spiro Davros is dressed in a crisp white shirt and immaculate black trousers, and his wife wears a light-brown dress set off by a broad leather belt that emphasises her narrow waist. They look like any ordinary couple as they try to enjoy the Volta.

Nico and I follow Spiros and Hanife, and Milos and

Alfie tag along behind. The stroll up and down the harbour is a mixture of pleasantries when we pass Cosmo's taverna, and unpleasantries (if you can have such a thing) as Hanife's unforgotten Turkish descent is depressingly mocked by the most ignorant Symiots, who deliberately turn away from the Davros' acknowledgements and blank them. Some even make the ultimate insult of spitting on the ground. Hanife has lived on the island for almost twenty-five years, but however decent a woman she has proved to be (and she is a marvellous mother and seems to be a fantastic wife), her acceptance and integration into the community is still far from complete. I feel guilty at my naivety in suggesting they join us.

Halfway along the first length, I can tell that Spiro already regrets the decision to attempt the Volta; but Hanife (encouraged by our foolish assurance that all will be well) feels that it is high time she and her husband held their heads high in Yiossos. She remains defiant.

By the third length her husband is at boiling point. One particular family, the Aristideses, deliberately block the couple's path and force them to make a detour via some heaps of rotting rubbish awaiting collection. Spiro has had enough. He turns to Nico and me.

'Stavros Aristides! We dismissed him from the family boat-building firm after a big discrepancy in the company's stock of brass fittings, and here he is, like a peacock, looking down on me and my Hanife. Scum.'

Hanife is agitated and clearly uncomfortable with the unwanted attention. She must realise that she had been wrong to accept the encouragement of this stupid English woman singing the joys of the Volta.

'We are residents of Yiossos and we are as entitled as anyone to enjoy a Sunday walk,' she says to nobody in particular but loud enough for plenty to hear. The awkward atmosphere is broken momentarily as the walkers are distracted by a warship that appears at the head of the harbour.

'Alfie, look!' says Milos, pointing excitedly and

seemingly unaware of the ordeal that his parents have been enduring. 'An Algerine-class minesweeper.'

I haven't been following the news, but Nico brings us up to date.

'There's some tension in Athens. A Turkish fighter jet strayed into our airspace the other day. Istanbul says it was accidental, but parliament has responded by sending that old wreck of a minesweeper. We bought it from the UK after the war to patrol the straits between Symos and the Turkish coast. It's usually out at sea.'

There's quite a clamour on the harbour side as the crowd watch the vessel anchor.

'The crew has been given leave to come ashore,' says Nico as about fifty young sailors in crisp white trousers and double-breasted white shirts arrive at the landing jetty by launch.

'Even more reason to think the Volta a mistake,' says Spiro.

The sailors are used to the promenading habits of the Dodecanese (even if each island and town has its own mildly different customs and practices), and the boisterous and happy crowd of young men soon bolster the Volta to a size that must have been unseen for years.

Spiro and Hanife seem to grow used to the continued hostility and turn the other cheek to the occasional insults. I don't think that they will be back in a hurry, but they are making the most of their first Volta and it's passing without any major problems. At least it is until I notice Stavros Aristides sidetrack one of the sailors. Nico and I have walked ahead of Spiro and Hanife, who are patiently waiting for the two boys. Alfie and Milo are still engrossed by the clapped-out old warship. Aristides grabs a sailor's shirt.

'See that tall guy down there in the white shirt?' Aristedes points back along the quayside.

'There are lots of white shirts,' says the sailor.

'Yeah, but the ugly one.' Aristides's opinion of Spiro's looks is not one that many would share.

'Ah, yes. Yes, I see him.'

Give Me Your Tomorrow

'Well. He's a Turk lover. He's a traitor. Watch out for him. He's a pig.'

We're too far ahead to offer any warning and we watch in horror as the sailor takes it upon himself to trail a foot lazily into the Turk lover's path, having a good laugh as he stumbles into some fishing nets left on the quay for repair and spoils his fancy outfit. But in grabbing out at the nets, his victim somehow slips on a wet patch on the pathway and slides sideways, feet first, off the wall and twenty feet into the sea. There's a nasty thud that even we can hear, yards further along the Volta, as the side of his forehead catches a wooden prow. The victim is left floating face down in the water. We run towards the commotion.

If Stavros Aristides had said 'See the tall handsome guy with the beautiful woman', it would have been Spiro and not poor Dr Kostis Palamas floundering dangerously in the deep waters of the harbour in his finest Sunday clothes.

Spiro and Hanife are closest to Dr Palamas and must be shocked to see the accident, but in an instant Hanife is in the harbour alongside the stricken man and holding his head above the water as a huge lump develops on his forehead. Lying back in the water, she holds Kostis firmly around his chest and with powerful strokes kicks back towards the nearby jetty. Cheers ring out as Spiro helps his wife to haul the doctor out of the water, but they soon subside as he starts to give him mouth-to-mouth resuscitation. But cheers rise again as Kostis coughs up a wave of seawater and starts to breathe unaided.

The sailors have a medical officer among them and he takes over from Spiro, leaving the proud husband, arms wrapped protectively around his bedraggled heroic wife, to head back along the jetty through the crowds. And for once the crowds are praising the Turkish woman, the woman who had so bravely rescued a pillar of the local community. And a group of sailors lift the couple (and Alfie and Milos) off their feet and ceremoniously march with them held high on their shoulders for a full three lengths of the Volta to the sounds of a hugely appreciative crowd.

'So how did you enjoy my sexy swimming?' I ask as Hanife changes into dry clothes provided by Cosmo's wife, Karena.

Hanife laughs. 'Well, the sexy bit wasn't too bad,' she says, nodding in the direction of the handsome young sailors, 'but I wasn't expecting quite so much swimming.'

Chapter Thirty-three

Liverpool

For the four weeks after the incident in the park, Fred locked himself away every night in his bedroom studying the scriptures and praying on his knees as usual for salvation, guidance and inspiration. He used a huge concordance – a sort of Christian's index to where to find every important word in the Bible – to help him to cross-reference passages throughout the holy works. Both his Bible and his concordance were covered in furiously underlined paragraphs and the pages were interleaved with bits of different-coloured paper to help him to move speedily around the texts.

Like every scholar before him, he had struggled to unravel the riddles of the Book of Revelation and the mysteries of the Book of Numbers. An American arm of the brethren had decided that they had the answer and had travelled to Turkey, where they intended to camp out on the summit of Mount Ararat in anticipation of a repeat of Noah's great flood. But they had been refused permission to even reach the foot of that great mountain and had taken refuge in a hotel where they prayed, cowering together in a huddled mass as the predicted deluge and doomsday approached. And when they awoke the next morning to sunshine and a cloudless Turkish sky, they returned to America for a complete rethink.

Fred's recent violent experience at the park had led him to have doubts. He was starting to feel isolated within the brethren. He wanted to be a 'fisher of men' but when he went on his fishing expeditions on his trusty soapbox, new disciples trailing in his wake, echoing Jesus's ragtag group of followers, none of the church elders wanted to join him. They were happy to believe that they alone held the Truth, but they did not have the courage of their convictions to go out of their way to take their message to the non-believers. Handing out leaflets anonymously or delivering them door to door was acceptable, but public lectures were just a bit too embarrassing for them. They had an image to uphold.

And Fred was unhappy with other aspects of his chosen church. 'It is easier for a camel to go through the eye of a needle than for a rich man to enter into the kingdom of God' (Matthew 19:24) – and yet there were two Jags and a Bentley parked outside the meeting room every Sunday morning.

There was talk of building a grand new purpose-built hall with a sizeable bequest from a recently deceased member of the congregation. For Fred, this was directly against the preaching of the Lord: 'For where two or three are gathered together in my name, there am I in the midst of them.' There was no need for fancy buildings and following down the ceremonial route of the C of E and Catholic faiths; but here were senior brethren so concerned with the building of a temple when any back room was all that the Lord required, ignoring the spreading of the Lord's word in favour of meetings with architects. The money could fund so many pamphlets, lectures and teachings to get the Truth across. Brother Fred with his constant objections was becoming a very sharp thorn in the brethren's side.

After many hours of prayer and contemplation, Fred reached a decision and announced to a puzzled Mary: 'Come on, Mother, get your glad rags on. We're going out.'

And out they went. The venue was a steakhouse in the city centre and Fred and Mary – looking completely out of place resplendent in their Sunday best, the only 'going-out clothes' they had – were seated in a private booth on red leatherette banquettes.

The food was the peak of culinary excellence: prawn cocktail served in a wine glass, followed by steak and chips with frozen peas and a single grilled mushroom and then peach melba, and was accompanied by a small glass each of red wine. It was the first time in sixteen years that either of them had consumed alcohol other than at the weekly ritual of the Holy Communion and breaking of bread. And even more adventurously, Fred went on to order Irish coffees – black coffees laced with a shot of brandy – again served in a wine glass and topped with double cream poured over the back of a cold spoon to float on the surface.

Mary was aware of the Whit Sunday incident, but had not known a great deal about Fred's rescue from the skinheads. Over the meal he explained everything in hushed tones.

'You know when I got this?' Fred said, fingering the still-red scar.

Mary said nothing but nodded.

Fred continued, 'Well, when I got this, do you know who rescued me – who my Good Samaritan was?'

'You said it was a boy called Tommy.'

'Yes, but I didn't tell you what he was.'

'You said that he was a nurse at the hospital.'

'Yes, I know I said he was a nurse, but I didn't tell you what else he was.'

'So what else was he?'

'You know.'

Mary looked confused. 'I'm sorry, Fred, but I don't know.'

'He was one of those. You know, one of *those*' – he couldn't say the word – 'one of those who go with men.'

There. He'd said it.

'Oh,' said Mary. 'And?'

'They made my flesh creep. The way that they looked at each other! When I left them, I swear they were holding hands.'

'And? What are you saying, Fred?'

'I'm saying, Mary, that the only people to help me were wicked.'

'Were they wicked if they helped you?'

'That's it. That's what I've been asking myself and praying for guidance about ever since. Are they wicked? Are they evil? Because if the brethren say they are wicked and they are evil, the brethren have to be wrong.'

'Fred!' Mary was shocked.

'I left as soon as I could, but how could I condemn them to eternal damnation? Of all those hundreds of people in the park, only Tommy helped me; and if those skinheads knew what he was then he risked an even worse attack.'

'You're right, Fred. But there's no arguing; the Bible says they are evil.'

'I know, Mary, I know. But I know that Tommy and Archie aren't evil, and if they aren't evil, the Bible is wrong.'

Mary was silent. The church obsession had worn her down over the years; now she was beginning to see a glimmer of light. Just listen, she thought. Let Fred make his own decisions.

He continued, 'I'm afraid that I have looked at it so many ways and keep coming to the same answer. The brethren are wrong. And if they are wrong, I have to give them up.'

Mary was shocked to hear the words that she had longed to hear and yet dreaded to hear. Sixteen or more years of zeal, passion and isolation were being dismissed just like that. Mary's whole life had revolved around her unyielding support for her husband and the brethren. Her joy at the thought of their connection with the church ending for good made her want to turn cartwheels through the restaurant. But the cartwheels were on hold. The church was her only social outlet; her own brothers and sisters had disowned her when she and Fred had wrapped themselves up in religion. What was she going to do now? Mary was nervous. What future lay ahead?

Fred explained that his weeks of soul-searching had led him to a heart-wrenching choice.

'I'm not saying that the Bible is wrong on everything, Mother. There's a lot in the New Testament that I agree with. But I've decided that I've got just two options: either I follow the Lord on the path to eternal life alone

Give Me Your Tomorrow

without the brethren, or I give up the Lord and live just the one life but live it to the full.'

Mary wiped a tear from her eye. 'Go on. I'm listening.'

'The only way to follow Christ completely would be to do as the disciples did and simply pack up my belongings and follow Him and gather more followers on the journey ahead. I could follow Him and be the way, the truth and the life for Him on earth ... but that would be selfish.'

'Not if that's what you want, Fred.'

'No, Mother. It would mean giving up everything: giving up you, giving up Maggie and giving up Alfie.'

'You've already lost them.'

'I know. But I'm going to get them back again. And I'm going to win you back too, Mary, and Maggie and Alfie. You watch.'

Mary knew Fred's determination.

'If you say so.' It was a lot to take in. The simple act of going out to a steakhouse was shock enough to the system; Fred's epiphany was too much for one night. 'Can we go home now, Father?'

'Of course, Mother. Did you enjoy the meal?'

And that was it; like turning off a tap, Fred would turn away from the brethren. And the senior members would be secretly glad to lose their leading recruiter and star speaker; while the confused newly baptised converts would never have the opportunity to ask Fred for an explanation, and without him their whole reason for attending the Sunday meetings would evaporate into thin air.

Like Ebenezer Scrooge after his night with the spirits, Fred had so much to do and so little time to do it. To start with there were bridges to mend with a daughter and grandson. So when he and Mary returned home from their steakhouse blowout, glowing slightly from the unfamiliar warmth of alcohol, Fred settled down to write a letter.

John Brassey

To Maggie Johnson
Care of Nicos Karteras
Symos
Greece

28th June 1969

Dear Maggie,

I don't really know how to start to tell you this, so I might as well just come out and say it.

I have taken the momentous decision to leave the brotherhood.

I am so terribly sorry for the effect that my fanaticism has had on my family's life, and it is my intention to do everything that I possibly can to make things up to you.

For a start, I would like Mother and I to come and see you both on your beautiful island. If we can sort out transport, I hope we can arrive in time to celebrate Alfie's birthday with you and I can start to put things right and show you both the love and affection that I failed to show you for so many years.

Don't worry about us. God willing, we'll find our own accommodation.
Hoping to see you soon.
With all my love and my deepest apologies,
Dad x

Chapter Thirty-four

Alfie

Mum's left me alone in the cottage. She's walked into town for some shopping, so I've got the place to myself and I've made the kitchen table into a desert from a couple of boxes covered with a cream-coloured blanket. There's a battle raging between the Desert Rats and the Afrika Korps.

I flipping love playing with these tiny plastic figures. They come in packs of fifty in cardboard boxes. The boxes have brilliant war pictures on them and the lids have a cellophane window so you can see the little uniformed men hanging from plastic frames inside. Each pack has two or three frames and when you open the box the first job is to twist the figures from the frame. That leaves them with plastic tufts, so they look like alien insects with antennae sprouting from the top of their heads.

The contents are listed on the back of every box: ten grenade throwers; one general; five riflemen crouching; five snipers. I don't mind that every grenade thrower is frozen in exactly the same position and every sniper's knee bends in exactly the same place. My soldiers are flipping well-drilled – synchronised grenade throwers, synchronised riflemen crouching, synchronised snipers. The boxes say you should paint the figures 'for your enjoyment' – Mum says 'more likely to sell paint', as the makers sell a big range of enamel paints in tiny pots. I tried it once. I bought a flipping tiny paintbrush and a little tiny tin with the word 'FLESH' on it. My platoon looked like their heads and hands had been dipped in calamine lotion. Mum looked at my work and said, 'Is it the clowns' battalion?'

'No, it's the candy-floss unit ... Perhaps they'll look better when they're dry,' I said. They didn't.

I hear Mum coming back and run to the door. She's carrying two heavy shopping baskets.

'I'd have come with you if I'd known you were getting all that, Mum.'

Mum puts the baskets down and slumps deeply into the settee with a loud 'Phew'.

I join her.

'So what have you been buying?'

'Well, with Nico coming tonight, I thought that I'd give him a taste of home.'

'This is home,' I say. I lift my hands apart, turn my palms upwards, and signal around the room and then towards the fireplace. I'm sure that Mr and Mrs Sunday give me a friendly nod.

Mum puts her arm around my shoulders and squeezes me towards her.

'Of course this is home. But do you know that Nico has never been further than Rhodes in his life and he has never eaten anything but Greek food?'

'Well, until we came here we'd never eaten anything but English.'

Mum puts me right. 'Don't forget the Chinese.'

'Okay. I'll give you that. So what's it to be? Beans on toast?'

Mum laughs. She's planning a meal for her 'boyfriend'; beans on toast would really bowl him over. 'I think we can do a bit better than that.'

'Is there anything better than beans on toast? I know: roast beef and Yorkshire pudding.'

'When did you last see a cow around here? But you're on the right lines.'

'Roast lamb with mint sauce?'

'I thought of that, but he eats a lot of lamb.'

'Spaghetti bolognese?'

'I said English. That's not English.

'Isn't it? Nana made it. Well, then it has to be fish and chips,' I say.

'You got it.'

'With mushy peas?'

'Steady on, Alfie. It was hard enough to find a nice piece of cod. We'll have to miss out the mushy peas, but

Give Me Your Tomorrow

we'll have plenty of salt and vinegar.'

'Can we serve it in newspaper?'

'If you like. And for pudding I'm making your very favourite.'

'Bread and butter pudding? Wow! Thanks, Mum.'

'Well, if Nico likes it as much as you do, I'll be onto a winner. Just one thing ...' Mum blushes slightly like she does every time she tells someone I'm her brother. 'Nico won't be able to make it until after your bedtime.'

'That's not like Nico, Mum. He usually comes at any time you ask. Aw.' I pull back with my arms folded.

'He said he's really sorry, but he has to put some shelves up for his mum. Don't worry; I've got enough for you too. You can be his taster.'

I brighten up at the thought of being a taster and imagine doing the job for a medieval king. Nice work if you could get it – as long as your king was popular, that is. When Mum puts the fish and chips in front of me, for a bit of fun I'll take one flipping bite and then hold my hands to my neck and make a strangled cry before banging my head down on the table.

Mum stands up and starts unpacking the shopping. 'I'm feeling more relaxed now,' she says. 'I had to do it as late as I could with us having no fridge and me cooking fish; I don't want to poison Nico.'

'I thought you said these thick walls keep the cottage cool.'

'Maybe. But cool's relative in Symos in June.'

'Uncle Cool, or Aunty Cool?'

Mum groans. I'm not sure that she always gets my jokes. 'Will you give me a hand? There's a lot to do,' she says.

'Sure, Mum. Can I have my records on?'

'Go on then.'

I clear away El Alamein and bring the Dansette Transit to the table. Mum says the battery-powered record player is her desert-island luxury, like on *Desert Island Discs*. That's a radio show that we pick up on the BBC World Service; it's been going for years and Mum listens to it every flipping week – without fail. The presenter asks people what their eight favourite records are and then he goes and sends them off to a desert island. Brilliant! It's been going so long that there can't be many islands left to send the castaways to. All the islands in the world must have someone camping out and listening to flipping classical music. If they run out of islands, they might choose ours. I'd be shouting, 'Hey, Castaway, keep that flipping noise down. I'm flipping sick to death of Beethoven and that Messiah thing "Come for tea".'

Mum may have her favourite programme, but I have mine too. We get my Saturday-morning show *Children's Favourites* on the World Service. I used to send in requests, but I haven't sent one lately. The stamps cost too much here. The record player holds eight forty-five records, so I can have my own episode of *Desert Island Discs*. As long as Mum doesn't send me to the island when I've finished.

'Is it okay to have the banned ones, Mum?'

Mum folds her arms across her chest and looks down her nose like Granddad whenever he caught me messing about. She's a great mimic. She does Granddad's voice: 'You're not playing that filth around here, young man.' And then her face creases into a smile. 'You play whatever you want,' she says.

It's not like I have the records that were banned by the BBC. I remember when that happened. I read the board outside the newsagents: 'BAN THIS BIRKIN FILTH'. I thought 'birkin' was a new word and I used it all the time for a week until I went into Sunday school and said, 'It's a birkin nice day today,' and Johnny Smith fell about laughing and said that Birkin was a singer. Johnny had heard the banned record. 'Je Tame', it was called. His big brother played it for him while his mum and dad were out.

'It's just a man singing and then a woman singing in a high voice and then she starts panting. My brother says she's having an organism.' We got out the dictionary and read the definition: 'an animal, plant, fungus – a living being'. We thought the BBC was a bit daft to ban her singing about that. 'It's probably just because she's singing in French,' Johnny said – which seemed a pretty good reason to ban it to me.

Johnny's brother had another banned record too. It was called 'Wet Dream'. Johnny knew some of the words. He said that the singer had said, 'It's about sleeping under a leaky roof.' He taught us the chorus and we made up a dance to go with it. When Miss Hargreaves came in and found Fiona lying on a table and the rest of us holding up a pretend ceiling to stop it falling on her while singing 'Lie down girl, let me push it up, push it up', she went bright red, hit Johnny with the ruler and said we should all wash our mouths out with soap and water. I told Granddad when I got home before flipping Miss Hargreaves said anything to him. But he didn't say much. He just said that he was going to have a word with Brother Smith.

Today Bernard Cribbins kicks off my choice with 'Right Said Fred'. Even Granddad didn't think there was much wrong with this one; although he didn't like that one of the useless workers in the song who spends all day drinking tea, more tea and yet another cup of tea is called Fred.

We hum along as we prepare Nico's feast.

'Let's get the batter ready nice and early,' says Mum, handing me the big mixing bowl. 'You can do the mixing.'

She starts to list the ingredients in military style.

'Flour,' she says, throwing a packet to me. I catch it with a cheerful 'Check' as the bag shoots a small puff of white powder into my face.

'Salt.'

'Check.'

'Beer.' Mum gives it a quick shake before throwing it to me.

Beer! That's not like Mum. I just manage to catch it.

'Check.'

'Okay,' says Mum, handing me a bottle opener, 'we start with pouring the beer into the bowl.'

I open the bottle. Mum explodes into a fit of flipping giggles as the beer sprays into my face.

'I'll get you for that,' I run towards her and chase her around the table.

The record has changed to the beep-beep song ('The Little Nash Rambler' by the Playmates) and by the time I start the chase it's getting near the end and the little car in the song is running faster and faster and faster. We go six times around the table before Mum collapses onto it and I catch her up and give her a playful pat on the bum.

After she stops laughing, Mum sieves the flour and salt and shows me how to mix the batter. Another of my favourites drops onto the turntable. It's 'Tie Me Kangaroo Down, Sport'.

'This one could have been made for mixing batter to,' she says as she holds my hand and together we sing as loud as we can — nobody can hear us — as we whip the batter into a perfect smooth gloop that drops off the spoon in exactly the way that she says it should. As we put the batter to one side, Mum dabs the wooden spoon against the tip of my nose, leaving a creamy white blob. I grab the spoon and do the same to her.

We laugh again and wipe the batter off our faces.

'Uh oh. Here's one of the banned ones.' I wink as 'Itsy Bitsy Teenie Weenie Yellow Polka Dot Bikini' fills the cottage. 'Bikinis! The *Devil's* swimming costumes,' says Mum, doing her Granddad impression again.

Mum looks at her watch.

'We'd better get a move on, young man.'

She tidies away the mess from the batter and helps me to grease the pie dish, then sets me to work buttering slices of bread that she has cut very thinly.

'One piece!' she says sternly as she catches me with my mouth full. 'When you finish that, will you set the table for me on the terrace?'

Mum hands me a starched white tablecloth that she

has found in the bottom of her wardrobe. 'I bet this used to be on Mr and Mrs Sunday's table,' she says.

'Only on Sundays,' I add.

I get together everything that Mum needs for the table: knives, forks, water glasses, wine glasses! Blimey, *wine glasses*, this *is* going to be special.

I set the table as nicely as I can. The lace-edged cloth is meant for a flipping square table, but I manage to position it so it fits the round table almost perfectly and none of it touches the floor. While I do the table I sing along to another of my favourites and look across to the Alamo where me and Milos are always playing 'Three Wheels on My Wagon'. Milos is the whooping Cherokee and I'm the frontiersman. 'Higgety, hoggety, haggety hi, pioneers we never say die.'

'How's that, Mum?' I say. Mum has tears in her eyes when she sees my finished job. 'I didn't think it was that bad, Mum,' I say, feeling a bit disappointed. Perhaps she doesn't like the little clump of wild flowers that I picked from cracks in the cliff edge and put in a jam jar.

'Don't be silly, Alfie. It's perfect.'

'I really want you to have a special time tonight, Mum.' The second banned song starts to play. 'Seven Little Girls (Sitting in the Back Seat)' used to get Granddad really worked up whenever it came on the radio; I've only got it because Mum got free samples of nearly everything from the shop where she worked. I've played this one so much that it's a bit scratched. Why didn't Granddad like it? I've no idea but perhaps it's all the 'kissing' and 'a-hugging' ... 'with *Fred*'. As the song gets to the end I sing along and change the words a bit for Mum: 'kissing and a-hugging with Nico'.

Mum goes bright red and flicks a tea towel at me. 'Alfie!'

'Is that what you'll be doing tonight, Mum? Kissing and hugging Nico? Cause I don't mind, Mum. Honest. I like Nico. Might he be my dad? Will you marry him?'

Mum's a bit flustered.

'Alfie, I've only known Nico for twelve weeks. How

can I marry him?'

'Because perhaps he's Mr Right, Mum. You always said you would wait for Mr Right. Perhaps it's Nico. Perhaps he's your Mr Right.'

'Let's have no more of that. Let's just see what happens.'

'But you do like him, Mum, don't you?'

'Of course I like him, sunshine. I've never met anybody gentler, kinder or more considerate. But remember, he thinks that you're my brother. I've got to tell him that you're not. I'm fed up with all the lying.'

'Me too. And if he is Mr Right, he'll be okay.'

'Do you think so?'

'He flipping better be.'

Mum cooks a small portion of fish and chips and serves them to me in the kitchen. I roll my eyes up into my head, make a gurgling noise and drop my head to the table. Mum plays along: 'Oh no! I've poisoned my son. Help! Help!' But the fish and chips smell too flipping good to carry on for long. I want to eat them while they're still hot. My plate's clean in a few minutes and the bread and butter pud disappears even quicker.

Mum clears away my dirty dishes. 'It's eight o'clock, Alfie. Time to get ready for bed.'

'Can't I stay up to see Nico, Mum? Please, *please*,' I put on my flipping best pleading voice, but she won't budge.

'What time is bedtime?' she says.

'Eight thirty.'

'And what time is Nico coming?'

'Nine o'clock.' I sulk a bit. I bet that's why she told him to come at nine.

She lifts the tin bath down from the wall and says, 'Sorry, sunshine. I've got a lot to do before Nico arrives. Now get ready for your bath.'

She fills the bath with cold water and adds a kettleful of hot just to take away the chill. I climb in and let her clean me with the golden sponge that Nico gave me on our first morning. 'I can do this myself, Mum.

Give Me Your Tomorrow

I'll be ten soon.'

'Okay, sunshine. It won't be long before you're a man.'

It's funny how she's not bothered about me having nothing on. In Liverpool, Granddad and Nana used to look away when they bathed me and wouldn't look back again until I had a towel round me. They were funny like that. I once went into Granddad's bedroom and saw him sitting on the bed with his back to me. I saw he had no shirt or pants on. As soon as he heard the door open he dived off the flipping bed onto the floor and hid out of view shouting at me to get out. It's much better here. Mum sometimes gets into my bath water after me and she doesn't mind if I'm around – there's no looking away.

As I dry myself off, Mum goes out onto the terrace to put a row of jam jars along the ground. She puts a candle inside every one; they're big candles – she must be planning a flipping late night. She comes back into the cottage and goes out again with the Dansette and puts it down near the table together with *her* choice of desert island discs.

'Are you dry?' she shouts. 'Hurry up. I want to get into your water when you're in bed. I want a bath before Nico comes.'

I go into my bedroom. I put on my pyjamas and walk back to where she's getting undressed by the bath.

'Boy, you're growing,' she says, looking at my stripy pyjama bottoms that only reach down to my calves and my jacket that make me looks like Frankenstein's flipping monster. 'They fitted perfectly when we got here.'

'Maybe you shrunk them in the wash,' I say. I put my cheek towards her for my goodnight kiss.

It's getting dark, but something flickers by the door. Has Mum lit the candles already? Surely not. I pull away from my kiss and go to investigate. I was right. It's not candles. At the end of the terrace the small light flickers again and goes right across the water towards the island.

And then there's another, and then another. It's like Tinkerbell and her fairies, or silent miniature fireworks; a magic light show just for me.

'Mum!' I shout. 'Mum! *Mum!* Come and look!'

Mum rushes out. She's wrapped in just a towel. 'What is it, Alfie? What?'

I point and she sees them. 'Oh, Alfie! Fireflies! I read about them in *My Family and Other Animals*, but I never thought that we would be lucky enough to see them – especially not here. How romantic. What a wonderful backdrop for our special dinner. I hope they stay around for Nico to see.'

We watch for a few more seconds, but now Mum's in a flipping hurry.

'Okay, you. Off to bed now.'

So off I go.

Chapter Thirty-five

Nico

The most memorable night of my life was the one I spent waiting to welcome mourners to the house. It's a night that I will never forget; a night of strong emotions; a night of unhappiness and sorrow; a night that condemned me to a life of loneliness. Now I'm anticipating another night that could mould my future – another night of strong emotions. I want it to be a very special night, another night that will stay with me for the rest of my life; but I want it to be a night of joy, not sorrow – a night to finally end my years of being alone. I've only known Maggie for twelve weeks. I can't believe that it is only twelve weeks since she walked down the gangplank in that torrential rain and I had the luckiest soaking ever. She has turned my life upside down.

Before Maggie came into my life, I spent some of my time in the fireworks workshop and helping out in Cosmo's taverna, but most of my time very much alone in my bedroom. Suddenly I'm a new man. Everyone in Yiossos wants my help. I'm now Cosmo's head waiter and all the other taverna owners are pleased when they see me. Rather than 'I'll give you a few drachma to take away all this rubbish', it's 'Will you look over our menu for me, please, Nico, and tell me if my English is right?' Now that we are seeing more tourists on Symos, they all want their menus translated. Although I was tempted to leave some of them with their 'Grumbled Eggs', 'Lamb Shops' and 'Fresh Crap, I've done my best, and most of the restaurants' menus are now printed in both perfect Greek and in perfect English.

Momma thinks I've changed for the worse, but nobody else does. I'm happy; my faint hope of a new life is now a strong hope; and maybe, just maybe, I will soon get married and have a son or daughter of my own. Yes, Maggie has changed my life, and if she accepts my proposal, we'll have the biggest ceremony the island has seen since the last time the sponge fleet sailed. If she accepts? *When* she accepts.

I dream about the ceremony: the dancing, the singing and the laughter. I dream about our first night together; I dream of our tenderness and passion; and I dream of the morning after our wedding night.

I can't wait to spend this evening with Maggie at the cottage. Nine o'clock is a late start, so Alfie will be in bed soon after I arrive. There won't be three of us like when Maggie came here. What's that English saying of Maggie's? 'Two's company – three's a crowd.' Momma's avgolemono, octopus and galaktoboureko might have tasted delicious, but that was an evening to forget.

I wash like never before. I scrub my hands until they are raw. I shave for the second time – not that I need to. No undertaker's suit tonight; I carefully remove my new shirt from its cellophane packet. Why do the shirt-makers insist upon so many pins?

I hold the shirt in front of me and look in the mirror. It's jet-black cotton; the creases from the packet will soon drop out. Or should I ask Momma to run her iron over it? I know exactly what she would say: 'How much did you spend on that shirt? *How much*? You must be stupid. She's got you wrapped around her little finger. What's wrong with cousin Agatha?' No, the creases will have to fall out by themselves.

I open the shopping bag on the bed and take out a pair of black-denim jeans in the latest style. They fit well. The waist is at least three sizes smaller than the ones I was wearing in March. I finish the outfit with a pair of smart, shiny black-patent shoes with just a hint of a raised heel. I look in the mirror again. 'Not bad,' I think. 'Not bad at all.' I sprinkle myself freely with the finest aftershave that I could find in the San Stefano general stores.

Maggie said to arrive at about nine. That means I will be heading home late at night, so to avoid the long walk in the dark I'll borrow Cosmo's boat. I bend down to pick up the brown-paper package beneath my bed and put it under my arm. I take a final look in the mirror and head downstairs.

Momma is sitting on the front doorstep chatting with our neighbour Mrs Sioufas. She breaks off her conversation and looks me up and down. 'What *are* you wearing, Nico?'

'Some new clothes, Momma. Do you like them?'

'Pah. You are dressed like one of the Ioannidis children,' she says, 'but I suppose *she* will like that. Costas Ioannidis is about her age.' She scowls and looks at her friend.

'You look very nice, Nico,' says Mrs Sioufas. 'Don't listen to your mother.'

I'm not listening. But is Momma right? Am I way too old for all this? Am I a stupid old fool? Should I go back inside and change into an outfit more suitable for someone old enough to be her father? No. I'm not letting this chance slip away.

I wish Momma and Mrs Sioufas a good night and head down towards Yiossos.

As I arrive at the taverna and walk into the kitchen, a cheer and a couple of whistles ring out.

'Oooh, look at Nico!'

Plump but feminine in her chef's whites, Karena stands with her hands on her hips and flutters her eyelashes at me. 'Go on. Turn around.'

Self-consciously, I turn a full three hundred and sixty degrees.

'Very nice. Very nice indeed,' says Karena, making a click-click noise with her mouth. 'Have you bought me a present?' she teases, looking at the parcel under my arm.

I laugh. 'For Maggie.'

Cosmo arrives with the key to the outboard motor and hands it to me. 'Ah, the mystery's solved at last,' he says.

'The mystery?' I give him a puzzled look and shrug. What the hell is Cosmo talking about? 'What mystery?'

'Zorro! He's finally been unmasked.'

I laugh out loud at the thought of me as Zorro the

masked swordsman and swashbuckling folk hero.

'Damn. I knew I'd forgotten something. I left the sword and cape at home ... and the mask.'

I worry slightly. Was the joke meant as a compliment – Zorro the mysterious handsome stranger? Or do I simply look ridiculous in my jet-black outfit?

Karena hustles me out of the kitchen.

'Come on, Nico. You better get out of here before that lovely scent turns into eau de moussaka.'

'Yes, I'd better go now,' I say, although it is really way too early.

As I set out on my journey from the harbour I keep reaching into my top pocket to touch the small silk-lined black box with its diamond solitaire ring snuggled inside. I feel compelled to check it is still there every couple of minutes.

I have been practising my speech in front of the mirror. I'm going to run through it once again as soon as I clear the headwater and leave the twinkling lights of Yiossos in the gathering dusk.

'Maggie.'

No: go down on one knee first. Start again.

'Maggie, I know I have known you only for a few months. But, Maggie, these are the happiest months of my life and I never want to lose that happiness. I want to be with you forever and I am happy for Alfie to grow up with us and he can be my little brother too and ... '

It's too long. How can I propose and go on about her brother? No: I need it to be short and to the point. Start again.

'Maggie, I love you. Will you marry me?'

That's it. I can't make it plainer or simpler.

I repeat, 'Maggie, I love you. Will you marry me?'

Yes. That's it. Plain and simple.

I say it again and again under my breath and then out loud, first whispered and then in a booming voice.

As I moor at the little cove behind the island I realise that although I detoured a little to kill time, I am hopelessly early. But Maggie won't mind. I can sit and listen to some of her music.

I cross the island, pausing to look up at the Alamo, where Zorba and Basil both stand with hands on hips looking out to sea. As I approach the bridge in the twilight I can see the terrace with the new woven straw awning that I made to replace the canvas – the canvas that caused such emotions on that other rainy day. What is it about Maggie and the rain?

On the terrace the cast-iron table is draped with a starched white cloth. Perhaps Maggie has bought it specially. Then I remember the cloth and how my aunt had been so proud of its fine lacework. I can see that the table is laid with enough cutlery and glasses for a feast. I see unlit candles in jars dotted around the terrace; Maggie must be expecting a long evening. I notice that Maggie's record player and some of her records are on the stone floor. I wonder which LPs she has selected: dance music, or romantic melodies?

When I reach the cliff edge, I look down at the channel below and pause to remember the last time I was so happy: the laughter and excitement of childhood as I and my big brother and cousins dived to the depths and explored the seabed almost thirty metres below the surface – such happy days. As I pause, I nervously finger the small black box in my shirt pocket and hold tighter the bundle under my arm. The brown paper holds a folded length of slightly faded, intricately and delicately patterned blue silk. To settle my nerves, I quietly sing a favourite song beneath my breath.

I step onto the bridge but hesitate as I spot Alfie coming through the front door. He isn't looking in my direction. Something at the end of the terrace has caught his eye. I am about to call him and catch his attention, but then I hear him shout to Maggie. His words shatter my future into tiny pieces.

'Mum! Mum! *Mum!* Come and look!'

I freeze. Did I mishear? The sea is choppy and small waves are breaking noisily beneath the bridge. But I know that I didn't mishear. With those six words, my hopes – the hopes that I had raised so very, very high – are completely smashed.

I watch in disgust as Maggie, wrapped in a towel, comes to share her son's delight at the flitting fireflies – the fairies that captivated me in the same way when I was a child. It's now dark; I am in black, and she doesn't spot me as she steers Alfie back inside the cottage.

'Mum'? How could anyone so young be Alfie's mother? What sort of person is she to lie and to lead me on for almost three months? Who is the father? Who is the man who ruined all my dreams? My dreams of me and my virgin bride losing our innocence together are gone – dissolved. I open my mouth, but my scream is silent. I slump to my knees. I wish I were dead. I want to be dead.

Life is no longer worth living.

Chapter Thirty-six

Nico

I stagger away aimlessly, blinded by tears. My wretched life that for a few brief weeks seemed to be worthwhile is back to normal; it's worthless again. I am at a place that I love, metres away from the woman who minutes earlier I worshipped and adored; now I hate her so very, very much.

Maggie disappears into the cottage. She is unaware of Zorro hiding in the shadows. She will be preparing for the excitement of the evening ahead. Perhaps she feels the way I felt when I practised my proposal. Can that only have been an hour ago?

I sit down on the island's dusty path – no need to worry about my smart new jeans now. What next? Another forty years of loneliness?

I don't know how long I've been sitting here. Perhaps half an hour has passed when I see Maggie come out of the door again and wander across the terrace. From the light of the door I see her peering into the dark. I know that she's looking for me and my heart aches to see her looking anxious. But why should I be bothered? She's cheated me for three months. Let her worry.

She walks across the terrace and lights all the candles. As they flicker into life I see the colourful long silky dress that she is wearing. I can't believe how fabulous she looks. She goes back inside. She's probably straining to see from the kitchen window whether I'm walking down the path.

I stand up and dust down my jeans. I cross the bridge and walk slowly up to the cottage. I toss the bundle of silk to the ground.

I bang on the door.

Maggie opens it and looks up at me.

'Nico. Where have you ...' Her voice trails off. 'What happened to you?'

'What happened to *me*? You're what happened to

me.'

'Me? What have I done?'

'You know what you have done.'

'What? What is it, Nico? What have I done?'

'You lied to me.' I spit the words out.

'*Lied?* When did I lie?'

'From the minute I met you and every day that I have known you. And you let Alfie and probably everybody else on the island lie for you too. They'll all be laughing behind my back at stupid Nico falling for the "He's my little brother" line from the English tart.'

I shudder, hating myself for using that word.

'"*Tart.*" You think I'm a tart?'

My cheek stings as Maggie swings her open palm ferociously across it.

'You're the one who suggested that Alfie was my brother. I'd just travelled a thousand miles from home on my own. I didn't have time for long explanations. I was going to tell you ...'

I raise my hand to feel my cheek. Maggie misunderstands and shrinks back, cowering, her arms above her head. She's shaking and starts to sob.

'No, Maggie, no, you ...' I reach forward to try to grab her arms but she screams: 'Get away from me!'

She steps backwards. I don't know how it happens – maybe her heel catches the hem of her dress – but she twists awkwardly and falls heavily to the floor. I try to help her off the ground but she pushes me away.

'I said *get away from me!*' She kicks out and I step backwards outside the door.

The door crashes shut and seconds later I hear the bolt slam into place. Her voice is muffled but there's no mistaking her final words.

'I never want to see you again.'

'You won't,' I say beneath my breath.

I've lost everything. How can I hold my head up in Symos again? The foolish cuckold who fell for a lying foreigner. How can I face Momma?

I lift a *skandalopetra* from beside the door. I put the

sixty-metre coil of fine rope over my shoulder. I walk back through the gate and onto the bridge to prepare for my final moments. This will not be a mad dash and leap into eternity. I don't want my body to disappear forever, to be left to the elements and eaten by fish. Burial is important; I want to be found.

I cross to the centre of the bridge, some ten metres above the waves. I pull apart two rope supports and sit between them with my feet dangling above the gentle swell. The moon has started to rise and there is enough light for me to see what I am doing.

'Maggie, I love you. Will you marry me?'

I spit out the words. My tears still blind me as I lift the heavy weight of the *skandalopetra* and place it across my thighs. I slowly move the stone from my thighs and lean forward, sliding it into position against my shins. I take the *skandalopetra* rope around my ankles several times, pulling tightly on each revolution.

'Maggie, I love you. Will you marry me?' I repeat. I'm laughing now.

I lean across to my right, where the bellstone's rope lies coiled. I find the end and tie it firmly to one of the planks.

'That's for you, Momma. You'll be able to find me now and put me in with Tata and Yianni. I'll be good company for them.'

I sit on the rope bridge for maybe five minutes, remembering my father and my brother. My mother will never forgive me ('Not for that foreigner!' she will weep when she keeps her vigil beside my open coffin), but at least I will leave a body to be found and buried in the church tradition.

By now the heavy bellstone is pulling on my ankles. The fifteen kilos are beckoning me towards the water.

'Come on, Nico, jump.' I remember Yianni's words as we held hands and leapt from the headland in those wonderful days of innocence. 'Come on, Nico, jump.' I see Agatha, Khristophoros and Spiro. They're standing at the cliff edge waving me forward. 'Jump, jump, jump,

jump, jump.' They stamp their feet and clap their hands. The noise deafens me. 'Jump, jump, jump, jump, jump.' I try to block out my senses. I put my hands to my ears and close my eyes. But I can still see them beckoning me and hear their words growing faster and faster: 'Jump, jump, jump, jump, jump.'

I sway gently forwards and backwards, sobbing, hugging my chest and patting the pocket that holds the now totally insignificant box. I take out the box and place it on the palm of my hand. I reach out over the sea, holding the box at eye level. I turn my hand over and it is gone.

The stone – the stone that Maggie likened to a giant teardrop – is weighing heavier and it is time for it to take me to my end. Yianni, Khristophoros, Agatha and Spiro are holding hands. They take two steps back from the cliff and then together, laughing, they rush forward and leap.

'Maggie, I love you. Will you marry me?' I shout in full voice and then I plunge downwards, feet first, into the void; down towards the deep Aegean, weighed down by a tear. My life does not flash before me, but in these few seconds my mind fills with thoughts of blue sharks, lavender scent and the most fabulous sponges. Ahead of me the small black silk-lined box holding the diamond solitaire ring sinks into oblivion.

Seconds later the rope is taut and points straight as an arrow to its miserable load, as if to say: 'This way to the body; this way to the loser.'

Chapter Thirty-seven

Alfie

It never takes me long to get to sleep. I'm usually in the land of nod before Mum finishes a chapter of my bedtime story. My dreams are full of our adventures on the Alamo. Milos chases me around the island. He's wearing his Sitting Hamster headdress and whooping a bloodthirsty war cry and then – beep-beep! – he chases me across the bridge and into the flipping cottage. The cottage turns into a blinking desert and now we're both struggling to walk through quicksand that feels like a thick blanket. We hide as giant plastic soldiers with candyfloss heads wage war with enormous insects and then a kangaroo bounces into view and squashes them all.

Mum's voice comes into my dream. 'Alfie. Alfie.' A clown soldier is shaking my shoulder. 'Alfie. Wake up. *Wake up!*'

I sit up and rub my eyes. 'What is it, Mum? Is it morning? Has Nico been?' But I can tell from her voice that it's important. She's panicking. She has tears in her voice and black streaks down her cheeks.

'Help me. One of the teardrops has gone.'

I know those stones are important to Nico – but important enough to wake me up in the middle of a brilliant dream? Uh oh. I'm worried. Did me and Milos put the stone back? After the newsreel about the 'adolescent initiation and fertility rites' of the teenage boys of the Pacific island of Vanuatu, we wanted to make it one of our games, and after Nico helped us to carry Basil and Zorba back to the cottage, we had a flipping great idea.

'I know where we can jump from,' Milos said.

'Top of the Alamo?' I said.

'Hmm. That's all of two metres.'

'Not the Alamo. What about the bridge?' Milos walked to the middle plank and looked over. 'Is this high enough for you?' He laughed as he said it. 'You can go first.'

'You must be flipping kidding. I'm not flipping jumping off there.' I stopped for a second. 'But I know who will.'

'Maggie?' said Milos.

'No.' I nodded towards the Alamo, where Basil and Zorba were keeping watch. 'Zorba and Basil!'

'Brilliant.'

Together we carried Basil and Zorba down from the platform. We took off all the dummies' clothes and dressed them in a couple of pairs of my flipping Y-fronts from the cottage, and for a real native look, we smeared them all over with brown boot polish.

'Have you got any rope?' Milos asked.

'There's tons of it on the stones by the front door.'

'Won't Nico mind?' said Milos.

'We're only borrowing it.'

I untied the rope from one of the teardrop stones. I cut a length and tied it to Basil's ankle. Milos did the same with Zorba, using one of his very best knots.

We tied the dummies to the bridge and started a countdown. 'Five, four, three, two, one.'

We threw Basil and Zorba forward and they dived towards the sea.

The first try was a flipping big flop. Zorba ended up six feet under the water and Basil was left dangling five flipping feet above it. We made a few changes with the knife and the ropes were soon just right.

'Wooo!' screamed Milos and 'Wahey!' I shouted as we launched Basil and Zorba off the bridge and they hurtled towards the sea. Now they both ended up just out of the water. Again and again we repeated their daredevil dive, and again and again the dummies ended up dangling above the water and we hauled them up, excited by the adventure (we imagined), to the top of the bridge.

When we were tired of the game, we took our brown natives back to their place at the top of the Alamo. We stowed the ropes away safely under my bed for the next time.

I tied the rest of the rope back to the bellstone. I was sure I hung it back up. Yes, I'm sure of it. I saw it by the door when I set the table.

'I'm sure it was there when I went to bed, Mum.'

'I know it was there. I've had an argument with Nico. Come quickly.' Mum's dragging me out of bed.

Chapter Thirty-eight

Maggie

I can't believe what's happened. How did Nico find out about Alfie? I should have told him months ago, but we were getting along so well I didn't want to spoil things. And now he thinks I'm a tart and I've slapped him with all the strength I could find. I've told him I never want to see him again. I knew it would all end in tears. It always does with me.

Time passes and my sobbing subsides. I check my watch. It's half an hour since Nico went. I thought he might come back, but he's probably in Yiossos now drowning his sorrows in Cosmo's. He might even have called on Agatha for a shoulder to cry on.

The light has almost completely gone. The last pink fingers of sunset are playing upon the horizon and the moon casts a pale glow as it rises above the island. I go outside to see if there is any sign of Nico licking his wounds or coming back to try to make up. On the terrace by the front door I see a torn brown-paper package, split to reveal a bundle of faded silk. As I stoop to pick it up I notice that one of the bellstones from beside the front door has gone. Something is very wrong. I feel sick. 'Nico!' I call out. 'Nico!' I hear only silence.

I clutch the bundle of silk to my chest and walk around the terrace with my heart pounding, fearing that something terrible must have happened. The missing bellstone is extremely worrying. It was definitely there while Alfie was laying the table in preparation for our feast; a feast that is now spoiling in the kitchen.

I rush into the cottage. 'Alfie. Alfie.' I shake Alfie from his dreams. 'Alfie. Wake up. *Wake up!*'

He sits up and rubs his eyes. 'What is it, Mum? Is it morning? Has Nico been? What is it?'

'Help me. One of the teardrops has gone.'

Alfie thinks for a moment. 'I'm sure it was there when

I went to bed, Mum.'

'I know it was there. I've had an argument with Nico. Come quickly.'

I almost drag Alfie out of bed. We walk around the cottage. We're both shouting: 'Nico!' The moon is higher now and the outhouse has a ghostly glow in the pale light. There's no sign of Nico. We walk back to the front and onto the terrace. We head for the gate. It's open. We walk onto the bridge.

'Whoa, Mum. Something's not right.' Alfie holds me tightly. He's right. Something is definitely wrong: there's an unfamiliar leaning to one side. I see the taut rope that is causing the tilt.

'Did you and Milos leave those dummies dangling from the bridge?'

'Dummies don't talk, Mum. Listen!'

Above the splash of the waves breaking against the foot of the cliff is the unmistakeable sound of Nico's voice cursing in Greek in between loud, heartbreaking sobs. I catch some of the words: 'Can't' – sob – 'even' – sob – 'kill myself.' I'm shocked at finding the love of my life in such awful circumstances and I'm horrified to realise that this could only have been a suicide attempt. I feel so ashamed that my white lie has driven him to such drastic action.

Before I heard Nico's woeful sobs, I was cross with Alfie and Milos for cutting the rope on one of the teardrops, but I'm so grateful that they did. It meant that when Nico made his suicidal plunge and plummeted towards his death on what he assumed to be sixty metres of fine rope, he was in reality tied to a length of just over twenty feet.

Looking down into the dark, Alfie gasps in shock. There's no doubt who is suspended from the bridge and causing it to sway increasingly violently.

'It's Nico, Mum. What the heck is he playing at?'

'I don't know, sunshine, but at least he's alive.'

The sway is getting worse; if we're not careful, it could send us both down to join him, and unlike Nico we have nothing to anchor us to safety. I'm pretty tough, but there's no way that I can haul a fourteen-stone man up twenty feet without assistance. It's time for my boy to become a man.

'Don't worry, Nico!'

Together we haul and heave and gradually bring our catch up from the deep. In order to avoid turning the bridge upside down, we need to sit at the opposite side to where Nico tied the rope so as to counterbalance him. A couple of times the rope slips and he drops a few feet back, but after about fifteen minutes of effort his ankles are within reach.

It is dark, but the moon gives enough light to show that those ankles are in a sorry mess. I wince and I hear a sharp intake of breath from Alfie. The fine nylon rope has gouged through Nico's trousers and cut deeply into his flesh. His legs are bleeding heavily. But he is almost there, almost saved.

'Almost there, Nico!' Alfie shouts.

'Come on, sunshine. Grab an ankle and, on three, heave. One, two, three ...'

We heave as hard as we can and manage to pull Nico close enough for Alfie to reach his belt. Then, with both of us taking a firm grip on the belt, we drag him and the heavy teardrop onto the now violently rocking bridge.

'Oh, Nico, Nico,' I cry. It is very dark and I am unable to make out his features clearly, but his misery is palpable. It's wretched to witness it.

Before we can haul him across the bridge to the safety of land, we have to untie the complex fisherman's knot that Nico used to secure the rope. It is difficult in the darkness, but Alfie manages to remember how Nico demonstrated the knot to him and Milos as he lashed together the planks of the Alamo. Eventually he succeeds in removing it.

We are nearer to the island than to the cottage, so together we manoeuvre him off the bridge and lay him gently onto the island surface. After untying the rope from around his ankles and taking away the bellstone, we try to help him to his feet.

'Nico, come back to the cottage.'

I want to get him back across the bridge where I can attend to his wounds. But despite his obvious disorientation and his badly shredded ankles, he is still a strong man and it is clear that he is determined to head towards the mooring.

He brushes us aside. 'Leave me. Just leave me, Maggie.'

Alfie looks up at his hero pleadingly. 'Nico, please. Please let us help you.' Alfie starts to cry. 'Please.'

Alfie doesn't know what caused Nico to leap headlong towards the deep; but he soon finds out. Nico limps away from us. We follow him, but he pushes away all our attempts to hold him back. As he reaches the stone steps above the mooring he turns and spits out his words.

'Goodbye, Maggie.' He pauses. 'Goodbye, Alfie. Look after Maggie. Look after *your mum.*'

We follow him down to the boat.

'Nico, please. Let me explain. Nico, please stay. Please don't leave me, Nico, please. Let me look after you.'

But he is in no mood for any explanations. I realise that in his eyes he has been cuckolded. His self-esteem will be as tattered as his trousers; his only wish will be to disappear into the night.

As he pushes the boat out into the waves he doesn't seem to hear my final parting cry.

'Nico, I love you.'

Chapter Thirty-nine

Nico

Costas Ioannidis is a troubled teenager. At seventeen, the outlook for him on Symos is bleak. With four younger brothers, a mother with a drink problem and a father who is away at sea for months on end, his life is going nowhere and he and his family are becoming outcasts due to the boys' tearaway behaviour.

But it seems that his terrifying experience in forty-five Kali Strata must have made him think about his life. It must have taken some time to pick up the nerve to do it, but at the start of July, Costas climbs the steps beyond the dogleg on the Kali Strata towards our whitewashed house in San Stefano.

When I answer the door, Costas seems surprised by how I look; I'm unshaven and dressed in a string vest and grubby black trousers. I am no longer the smart, broadly smiling man who was briefly the talk of the Volta with his pretty English friend. No, I probably remind Costas of his mother after a particularly heavy drinking session. But there is no smell of booze on my breath. This is a hangover from love, not alcohol.

I am surprised to see my visitor and also slightly alarmed. Costas is a well-built lad; perhaps he wants to continue the feud. The state I am in, I have little doubt which of us will come off the worst.

But Costas is uncharacteristically polite. 'Good evening, Nico. May I come in?'

I let Costas inside. I shuffle with my uncomfortable limp. Costas nods at Momma, who is sitting watching television. Glued to the grey flickering screen, my sad-eyed mother stirs only to swat with a small paddle at the little black flies that buzz annoyingly around the room.

I lead Costas up the stairs to my bedroom – my only private space.

'So?' I ask.

'I've been thinking, Nico. Everybody hates us on this

bloody island. I can't read and write. Nobody will give me a job. I've done nothing but cause trouble all my life. The only thing I was ever any good at was the fireworks, and you fucking ruined that when you kicked me out.'

'What did you expect? You wanted me to be responsible for you blowing up the whole bloody island? Enough stuff went missing for you and your brothers to start World War Three.'

'I know, I know.' Costas shakes his head. 'And I'm sorry for that, Nico, really sorry. But if I don't get a break soon I'm going to end up behind bars, and I need you to give me that break.'

'How can I help you?'

'By taking me back and putting me on the team for the moon mission fireworks.'

'The Apollo 11 show?'

'Yeah.'

'How's that going to help? There's no money in it.'

'Respect. That's all. Respect. Everyone respects the firework team.'

I pause and think long and hard. I spent weeks planning revenge on this yob and his brothers for attacking those kids, but here he is pleading for my help. And he has made an effort. He's wearing a clean white T-shirt and smart blue jeans (even if they are probably stolen) and he has his black hair smartly slicked back with Brylcreem. I see desperation in Costas's brown eyes, and I know that feeling well. I have seen the dark dog of depression so many times since my headlong plunge from the bridge. If I don't help him, what is left for him and the Dave Clarke Five?

The exact date of the moon landing is not known. If the weather is bad at Cape Canaveral, the launch could be postponed, but everyone knows that it is imminent. I have let things slide badly; I haven't been to the fireworks factory since my suicide attempt and things will be running well behind schedule. Another pair of hands would certainly help. And, thieving apart, Costas is a very talented pyrotechnician.

'Okay, Costas. Okay.'

Costas hugs me tightly. 'You won't regret this, Nico.'

He leaves quickly before I have time to change my mind.

~

My legs are troubling me. The doctor advised rest, but there is no time for relaxation. The nasty gash in my left ankle is taking an age to heal and has not been helped by a mosquito that decided it was the perfect feeding ground. It is impossible for me to lead a donkey to the fireworks factory, so that will be Costas' first task. That long trek will test the boy's willingness and will certainly prove his reliability. If he can resist the temptation of two huge panniers of chemicals, that will be a good start on his road to being accepted. He passes the test with flying colours, arriving at the little church with its neighbouring house way ahead of time.

The plan is to theme the next display around the Apollo mission. The Easter show paved the way, but that had been more of a rocket spectacular; I want something more refined for the most important event of the century. I have a responsibility to the townspeople and, however bleak I am feeling, I am not going to let them down.

I pin my sketches onto the factory wall as I plan the display. One huge rocket representing the lift-off to the moon to start; mortars full of bismuth subcarbonate to signify crackling shooting stars; some slow-falling calcium carbonate for a hundred lunar modules; and then a finale of strontium nitrate, copper sulphate and barium carbonate for the red, white and blue of the stars and stripes. I would have loved to be able to recreate the flag in fireworks, but that would be impossible unless it was designed as a flag turned on end – with streaks of red and white sprinkled with stars and blue smoke. I decide against that, as anything that needs to be explained to the crowd will not be worth doing.

It is a simple display and one that will depend upon the sheer size, power and number of fireworks to make it worthy of the event that it will celebrate.

The team gets together in a simple production line. There are half a dozen volunteers including Costas and me. The four others are old-timers in their seventies who have been helping out for years. They can be relied upon to filter and grind the black powder to just the right consistency for each different payload. Their kaolin stoppers are perfectly formed and the exhaust holes drilled to just the right depth and at just the right diameter. But however expert the old men are in constructing the rockets, even after years of practice they don't have the skill to combine exactly the right ingredients to produce the desired artistic effect. Fortunately, I have that skill, and now Costas does too.

As each batch of finished fireworks is completed, it is stored in one of the lockable cages in preparation for the main event.

Chapter Forty

Maggie

We hardly leave the cottage now. We go out to Yiossos only when we need provisions. I assumed that after I destroyed Nico, we would be unwelcome in the town and all the old insults that we left behind in Liverpool would start to ring in our ears again. But I seem to have assumed wrongly. Everyone is still fine with us. Perhaps Nico is not one to air his problems in public. When I ask after him at the post office or at Cosmo's, everyone tells me that he looked untidy on the few occasions that they have seen him and he hasn't been working at the taverna. They say that they miss us at the Volta, and the nosy ones try to ask what has happened between us. I think they have simply put this down to a lover's tiff. The biggest gossip, Mrs Constanides, says that, however much she has probed on the rare occasions that she has been able to corner him, Nico's lips have remained tightly sealed. 'Ask Maggie,' is all that he says.

During my lonely sojourn, I type up my dossier on the island using a small machine that I bought in Yiossos; but although my research has been incredibly thorough, my enthusiasm for the job has waned. I only get through a few pages each day as the thought 'Why bother?' is always uppermost in my mind.

My whole plan for our future has been ruined by just one indiscretion. If only I had put Nico right as soon as he had called Alfie 'your brother'. Then I would be feeling none of the pain that causes my stomach to churn constantly, and I would not have lost the twelve pounds that my small frame could ill afford to lose. Perhaps I would never have experienced the joy of Nico's attention and affection, but I would not be suffering the grief and anguish that now fill my every waking hour – and as I am sleeping so little, that is a lot of waking hours.

We paid our six months' rent in advance, so Nico

hasn't thrown us out. I don't know what will happen when it's due again. We've got some time before then. When I am not typing or sitting with Alfie on top of the Alamo looking out to sea, I work on a dress. The blue silk is a reminder of Nico's final visit to the cottage; I remember how he told me that his mother had planned to use the material to create a ball gown when he found a bride. I have no doubt about the significance of his bringing that silk with him on that dreadful night.

I am no seamstress, but I have some sewing experience and have chosen to model my dress on a magazine photo of a film starlet attending a movie premiere. I have lost the opportunity to model the dress for my beloved Nico; but I will wear it for Alfie, the other man in my life, on his tenth birthday.

~

Liverpool

Excitement reigned in Liverpool. Mary had never flown in her life, and Fred had flown only in a troop carrier. Passports were required. Clothes for hot weather and swimming costumes were bought, along with sun lotion, insect repellent and travellers' cheques. There was no airport on Symos, and as far as most of the travel agents were concerned the island did not exist. 'How about Corfu or Mallorca?' they would say. But no. Maggie and Fred insisted. Symos was where the family was. Symos it had to be.

However, when they realised the complexity of the journey and the near impossibility of booking a hotel on the island, they opted to stay on Rhodes. From there they would travel to visit Maggie and Alfie by boat, and maybe they would be able to stay with them in their idyllic cottage for a night or two.

When a letter addressed to Maggie and Alfie care of Nico arrived in San Stefano, Nico was at the fireworks factory and the postman handed it to Anna Karteras. Recognising the English stamp and knowing who had caused her darling son such torment, Anna used it to light the stove.

Chapter Forty-one

Nico

Apollo 11 is in space. After a successful launch on the sixteenth of July, Aldrin, Armstrong and Collins are on their way to the moon.

I tell the Ioannidis boys to put the posters up. Within hours, every spare centimetre of space in and around Yiossos harbour, in all the bars and tavernas, on every lamppost and all around the San Stefano square is being used to advertise our planned spectacular. The Apollo 11 firework display will take place the night of a successful landing, at around midnight. The mission is expected to land on Sunday.

My ankle is still causing me trouble and I need help. I go back to see Doctor Theophilus. He unwraps my bandage, shakes his head and draws a deep breath.

'I thought I told you to relax, Nicos. This ankle does not look like it has had much relaxation.'

I shrug. 'I've got the fireworks to plan, doctor.'

'What is more important? Fireworks or your leg?'

I'm tempted to say 'fireworks', but I know that it is not what he wants to hear.

'My leg.'

'Yes, your leg. And if you are not very careful, you might lose it.' He shakes his head. 'I need to send you to see a specialist.'

I know that there are no specialists on Symos. Where is he going to send me? He picks up the telephone and phones the private clinic in Rhodes. There's a brief discussion with someone at the other end and Dr T. puts the telephone back on its cradle.

'I've arranged a private appointment for you on Saturday the nineteenth of July.'

He sees me shake my head.

'Don't worry, Nicos. The specialist owes me a few favours. There won't be any charge.'

'It's not the money, doctor. I can't do it. What about

the fireworks?'

'Remember what we just agreed? What's more important: fireworks or your ankle?'

'Okay, doctor.' I can't win. But if the appointment is early enough, I will be able to catch the afternoon ferry back home.

As the astronauts go into orbit, I explain to my team that I will be going to the hospital in Rhodes on the Saturday morning. I give the all-clear for the display fireworks to be taken down from the mountaintop on Sunday morning, but I tell them not to worry as I will be back in plenty of time to supervise. The plan is to store the fireworks at forty-five Kali Strata for the day and move them to the harbour during the evening in time for the anticipated moon landing late on Sunday night. As soon as the television announces the landing, the fuses will be lit and the celebrations will commence. That is the plan, but in recent weeks where I have been involved things have not always run to plan.

I head off to Rhodes on the early Saturday ferry and arrive in good time for my appointment. The specialist is unhappy that I have not relaxed as instructed by Dr Theophilus, but the mass of mosquito bites and the swelling that they caused has misled the village doctor; I have nothing more than a very bad sprain and a slowly healing wound.

I head back to the ferry terminal with a spring in my step despite the searing pain in my ankle. Arriving at the port, I am taken aback to find a clamour around the ticket office. I am horrified to find that the Saturday-evening sailing has been cancelled due to mechanical difficulties. I have no choice but to stay overnight in Rhodes.

Hot, tired and thirsty, I head for a bar on the promenade alongside the ferry berths. I order a beer and wonder how Sunday will unfold. Worried about how the fireworks team will cope without me, I ask at the bar for permission to use the phone and dial Cosmo's taverna.

'Cosmo?'

Give Me Your Tomorrow

'Yep.'

'Nico here.'

'Nico, where have you been? Everyone's been asking about you.'

'It's a long story, Cosmo, but look, can you get a message through to Costas Ioannidis and tell him I've been stranded in Rhodes?'

'Ioannidis?'

I can hear the disapproval in Cosmo's voice, but I know that I can rely on my friend to do as I ask. I brief him fully and I am confident that my message will get through. Feeling more relieved now that I have got a message to Symos, I sip my beer and watch the crowds on the quayside. It is quite easy to find a place to stay; I choose a clean room at a nearby taverna and enjoy a decent meal before turning in early.

~

Costas Ioannidis

Such is the change in Costas Ioannidis that he is delighted when Cosmo's message comes through. He is told that he has been chosen to lead the procession of five donkeys down the mountain track, and, what's more, Nico has suggested that the rest of the Ioannidis quintet should assist him.

Costas and his brothers arrive early on Sunday at the fireworks factory, faithful train of donkeys at their sides. Despite his recent heartbreak, Nico still has his sense of humour and has named the donkeys Dave Dee, Dozy, Beaky, Mick and Tich. It is going to be a huge display and Costas suggests that two trips would be sensible: the first with the massive launch rocket and accompanying shooting stars in the morning; the rest in the afternoon. It is an uneventful morning and the first fireworks are safely stored in the huge hall at forty-five Kali Strata.

The heat on Symos on that Sunday is oppressive. The boys are exhausted when they return to the factory for the final journey. Dave Dee, Dozy, Beaky, Mick and Tich are carefully loaded with their precious cargo.

Snakes are rare on Symos, but visitors sometimes see one, perhaps squashed by a moped at the side of a track. Unfortunately, on the day that Costas has the most responsible job of his life and is proudly leading his brothers and five heavily laden donkeys down that rutted mountain track for the second time, a black whip snake decides to sun itself out in the open. Instead of choosing any number of smooth, flat, white rocks strewn across the mountainside, the snake finds a much more suitable spot slap-bang in the middle of the track.

True to his name, Dozy passes the snake without noticing it, but Beaky lurches to a nervous halt, clearly spooked and braying furiously. The donkey might as well have shouted 'Charge!' as within seconds all five donkeys have fled from the path and into the steep stony undergrowth with five youths in hot pursuit.

Donkeys aren't known as being God's fastest creatures, but in the right terrain a donkey can easily outrun an exhausted boy, as the lads soon discover. After a fifteen-minute chase, Costas sinks to his knees in desperation.

'What the fuck are we going to do? We're screwed. If we mess this up, we might as well emigrate.'

By now the donkeys are just a cloud of dust in the distance. And to make matters worse, they are heading towards the summit rather than in the direction of Yiossos. So much for Costas finally earning the respect of Symos.

Chapter Forty-two

Nico

I rise early on the Sunday morning, but I might as well not have bothered. Repairs on the ferry engine are incomplete and the morning sailing is also cancelled. The Sunday service is limited, and there will be just one ferry today at four o'clock. I sigh; but at least I will be in Yiossos by seven.

I spend the day wandering around the streets of Lindos, where most of the shops are shut for the Sabbath. I stroll around the ruins of the ancient citadel and marvel at the thickness of the walls, built to keep out marauders from the seas. The day is stiflingly hot, and after I have completed the circuit of the town I rest in the shade of an ancient plane tree. I am not alone: I enjoy watching the local men playing backgammon and chess in the dappled light.

I make sure that I am back at the ferry terminal in plenty of time for the boat. The sky looks ominous as I turn up at the jetty. The stifling heat has brewed up huge black clouds over the island and these are heading in the direction of the port, dragging nothing but blackness behind them. White spume tops the waves and the sea has a heavy swell. At first I imagine it is just the wake of a distant cruise liner, but the waves grow higher and higher and start to slam into the seafront.

The first bolt of lightning flashes across the horizon and within minutes it is followed by another and another. At the terminal the ticket-kiosk window is slammed shut. The ticket seller comes out of her booth and on the board that states 'Next Sailing Symos 16.00' she sticks a large label that simply reads 'CANCELLED'.

I don't blame them. I have almost forty years' experience of the seas around Rhodes, and while they are mostly calm waters, they can rock and roll as well as anything that the great Capes can dish up.

What can I do? How can the fireworks go on without

me? Damn that Theophilus. What sort of doctor can't get a sprain and a few mosquito bites right? What now? I don't have that much time to think clearly, as by now the rain is falling in torrents and I need to run from the quayside to find shelter. Shaking myself down, I open the glass door of a hotel opposite and tumble into the residents' bar. I am not alone: it seems that every prospective ferry passenger has sought refuge in the same bar, crammed together like sardines.

As the storm crashes on, it dawns upon all of us in the packed bar that we will not be spending the evening on Symos, or any other nearby island (all of the ferries are cancelled), and the crowd starts to thin. I am resigned to missing a fireworks display for the first time in maybe twenty years. I will be letting down the whole island. Yet another abject failure.

I use the hotel pay phone to contact Cosmo.

'Cosmo?'

'Nico, where are you?'

'Still in Rhodes. Bloody weather. We can't sail tonight.'

'It's still clear here. No sign of clouds.'

'Well, at least that's something. You're going to have to tell Costas to go it alone tonight.'

'If I can find him. Everyone's saying that he and his brothers disappeared up towards the factory hours ago and haven't been seen since.'

'Shit. That's all I need.'

My heart sinks. Once again my faith in human nature has been misplaced. Once a tearaway, always a tearaway.

~

Costas Ioannidis

As Nico is replacing the receiver, Costas Ioannidis is within touching distance of Tich.

The boys have been led on a chase backwards and forwards across the barren mountainside, and by now both they and the donkeys are totally exhausted. The terrain was steep in places and the boys are covered in dust, their clothes tattered by the thorny shrubs, and the legs of the youngest two, Spiro and Dimitri, who are wearing shorts, are covered in a mass of cuts, bruises and grazes.

'Got one!' Costas yells in triumph as he finally grabs Tich's bridle. His brothers come running to share in his celebration.

'One down; four to go. At this rate there'll be a man on the moon before we've got all of them.'

He looks down to the harbour below. A lot of people down there are going to be very disappointed, and who will they blame? Nico? No. Costas Ioannidis.

And where is Nico? Surely he should have come looking for them by now.

Costas is proud of his organisation of the donkey hunt. After a few hours, he detailed the eldest of his four siblings, Hero, to stand guard at the factory. The logic is that either Nico or at least one of the crew will come to check things out. And maybe the donkeys will find their way back there.

Looking down on the harbour again, Costas decides that if he is going to fail, he will at least go down trying.

'Spiro, stand with Tich. Water him, feed him and try to keep him calm. We'll show them we're not useless.'

Costas looks into Tich's pannier. 'Thank you, God.' He waves an arm skywards. The fireworks team have five torches. They could be in any of the five panniers, but they are here.

'Okay, Dimitri. Come on, Stefano. Let's find the others.'

By now night is closing in. The harbour lights are bright and music drifts up the hillside from the filling bars and tavernas. And the way to guarantee a full bar or taverna on this evening is to be sure that there is a television for the customers.

~

Nico

There is no television in the residents' bar when I return from the pay phone in reception. That's why there are now plenty of seats. It is around five thirty and the incredible storm is passing and its tail is heading out to sea. Why can't the ferry sail now? Because by now the crew will have been sent home. There will be no sailings this evening.

I've yet another night on Rhodes to kill. What am I going to do? I sit at the bar and order a snack of dolmas. As I start to eat, I sense a presence alongside me. I smell an unfamiliar scent; a heady perfume. A hand touches my arm.

'Beer to go with those dolmas?'

The voice, though speaking Greek, has an English accent, and for a second my heart leapt at the thought of Maggie. But this is not Maggie. The English girl has straight blonde hair with a fringe across her eyebrows above dark-brown eyes and lashes with way too much mascara. She is wearing an ankle-length strappy white-cotton sundress, buttoned from top to bottom in a modest style that conceals her bosom. Beneath her shiny silk-stockinged ankles are white patent leather high heels. The dress straps, a couple of inches wide, hang on tanned shoulders. I recognise the touch as one that has tempted me so much on previous visits to Rhodes while collecting my chemicals, but this time my body doesn't stiffen and – strangely – I feel relaxed.

'Why not?' I hear myself say.

The girl – she says her name is Samantha – gestures to the barman, who brings over two beers. She senses my grasp of English. That will probably make our transaction much easier than usual for her. I put my hand in my pocket to find change for the beer.

'No. They're on me.' She dips into her bag and settles up with the barman. I'm sure she will be making a note to add the beer to her price. 'Would you like to spend some time with me?' she asks. She smiles attentively and tosses her head and flutters her eyelashes.

I think hard. I look down at the silky ankles and then up at her face. She smiles again. It's a tempting proposal.

'Well?' she says. She slowly runs her fingers up her bottle of beer; she puts her thumb and forefinger around the neck and moves her hand downwards and then back up before picking up the bottle and taking a swig.

'Maybe.'

I can't believe what I have just said. I start to sweat and take a swig of my own beer to try to cool myself down.

Samantha squeezes the top of my leg, her hand provocatively close to my crotch.

'Only maybe?'

I want to pull away, but at the same time I want her hand to stay. She moves it closer.

'Okay.' The temptation is simply too much. 'Okay.'

'You won't regret it.' Samantha moves her hand away and bends down to pick up her bag. I drink the remaining beer in one swig and look anxiously around the bar to see who is witnessing my downfall. It is empty. The barman, studiously cleaning glasses and holding each one up to the light for inspection, is my only witness. He smiles across at me and winks.

'Come on then.' She holds her hand out to me.

I slide off the bar stool and take it.

She whispers into my ear. A price is mentioned. Expensive, but my mind is no longer in rational mode. I have given in. I am past the point of no return.

The sun is now warming the promenade that runs alongside the boat piers. Other women have started to look for business, but these more blatant hookers lack the sophistication of the sleek cotton dress and the heady perfume that is now leading me towards moments that I will never forget. Only the silken ankles and stilettos hint at what pleasures await. The yearnings I have nurtured for so long are finally to be fulfilled.

Samantha crosses the road away from the sea and

leads me down an alleyway. Surely not here; after waiting all these years, am I going to be deflowered against a wall in a grimy alleyway? But no. Samantha opens a door along the alley and leads me inside. We climb some stairs, past a dirty-looking WC and bathroom, along a landing to a room at the very end. Samantha unlocks the door and opens it.

'Welcome to my humble abode.'

She probably hates the punters. But she knows how to turn on her charms; her words seem genuinely inviting.

I look around the room that frames my destiny. A double bed with ornate brass-topped bedstead and a crimson-silk bedcover stands in the centre of the room. To the left is a small stove and a table, to the right is a dressing screen. Behind the bed is a shuttered window.

'Let's have some light.' Samantha opens the shutter and the sun's rays stream through. I see the shape of her legs outlined through the flimsy white cotton. And as I see the curvy frame swathed in a long white dress silhouetted against the sun, I see Maggie in a long white dress, smiling and holding a small floral bouquet in her hands. I blink briefly and my vision is gone.

The girl unbuttons the dress slowly. She has quoted a far higher price than I expected, so slowly is good. She's making sure that I have my money's worth. She might hope I become a regular. Although she could have removed the garment easily after just a few buttons, she carries on to the last and then slips the dress back off her shoulders.

I gasp as I see the firm brown breasts, the dark seductive nipples, the slim waist and flat stomach. She is wearing only a suspender belt and white stockings beneath the dress and I look down to see a thicket of brown hair marking the place of my desire. Few men could fail to be aroused by Samantha's body, but I feel strangely detached as I look for the very first time in my life on female nakedness.

Naked but for the stockings and stilettos, Samantha

Give Me Your Tomorrow

takes my hand and leads me to the bed. I wonder if I am much slower to respond than her regulars. I wonder if she can sense that this is my first time. I sit on the bed and wait for my temptress to take the lead.

As she unbuttons my shirt I hear a distinctive sound. There is no doubting an infant's cry. And it is in the room. Samantha puts a finger to her lips. 'Ssshhh,' she says and, backing away, steps quietly behind the screen.

And when she returns from behind the screen, she finds her client gone.

'Shit, shit, shit, shit, *shit*!' I hear from the open door. I look back and see her naked on the landing. She tears the blonde wig from her head and throws it to the floor, weeping. She looks at me with eyes full of hate and shouts, 'You *bastard*!' But her tears will soon dry when she finds the pile of notes on the bedspread. More than she has ever earned before for a trick. And by then the punter will have disappeared.

Now that *is* a trick.

Chapter Forty-three

Costas Ioannidis

Midnight approaches. The boys have rounded up the last donkey and have led them all to the spot where Spiro has been carefully watching over Tich. Hero has long given up on help from Nico or from the rest of the fireworks crew and has followed the torch beams to help his brothers on the dangerous hillside.

It's late at night. Costas has big decisions to make. Hero has a transistor radio and has been monitoring the progress of the astronauts on the national news channel.

'It won't be long now. They're in the lunar module and they're going to land any time.'

That's it. Costas's decision has been made for him.

'Okay. We've got to find the spot now.'

He scours the scrubland for a flat, clear patch of mountainside and before long he has found one. The donkey's loads are carefully taken from the panniers and spread along the small plateau.

'Now, Stefano, get those donkeys somewhere safe.' Costas is enjoying his new role as leader.

Stefano leads the donkeys back to the track, pats Dave Dee on the haunches and sends him trotting down towards Yiossos, followed faithfully by the others.

The message comes through on Hero's transistor radio. 'Houston. Tranquillity Base here. The eagle has landed.'

And within seconds of the message being received, the mountainside above Yiossos explodes in a mesmerising sea of noise and colour. Rocket after rocket pierces the sky with screeching bangs, and as each explosion recedes a louder cheer and more fervent applause drifts up from the harbour. The grand finale, the red, white and blue of the American flag, is as magnificent as Nico had planned. The whole of the mountain is lit up with wonderful streaks of colour.

The general view on the harbour? Fancy that Nico

sneaking back without any of us spotting him. It might not quite have matched the Apollo Extravaganza at Easter, but what a brilliant idea to use the moon-like landscape of the barren mountainside for a launch pad. The crowd cheers, claps and hoots its approval.

Costas bows to his brothers and smiles.

'Respect for the Ioannidis brothers. At last.'

For once the Dave Clarke Five really are feeling glad all over.

Chapter Forty-four

Nico

After my brief brush with temptation, I head back to the taverna where I spent Saturday night and luckily the landlord still has a room available.

With no change of clothes, I feel unwashed. This is not a particularly strange feeling for me as I have been dishevelled for a good part of the last month; but my close encounter, though unfulfilled, has left me feeling dirty and I feel an urge to cleanse myself and wash away the experience. As a guest of the taverna I also feel that I should smarten up. After showering thoroughly, I wash my shirt and underwear in the taverna bathroom and hang them from the window. Now that the storm has passed, the sun is back and shining directly towards my room.

I lie naked on the bed, thinking of the events of the last few weeks and wondering what will happen without me on Symos tonight. But the firework display plays only a minor part in my thoughts. Over and over again I see the vision of Maggie against the sunlit window, dressed in white before a double bed. I remember the months of pleasure we shared: the laughter over getting drenched under the split awning; the journeys around the island's secret places; building the Alamo; my poetry reading. And I can think of nothing bad about any of it. Why has it all changed just because of Alfie? What makes Maggie different now?

I think of Samantha, and how I felt unmoved by her glorious curves and her long legs in the seductive silk stockings. Am I homosexual? I wouldn't be the first to suggest it after years of being at my mother's side. But no, I know that is most definitely not the problem. The problem is that I am beginning to understand the difference between love and lust, and love has kicked lust to the back of my mind.

How can I love Maggie? Is she not as bad as the

whore with the hidden child? Who was the man who enjoyed the warmth of her body? What happened to the sanctity of virginity? I have so many questions, but very few answers.

As the sun goes down, I gather my clothes from the window. They are still slightly damp, but they will have to do.

The taverna is packed. The landlord has a television and it seems that most of the local street has packed into the place to witness the men on the moon. But as a taverna resident I have priority and I am shown to a table with a good view of the screen. As I sit deciding what to eat, I glance around the taverna. The walls are filled with the paraphernalia of sponges, for this is one of the places that those brave swaggering crews had stopped at all those years ago before setting off on their perilous journeys. And I look at the black and white photos and wonder if any of my ancestors are among the men proudly holding the most gigantic sponges aloft or looking adoringly on the diver in his *skafandro*.

I notice a couple of foreigners entering the room. They're in their late forties and judging by the colour of their skin they must be English – you don't see that lobster pink on a Greek. They present meal vouchers to the proprietor. I recognise the vouchers – tourists who stay in hotels without restaurants are given them by their tour operators to buy evening meals at tavernas nearby. The proprietor shrugs his shoulders as if to say 'No room at the inn'. But wait: I am taking up a table for four. I don't mind the middle-aged pink foreigners joining me. I wave him across.

'They can sit here.'

'Thank you, Nico. You sure you don't mind?'

The couple smile as they sit down. I look up briefly. I think the woman's face looks vaguely familiar, but I look back down, concentrating on my grilled octopus salad. It is dark by now and the television reporters are excitedly spinning out what is going to be a long night. Nobody could fail to be impressed by the pictures being relayed back to the earth.

As I eat, I can't help but listen in to the foreigners' conversation.

It seems that their holiday is not going to plan. The journey was long and uncomfortable and they are not looking forward to repeating it at the end of the fortnight. Despite copious amounts of sun lotion, the woman had totally underestimated the strength of the Mediterranean sun; it seems that they burned themselves four days ago and the throbbing has only just started to subside.

Their hotel near to the citadel is 'nice enough': only two storeys, but with their own bathroom and a balcony that looks out over the deep blue sea. It seems that this is their first-ever stay in a hotel and they were delighted when they realised that if their beds were left unmade someone would make them up. They're unimpressed with the breakfast of bread and jam served in the hotel reception, and they are definitely uncomfortable with the instructions not to put toilet paper in the pan but into a bin alongside the WC instead.

The man looks up at the television.

'Messing with nature, eh, Mother? If God had meant us to go into space, he'd have given us wings. I wish they'd just stop interfering with things that are too big for them.'

'Well, they're almost there now, Father. We can't do anything about it now.'

'No,' he growls. 'Well, Mother, what do you fancy?'

'I thought we had to have the set menu with the vouchers.'

'Blow that. Let's push the boat out. How about some nice lamb chops?'

'Yes, that would be lovely. You know, I've not enjoyed eating the set menus. The food that the locals have looks much nicer. They get welcomed into the tavernas like old friends and taken through to the kitchen to inspect everything that's on offer. We get soup, moussaka and watery wine.'

Give Me Your Tomorrow

The waiter arrives. There is no menu. He tries to explain what is available, but the man only knows how to communicate in that typical English tourist way: speak loudly and slowly and the message will sink in. 'Lamb chops, please,' he says.

The waiter looks puzzled.

The Englishman repeats himself: '*Lamb chops!*'

Another quizzical response.

He's determined to get the message through. 'Look,' he says, 'lamb – *baaa*,' and as he says it he clasps both hands together and makes a chopping motion like a lumberjack, then, just to be sure, he turns towards the woman, cups her face and slaps her cheeks gently and adds, '*chops*.'

I struggle to control my laughter and mutter beneath my breath, '*Paidakia*.'

The waiter catches this and a look of recognition comes over his face. 'Ahhh – lamb chops,' he says.

'There you go, Mother. That did the trick.'

As the couple enjoy their lamb chops, I, their silent companion, appear to concentrate on the events going on in space. But, as I listen to their chatter, it is only a short while before their identity sinks in. The mention of Alfie and a birthday seals it. They hope that her landlord has given her the letter (letter? what letter?), and they worry about how sad she seemed in her last brief note home. There was no explanation, but the overflowing passion she expressed for the island had become subdued, and there was no mention of 'the landlord' who had featured so prominently in her April, May and June epistles. 'Perhaps he's gone on holiday,' is the woman's view. 'I got the impression that there were feelings there.' Both agree that they had never known her to sound so happy. For the first time since Alfie had been born, she seemed to be alive.

So Maggie has been unhappy since Alfie was born. No mention of a husband; no sign of a string of lovers. And, as I listen to this nice but distinctly naïve middle-aged pair, I realise that I have made a terrible mistake. Will she ever forgive me?

Chapter Forty-five

Maggie

Alfie and Milos were both as excited as any small boy about the moon mission. They spent hours gazing skywards from the top of the Alamo. Alfie wondered if the astronauts needed to wait for a full moon before they landed so that they would have more to aim at, but Milos had learned all about it at school and assured him that that was not the case – they wouldn't even have to wait until it was dark!

It was a difficult decision, going to watch the moon landing at Cosmo's. I feel uneasy about going into Yiossos and spoiling Nico's big night for him; but it's Alfie's birthday on Monday and I decided that as a very special treat he can stay up to witness the moon landing on TV. It's something he'll remember for the rest of his life. Spiro and Hanife agreed to let Milos join Alfie and me, so at the latest hour any of us have ever been out, we sit in Cosmo's, eyes glued firmly to the black and white TV. From time to time we glance upwards at the moon, where history is unfolding.

The place is crowded. 'What's happening with the fireworks?' is on a few lips. 'Ask *her*,' is the frequent response, with a nod in my direction. But I can throw no light whatsoever on the subject.

It's already two in the morning and well into Alfie's birthday now. I am not only responsible for him but for Milos too – he will be staying the night with us at the cottage. I worry that it's getting too late.

But at last things happen. Astronauts land on the moon. We watch the grainy grey pictures in awe. I feel myself welling up at the magnitude of it all, but I don't have time for tears. Moments later we rush outside with the crowd as Nico's spectacular firework display booms out from the mountainside. He was right: he is a real genius at pyrotechnics. I've never seen a display like that before.

Now the word is out that the astronauts are shortly going to walk on the moon. This is one of the most important moments in history and it is going to be played out live on television. But can I justify keeping my neighbour's child out until dawn?

Luckily the decision is made for me. And it's God that makes it. The storms that the TV weatherman reported rumbling around the Dodecanese all night have been kind to Symos. Distant lightning flashes had supplemented the fireworks, but now they are finally heading towards the island. It feels as if God is displaying displeasure at the violation of His universe.

The storm is brief and passes over the island in just a few minutes. But what a few minutes! There are no more than ten bolts of lightning and rumbles of thunder, but one of those bolts scores a direct hit on the TV mast and seconds later the television is showing only a white fuzz.

What a commotion! Cosmo immediately starts recruiting a team to scale the mountain straight away to fix the mast, but when the last flash of lightning illuminates the summit for a brief second, it is clear that there is going to be no more TV today – the top twenty feet of the mast is now leaning at quite a jaunty angle.

A wave of disappointment washes over the assembled throng, but realism soon sets in and the harbour clears as the tired revellers head for their beds. I am fortunate to collar one of the water taxis. The boatman, Stephano, is off duty, but is heading home to Agios Giorgios after all the excitement. He's delighted to have the prospect of a contribution towards the ouzos that he has downed during the night.

I only notice his uncertain gait as we are well past the breakwater. It has been an exciting night for everyone, but Stephano is more than excited. 'Giddy' would be a better word, I think as he starts roaring with laughter, pointing at the moon and making unintelligible jokes. The boys think this is great fun and chuckle merrily at his every word, encouraging him to repeat and embellish everything he says.

Stephano stands up, shouting something about Apollo being Greek and not American, and starts to shake his fist at the moon. His shaking, interspersed with drunken laughter, starts the boat rocking and a wave laps over the bows and into the hull. 'Oops,' says the drunken Stephano, stopping his swaying and slumping into his seat beside the tiller. This is followed by a series of belches, interspersed with giggles and another 'Oops' as the pool of water in the bottom of the boat sloshes around and splashes his feet.

I can see that the boat is perilously near to land. I have sailed these waters many times with Nico and I know that jagged rocks pepper the coastline. How have I managed to get us into this predicament? I turn to Stephano and find to my horror that my gondolier is now fast asleep at the helm, head slumped along the tiller and snoring fitfully.

The boys are in the prow looking seawards as I shout for them to join me in the stern. They are no longer laughing as they watch me slapping Stephano around the face to try to rouse him. But it is no good. Stephano is dead to the world. I am going to have to take control.

Nico sometimes allowed me to steer Cosmo's small dinghy during our days of research, so I know the general principle of pointing the tiller in the opposite direction to the one I want to travel, but the water taxi is a much larger vessel and responds differently to my touch. Soon the boat is smashing into the waves and I am frightened that we will end up impaled on one of the deadly razor-sharp traps that lurk inches below the surface.

Milos sees my face; it must have sheer terror etched on it. He's only a little kid, but he pushes me aside with all the confidence of a man.

'Don't worry, Maggie. You will be safe with me.'

He comes from the oldest boat-building family on the island. Boats are in his blood. Hanife told me that he had learned to sail not long after he learned to walk.

'My father built this boat,' he says, and within a few

minutes the water taxi is back under control and heading for deeper water away from the dangerous rocks.

The journey is mercifully short, and Milos is a competent and extremely able sailor. He manoeuvres the water taxi towards the cove and Alfie jumps ashore and holds the rope, allowing me to alight in comfort. We tie the water taxi to the mooring ring.

'What are we going to do with Stephano?' says Alfie.

Milos fills the bailer with water and empties its contents over the stupefied mariner's head. It has the desired effect: Stephano bursts into life with a loud shriek.

'Stephano, listen,' I slap his face to try and get his attention. 'We're back at the island. You can't carry on to Agios Giorgios like this.'

'I'll sail him home. I know where he lives,' Milos offers.

'If your mother knew what I've just put you through, she would be horrified. You're staying on dry land, young man. Nobody is going out on the sea again tonight.'

With great difficulty, we help Stephano up the stone stairway to the top of the island. He starts to come round a little and is keen to explore the Alamo, but together we manage to get him over the perilous bridge crossing and onto the terrace, where he slumps exhausted to the ground. Within seconds he is snoring again. I decide that he's in a safe place to sleep off his stupor.

There's a feeling of anti-climax as we enter the cottage. The night has been so memorable, but watching men walk on the surface of the moon would have been even more incredible. We look through the window at the moon bathing the surrounding sea in pale light, and I feel humbled by the astronauts' bravery – so, so far away.

The radio is still receiving a strong signal, and I let the boys listen in bed as events unfold in the heavens above them. But by the time Armstrong says the words that will surely become immortal, the boys are fast asleep in their own sea of tranquillity.

I hear the whole thing. The sun is dawning over Symos when I finally drift off to sleep.

Chapter Forty-six

Nico

As soon as I wake, I phone Cosmo to ask about the fireworks.

'Yes, Nico, they went well.'

I'm relieved. Cosmo describes the display and it's clear that things didn't go completely to plan – there's no mention of the giant opening rocket that should have been the talk of the island for months – but at least my reputation is not ruined. Cosmo says that the islanders were pleased with the show.

It is third day lucky with the ferry for me. As I arrive at the quayside, the sun is up and the sea is flat and calm. With two extra days' worth of passengers, the boat is full, but I find a seat on a bench on the top deck of the ferry. I spot the pink couple, Maggie's parents, among the crowd. They are carrying a small suitcase and a brightly wrapped parcel.

News of the damaged TV mast on Symos has filtered through to the crew and the passengers. Maybe the cancelled sailings were a good thing; I was able to stay awake at the taverna and watched the whole moon landing and the incredible walk. Maggie's parents left shortly after eating their lamb chops, which Maggie's dad had declared 'fit for a king'. They must have known that something extremely important was about to take place; but Maggie's dad kept looking at his watch and said that nothing should interfere with their daily seven hours' sleep, and anyway the hotel locked its front door at midnight. I imagine that the proprietors were wide awake and in their private quarters watching TV.

As soon as the harbour comes into view and the new visitors (and not a few returning travellers) have taken it in with the customary gasp of delight at its beauty, the broken TV mast high above Yiossos is obvious to everyone. The journey has run smoothly and the ferry docks in Symos at eleven o'clock on the dot. I see

Give Me Your Tomorrow

Maggie's parents showing a photo to some of the locals greeting the ferry; judging by the arms pointing, I can see that they have made themselves understood and will find their way to the cottage.

I am in a hurry. Throughout the two-hour journey I have been making a plan, and I will need every minute of the day if I am to fulfil it.

Chapter Forty-seven

Maggie

I'm watching fireworks soaring into a black sky and exploding loudly. The rat-a-tat-tat of the firecrackers blends into a knocking at the door. Coming round, I look at my watch. It's past one o'clock. I have never slept this late before in my life and wonder if the watch has stopped; but no, I can tell from the angle of the sun that the day is well under way. I quickly put on a dressing gown and answer the door.

Apart from Nico coming for his lessons and Milos asking if Alfie can come out to play, we never have visitors; not one since we arrived. Who can it be? Has Stephano recovered from his overindulgence and decided to ask for his fare, or maybe he wants to apologise for putting our lives in peril? Is Nico finally collecting the next rent instalment, or perhaps coming to tell us that it's time to pack our bags and leave? I blink as I open the door but there is no mistaking the man in a wide-brimmed hat with a woman carrying a parasol.

'Mum! Dad! What are *you* doing here?'
'Alfie's birthday. Didn't you get the letter? We said we'd come for his birthday.'

I'm totally shocked.

'Letter? No, I've had no letter. But please, come in.'

I lead them inside and go to Alfie's room to find the boys just stirring from hearing the voices.

'Happy birthday, Alfie!' I had already said it at midnight, but somehow a birthday is not really a birthday until daylight. 'You've got some visitors.'

'Nana! Granddad!' Alfie is speechless for a second and then runs towards his grandparents and gives Mum a tight hug. Dad tries to hug Alfie too, but there is a stiffness to Alfie and Dad gives up.

There are presents to open. Mum hands Alfie a brightly wrapped parcel and he opens it to find two wonderful Airfix model-aeroplane kits – a Spitfire and a Lancaster Bomber.

'Granddad didn't think you'd want one of them Jerry Messerschmitts,' says Mum.

'Come on, Mother. You know *you* chose them. I'm the one who kept suggesting socks and hankies. I've not been the best Granddad, have I Maggie?'

I squeeze his hand. 'Perhaps not, Dad. But he's only ten. There's plenty of time.'

'Thanks, Nana. Thanks, Granddad.' Alfie is amazed at his grandparents' choice. Dad never approved of Alfie's interest in the war.

'Think nothing of it, Alfie.'

I give him a book on cinema that I ordered from England. It arrived just in time for the celebration. Milos gives him a cap gun that he has saved long and hard for and bought from the toy and general store in Yiossos with his own pocket money.

The boys play at the Alamo while we adults sit on the terrace (long vacated by Stephano, who will by now be nursing an Apollo-sized hangover in Agios Giorgios).

I can tell that Mum's very excited. 'What a beautiful place you've found here. The walk across from the town was wonderful – the scent of the shrubs, the noise of the cicadas and the blue of the sea and sky. Just amazing. And the cottage is lovely too.'

'So, Maggie, what were you doing asleep at this time of day?' Same old Dad.

'Fred, it's none of our business.' Mum gently slaps his wrist. 'She's a grown woman. She can sleep when she wants.'

'It's all right, Mum.' I laugh. 'Something huge happened last night, Dad. Didn't you hear?'

'And you stayed up to watch it?'

'Yes, we all went into Yiossos and sat in Cosmo's taverna.'

Dad's jaw drops. 'A taverna? At midnight?'

'Fred, you should know by now; we've been here nearly a week. A taverna is not a tavern – and how many times have men landed on the moon? Don't you think Alfie will always remember actually seeing the first men on the moon, instead of reading about it?'

I am thrilled to see my mother taking control. It's something I have never witnessed before.

Mum continues: 'You'll have to forgive your dad, love. He's been through a lot lately.'

'Okay, Dad. You're forgiven. But as it happens, we didn't see the men on the moon. Did you see what had happened to the TV mast when you arrived?'

'You couldn't miss it. Everyone was very excited about it on the ferry – they were all pointing to the mast.'

Mum and I talk on for hours. Dad remains relatively silent. Mum explains the upheaval in his life and how he is trying to come to terms with it.

'It's good to see you two chatting,' he says. 'Your poor mother has had nobody to talk to for ages.'

Milos leaves for home, but I invite him to come back for Alfie's birthday tea. It's scheduled for around seven thirty. That leaves our reunited family a few hours to get to know each other once again.

Chapter Forty-eight

Nico

I know Maggie's daily routine. She will be eating inside at the table with Alfie at around seven forty-five. No doubt her parents will be joining them. That leaves me about eight hours. It is going to be tight, but I reckon that I can just do it.

Laden with all sorts of stuff, I walk down from forty-five Kali Strata towards the harbour. I worry that Cosmo's boat might be too small, but with good organisation I will just manage. It takes me several journeys up and down the steps to get everything I need safely stowed away, and it is past eight o'clock when I finally chug out of the harbour.

As I pass the cottage, the sun is sinking. Maggie's parents are taking in the beautiful sunset from the terrace and pay no attention to my little boat passing. They have probably seen a few fishing boats pass by during their day at the cottage.

While the family and Milos are sitting down to Alfie's birthday tea, I carry the fruits of my day's labour towards the Alamo. Three or four journeys from the cove and up the stone steps are needed, but everything is running to plan. I can hear the buzz of conversation from the house, and I notice that Maggie is playing her favourite Simon and Garfunkel LP.

Among my equipment I have a small, petrol-driven electric generator, a spotlight, a reel-to-reel tape recorder and two speakers borrowed from Cosmo's taverna. Once I am sure that the party tea is well under way indoors, I set to work.

Everything is loaded onto the Alamo's platform. I mentally divide the platform into four squares and in the centre of each square I push a long, thin cardboard tube down between the planks, so that each one ends below the branches but about four feet off the ground.

Next, I erect a frame at the front of the platform,

facing directly towards the terrace. The frame is the width of the Alamo, about six feet high and made of thin plywood. From the top of the frame I hang a white sheet, pull it taut and fasten it securely top and bottom. The sheet has writing on it in bold black letters.

Next, I put Basil and Zorba into position, seating them at opposite sides of the Alamo each facing seawards behind my makeshift screen. Finally, I place the speakers at the back of the platform with the tape recorder in between and the spotlight pointing directly towards the sheet. In the centre are more boxes that will help me to complete my master plan.

It is approaching a very late nine thirty when a chorus of 'Happy birthday, dear Alfie' comes from the cottage.

Okay, that's the signal. This is it. I set the generator running and light a small rocket.

Chapter Forty-nine

Maggie

It's been a wonderful day. I'm so pleased to see that my parents are attempting to start a new life together and putting the church behind them. It's going to be a struggle, but Mum seems to be coping well and Dad – well, he's been through a lot and he's doing his best. They seem to have accepted that Alfie and I are not coming back and that we are making a life for ourselves here in Greece; Dad hasn't even tried to suggest otherwise.

I've put on my blue-silk dress for Alfie's birthday tea. I'm pleased with the results. It's an eclectic mix of his favourites; it's strange to see the table laden with a sort of meze of Liverpool and Symos: taramasalata jostles for space with pitta-bread jam butties, there's tzatziki alongside jelly and cold chicken drumsticks with olives (he hates olives, but Milos loves them). To complete the feast, I've prepared a cake while Alfie's been out playing. I go to where it is hidden in my bedroom wardrobe, light the candles and bring it to the table.

'Wow, Mum! An Alamo cake.'

I'm pleased that the results of my artistic attempts are recognisable. It's a square fruitcake iced to look like the white rocky island. In the middle is a marzipan tree, and propped up by carefully trimmed drinking straws is the Alamo, built from my own handmade biscuits – a KitKat would have been better, but even if I could have found one it would have melted in seconds. I made the Alamo sign and Alfie's red-jumper flag from marzipan, and there's a mini Alfie and Milos too.

I can see that Milo is impressed – I made both boys the same size.

'Okay, everyone.' On cue, we all start to sing. 'Happy birthday to you. Happy birthday to you.'

As we reach 'Happy birthday dear Alfie', we are interrupted by a loud explosion.

'What was that?'

'It came from outside,' says Alfie.

'Well, that's pretty obvious, sunshine.' A shiver runs through me. 'It sounded like a rocket!' My voice is shaking.

'Come on, Milo. Let's go and look.' Alfie grabs Milos's hand and rushes from the table onto the terrace. I follow with Mum and Dad.

'My cake!' says Alfie suddenly. 'I've forgotten to blow out my candles.' He rushes back inside.

'Don't forget to make a wish!' I shout from the door.

He comes back out.

'So did you make one?'

'I sure did.'

Alfie hurries to join us on the terrace. It is dark, but there is some moonlight. There's no visual sign of what caused the explosion, but a pungent cordite smell hangs in the air. Milos points excitedly towards the island.

'What's happened to the Alamo?'

Where there's usually only Alfie's jumper on a pole, in the dim light we can just make out a large white square above the tree.

'Spooky,' says Alfie.

'What's going on?' asks Dad.

The air is still and silent. But then a drone starts up.

'That sounds like our generator,' says Alfie. 'But it can't be ours.'

'Shush a second, sunshine.'

'Happy birthday, Alfie,' booms loudly and clearly from the island.

'It's Nico!' Alfie tugs at Mum's sleeve.

I grab Alfie's hand.

There's a brief pause. And now music – brass. Daaa – daaa – daaaaaa. Da daa! Then rolling timpani. I recognise it as *Also sprach Zarathustra*, the theme to Kubrick's film *2001: A Space Odyssey*. Several bars play, building up an air of excited anticipation on the terrace. As the music dies down, a cod American accent starts a countdown.

Give Me Your Tomorrow

'Ten, nine, eight, seven, six, five, four, three, two, one. Lift-off!'

And at 'lift-off', an enormous rocket blasts skywards with an almighty whoosh. It is so powerful that the kids might think it's a real Apollo spaceship. We watch in awe as the cleverly designed rocket breaks into stages, just like Apollo 11, but thankfully the real Apollo 11 didn't explode like this one into a million green flashes upon reaching its orbit.

As our gasps of delight die down, a spotlight lights up behind the white square on the Alamo. There, silhouetted by the light we can make out the words 'Apollo 11'.

'It's the lunar landing module!' says Milos.

We can see two small astronauts sitting very still inside the lunar landing module, while a bigger astronaut is clearly busy doing all the work. From the base of Apollo 11 come four shafts of orange light, producing a mass of orange smoke. As the smoke subsides, the light inside the spacecraft goes out and the American accent returns.

'Houston. Moon calling.' (Well, Armstrong fluffed his words, so we can excuse that.) 'The Eagle has landed.'

What next? A minute's silence, and then the ladder drops down from the tree and the spotlight returns. Down comes Nico Armstrong.

What must be the white *skafandro*, emblazoned with the stars and stripes, makes a perfect space suit. Slowly Nico steps down. His outfit is topped with a fabulous diving helmet, now painted white, and there's a white pack strapped on his back. As he reaches terra firma, the thunderous voice is back.

'One small step for man. One giant leap for mankind.'

And once on the moon, Nico Armstrong circles the surface in his best slow-motion gravity-defying steps, bounding across the lunar landscape with just the slightest hint of a limp.

After the disappointment of having missed the TV spectacle, we have now witnessed our very own exclusive launch, landing and live moonwalk for ourselves. My heart is pounding.

Nico returns to the lunar module and reappears a few seconds later with an American flag attached to a broom handle. He climbs back down and plants it firmly in a crack in the rocks below the Alamo. The voice booms out once again. This time it's Nico without the American accent. First in Greek and then in English, he says, 'Finally, a very special request for my Maggie.'

More music starts – it's the Four Tops. So many singers have covered Tim Hardin's wonderful song (even Dave Dee, Dozy, Beaky, Mick and Tich have released it), but Nico has chosen my favourite version. I recognise it from the very first chords and know that those fabulous soul voices are going to ask me a question that I thought I would never hear. Although I have heard enough at the opening note of 'If I Were a Carpenter' to understand the meaning exactly, I wait to hear the whole song. The group sings about marriage and having a baby and I savour every single word of Nico's proposal. It isn't every night of my life that a fabulous soul group sings a proposal just for me – on the moon.

As the Four Tops fade out, I walk to the gate and cross the bridge – the film starlet in a beautiful dress of faded blue silk. As I arrive on the moon, Nico the astronaut is waiting for me with arms outstretched. I stand on tiptoe, lift off the fabulous helmet and put it down. I put my arms around his neck and kiss him tenderly on the lips.

Then I sing in a gentle voice, paraphrasing the song.

'You've given me your only-ness. I'll give my tomorrow.'

Chapter Fifty

Alfie

I run across the bridge with Milos behind me. We reach Nico and Mum, who are still stuck together like flipping glue. I tug at the sleeve of Nico's space suit.

'Wow, Nico. That was fabulous. You did all that just for my birthday?'

'Of course, Alfie.' Nico looks down into Mum's eyes and smiles. 'Just for your birthday.'

'Are you going to be my dad?'

'It looks like it.'

I am thrilled. Has any wish ever been granted this fast in the whole history of birthday-cake wishes?

'Brilliant! Can we go on Apollo 11? Or is it Alamo 11?'

'It's your spaceship, Alfie.' Nico hands me the astronaut helmet.

'Blimey. It's flipping heavy.'

I climb the ladder, followed by Milos.

'Can we have the light back?' Milos calls down from the platform.

Nico tells us how to power the light back up. As the light returns, from our position on the island we can see Nana and Granddad on the terrace. Granddad is holding Nana tightly. Blimey: they've all gone flipping bananas! He bends and kisses her gently on the forehead. In the quiet his voice is loud and it carries to the island.

'I love you, Mother,' he says.

Nana looks up, 'I love you too, Fred – and I'm not your mother!'

Good old Nana.

I put the helmet on Milos.

'Right, Space Cadets Zorba and Basil and Captain Milos, we've got two minutes to get us out of here before the air supply on this planet runs out.'

'But Major Alfie, what will happen to the aliens?'

'Don't worry about them.' I look down at Nico and Mum, still flipping kissing. 'They're like sponges. They don't need air. Now. Thrusters ready?'

'Yes, Major.'

'Fasten your seatbelts everybody. Ten, nine, eight ...'

Apollo 11 heads earthwards with Major Alfie in complete control.

Epilogue

Nico and Maggie married in autumn 1969. At Easter 1970 they welcomed the very first Apollo Cottages customers to Symos. The business is run from their home at forty-five Kali Strata, and the now modernised Bellstones Villa has always been the most popular of their wide portfolio of properties. Visitors return year after year to take advantage of the warm Symos hospitality, their stays made so much easier by the helpful dossiers constantly updated by Maggie.

The business now makes wide use of the Internet, with the innovative Maggie setting up Apollo's website way ahead of the competition. She is due to retire soon, but is confident that her manager, Costas Ioannidis, will continue to run the business smoothly, along with his bachelor brother Hero, their most popular tour rep.

Alfie went to university in Athens. Then, on a trip to visit Nico's distant cousins in Florida, he fell in love with a dark-eyed beauty and with the country itself. His vivid imagination and love of cinema never left him, and he is now a creative with one of the major Florida film-studio theme parks.

Alfie's half-brothers and half-sisters grew up happily on Symos. They have left the island but frequently return to see their mum and dad.

Fred and Mary managed to enjoy the last years of their lives and became regular visitors to the Greek islands.

Milos is the projectionist at Symos's (now open-air) cinema. Today the Odeon is a museum of sponge diving in Greece.

Nico recently celebrated his eightieth birthday – with fireworks, of course. He and Maggie enjoy sitting on the balcony of forty-five Kali Strata, watching the sea as the sun goes down while listening to their favourite playlist on the iPod. I don't need to tell you which song is at the top of that list.

Author's Note

Any regular visitor to the Greek islands will immediately recognise that Symos is based upon the beautiful Dodecanese island of Symi. For this reason, I have made little attempt at disguising its name. But if you go to Symi and search for the white cottage with the small island opposite, you will be disappointed. You will certainly find the most beautiful harbour in Greece and two towns split by hundreds of steps on a street called the Kali Strata; but number forty-five is purely a figment of my imagination. The remainder of my island is a mixture of fiction and reality.

I appreciate that during 1969 Greece was under military rule and life may not have been as carefree as I depict; but it was my intention to create a story and not a historically accurate reference work. In the same way, my accounts of German and Italian occupation and the growth of the sponge industry are all subject to artistic licence.

I apologise to Rhodes for my depiction of its harbour as a haunt for prostitutes; but I think it is safe to assume that there may be one or two plying their trade around the port.

Acknowledgements

I am indebted to Karen Ings and Caroline Goldsmith for their excellent editing and professional support and to Charlie Wilson of perfectlywrite.co.uk for her invaluable help and guidance. I would also like to thank Scott Pack for his advice and words of encouragement.

I must thank Michael N Kalafatas for the background information on sponge diving presented in his book *The Bellstone: The Greek Sponge Divers of the Aegean*; to Faith Warn for her book *Bitter Sea: The Real Story of Greek Sponge Diving*; and to Dr Nikolas Tricolis for an Internet article on the subject.

I must also acknowledge the websites www.pyroguide.com and www.targetwoman.com for their information on fireworks and on Greek food. Thanks also to the Hal Leonard Corporation and Allan Stanton Productions for their kind permission to reproduce lyrics from the song *If I Were A Carpenter* by Tim Hardin.

Thanks to Spiffing Covers for creating such a lovely cover which certainly lives up to their name.

Finally, I must thank my darling wife, Marion, for bearing with me during the hours spent locked away writing this novel. It is to her that I dedicate this story.

About the Author

John Brassey was born in Heswall in 1953 and grew up in the Lancashire seaside resort of Southport where he attended King George V Grammar School. He left school after completing his A' Levels and joined one of the high street banks working in many branches and offices throughout Merseyside before moving to London as a secondee to the Department Of Trade And Industry.

After his secondment he switched careers and used his banking and DTI experience to join Instanta Ltd, his parent's catering equipment manufacturing business in Southport, which he ran initially with his brother Peter and then with his wife Marion after Peter retired. He and Marion sold the business in 2010 and recently retired to Framlingham in Suffolk.

John is an avid reader who has always enjoyed writing. He wrote a regular blog for the Instanta website and, upon retirement continued blogging in "Notes From Retirement...Where Did The Years Go?" in which he has charted the adventures of moving to a completely new and unknown area.

When not reading or writing he is a regular cinema and gym goer, a cyclist and he also enjoys searching local farms with his metal detector. He is also a voluntary business mentor for Suffolk Chamber Of Commerce and a volunteer for the Framlingham Hour Community.

He has two children, Sarah who is a teacher living in St Andrews and Paul a TV Producer living in Kent. Since retirement John and Marion have been blessed with three granddaughters Rose, Catherine and Melody and a lot of their time is now spent travelling to Kent and to Fife where they have bought a caravan to be close to the family.

Printed in Great Britain
by Amazon